Ethan Mordden

WAVES

An Anthology of New Gay Fiction

Ethan Mordden spent his youth in Heavensville, Pennsylvania, in Venice, Italy, and on suburban Long Island. A graduate of Friends Academy in Locust Valley, New York, and of the University of Pennsylvania, he worked as a music director off-Broadway and as the Assistant Editor of *Opera News* magazine before launching his writing career. A regular contributor to *The New Yorker*, he is the author of numerous books on music, theater, and film, including *Opera in the Twentieth Century*, *Demented: The World of the Opera Diva*, *The Hollywood Studios*, and *The Hollywood Musical*. In fiction, he is the author of the novel *One Last Waltz* and the more-or-less celebrated cycle of short stories known as the *Buddies Trilogy*. He won the National Magazine Award for fiction in 1989.

Also by Ethan Mordden

WAVES

An

Anthology of

New Gay Fiction

Edited and with an Introduction by

Ethan Mordden

Vintage Books / A Division of Random House, Inc. / New York

A Vintage Original, July 1994
First Edition

Compilation, Introduction, and "The Hunt for Red October"
Copyright © 1994 by Ethan Mordden

Library of Congress Cataloging-in-Publication Data
Waves : an anthology of new gay fiction / edited and with an intro-
    duction by Ethan Mordden. —1st. ed.
        p.   cm.
    "A Vintage original"—T.p. verso.
    ISBN 0-679-74477-0
    1. Gay men—United States—Fiction.   2. Short stories,
American—Men authors.   3. American fiction—20th
century.   4. Gay men's writings, American.   I. Mordden, Ethan.
PS648.H57W38   1994
813'.01089206642—dc20   93-40349
                                        CIP

Book design by Chris Welch

Cover photography (front—left to right, top to bottom): Anthony
Knight, Christopher Makos, John Skalicky, Rory McNamara, Douglas
Keeve, Francis Hauert, Lisa Barlow; (back—top to bottom): Rick
Gerharter, James Mordden, Don Press, courtesy of the author,
Brandon Troy Smith, Dennis Dermody, James Farnum.

Manufactured in the United States of America

10   9   8   7   6   5   4   3   2   1

ACKNOWLEDGMENTS

Of my ever-sharp copy editor, Benjamin Dreyer; of the tireless Edward Kastenmeier; of my editor, Marty Asher; and especially of my encompassing and ingenious agent, Joe Spieler.

CONTENTS

INTRODUCTION

*I*n his book *Talents and Technicians: Literary Chic and the New Assembly-Line Fiction*, John W. Aldridge singles out American authors in particular as having been

> provoked into becoming writers by their sense of estrangement from a culture that has been provincially inhospitable, if not downright hostile, to the kind of human beings they found themselves to be or that subscribed to a system of values that they saw either as irrelevant to their deepest concerns or as utterly monstrous.

Aldridge is speaking generally, but he could easily have been explaining one of the most remarkable developments in contemporary American literature: the rise of gay fiction in the past quarter century, the so-called era of Stonewall.

Partly to combat hostility and to propose a more tolerant social contract but mainly to identify the gay condition for gay readers, the authors of Stonewall have in effect created themselves by inventing a literature. They have not built on Herman Melville, Walt Whitman, or Tennessee Williams in tone or subject matter; nor have they adapted the models of contemporary American fiction. Gay writing is a thing-in-itself, counting such a variety of voices and points of view that the anthology of short gay fiction—whether by men or by women or by both in a single volume—has become essential simply to introduce the wide range of experiences, of estrangements from the inhospitable culture. There is an air of urgency about these collections that one misses in the usual "best of" omnibus—a feeling that gay writers are recording and analyzing their lives because, if they didn't, no one would know that they had been here, including themselves. The gay anthology might well be an epitome of gay lit, omnivorous, contentious, self-righteous: insisting upon a definition of gay life even as it reveals how many different kinds of lives gay men and women lead.

Consider the typical gay books: There aren't any. The works of Stonewall—to limit the discussion to the men's books—have included an epistolary novel from a medical corpsman serving in Vietnam (Charles Nelson's *The Boy Who Picked the Bullets Up*); a deviously savage satire of operamania in which fans of rival divas do battle in something like the old Met (James McCourt's *Mawrdew Czgowchwz*); a deadpan mystery series on the life and work of an insurance investigator (Joseph Hansen's Dave Brandstetter books); the adventures of a college-educated hustler on the lam from having murdered a john (Steven

Simmons's *Body Blows*); a lazy comedy on a man's return
to his East Texas hometown, disguised as a woman (Edward Swift's *Splendora*); a gentle look at young men in
Toronto mating and breaking up, changing jobs, and
renting apartments (Peter McGehee's *Boys Like Us*).

Whether describing the gay scene or simply depicting
the life of a particular gay man, these books are of course
using the specific to illuminate the general: A persuasive
view of any human condition helps us to comprehend hu-
manity. Some heterosexual readers cannot fathom this.
Despite his discerning observation on how social con-
frontation impels the writer, John W. Aldridge fails to see
why this would lead a gay writer to write about gay life.
In a discussion of David Leavitt, Aldridge remarks that
homosexuality "becomes an increasingly large preoccu-
pation in his work"—as if Leavitt's sexuality were a tic or
a hobby rather than the construction that generates his
social life, his romantic life, his politics, his very identity.
Leavitt, says Aldridge, "will need to broaden his range
and sympathies and come to understand that sexual ori-
entation is not by itself a sufficient basis for the creation
of meaningful portraits of the immensely complicated
human condition." This is not unlike chiding Isaac Ba-
shevis Singer for concentrating on ghetto life, or Richard
Wright for hammering away at black options in a white
racist society. A gay book will present gay people—even
nothing but gay people—because the quality of a work of
fiction depends upon its author's imagination and observation, not upon a predominance of heterosexual characters.

Oddly, at the dawn of the Stonewall era, in 1969, gay
writers themselves were not sure what a gay book might
consist of. Their predecessors were questionable. Consider the Englishmen of established reputation: Ronald
Firbank was languorously overheated, a queen speaking

in tongues, and Christopher Isherwood was all boarded up in codes. (Isn't Sally Bowles supposed to be a man?) E. M. Forster's almost shockingly forthright *Maurice*, written near the start of World War I but not published till 1971, a year after its author's death, had little impact among American gay writers, partly because of its by-then antique setting and partly because Forster came off as something of a sneak for insisting upon posthumous publication.

True, Isherwood had produced *A Single Man* in 1964. This is a very out work—and a virtually American one, for while it examines, from dawn to following dawn, the soul of an English academic, he is an expatriate living in that ultimate New World address, southern California. Mourning his dead lover, alienated from his surround-ings, taking a moonlit ocean swim with a straight student to whom he is attracted, and masturbating to a kaleido-scope of erotic images, Isherwood's protagonist did offer a fully developed gay viewpoint. Still, this drearily iso-lated figure was not one that young gay writers identified easily with. Half a decade later, Stonewall had exploded: Suddenly there were gay clothes, gay gyms, gay dance rit-uals, even gay neighborhoods, not to mention gay politics and, best of all, gay haircuts. Where in lit was the energy, the facetious ingenuity, the sexuality of gay life?

The classic American titles offered a highly various set of potential models. Gore Vidal's *The City and the Pillar*, published in 1948, is perhaps the most fearlessly honest pre-Stonewall work, so much so that the homophobic *New York Times* critic Orville Prescott refused to review not only this book but any other book that Vidal hence-forth might write. Forty-five years later, *The City and the Pillar* cannot shock as it once did, for its milieu of dark bars, Hollywood "guest" rooms, and arty parties—the world where closeted men share secret smiles with their confederates—has been outed many times since. But, considering how far authors were permitted to take sexual material of any kind in 1948, Vidal's fearlessness is astonishing in a writer who had yet to establish his reputation and knew he could scarcely do so without straight approval. Readers of 1948 took his tale as autobiography, though Vidal claims that, like any storyteller, he made it all up. If so, his imagination is acutely reportorial, for we have all noted these bars and parties and smiles.

Lot's wife was turned into a pillar of salt for looking back upon the destruction of Sodom and Gomorrah; Vidal's young hero Jim Willard suffers a petrifaction of the heart for looking back, obsessively and idealistically, upon a weekend camping trip with a schoolmate. At the book's end, he finally meets up again with his comrade, now about to be married. They fall into bed, the friend rejects Jim's advances, and Jim rapes and kills him. Gay folklore tells us that Vidal's publisher demanded the violent ending as a cautionary horror; no, again, Vidal made it up. It's a psychological device, for in killing his impossible dream Jim at length frees himself of having to believe in it, and immediately after the murder he coldly repairs to a bar to pick up a sailor and launch a career of drifting promiscuity. Revising the novel in 1965, Vidal retained the rape but dropped the murder. Nonetheless, Vidal's delineation of how Jim chases down his shadow is less telling than the revelation that Jims exist: not transvestites or hairdressers, straight America, but your sons and brothers and you. Back in the days of the parties and smiles, *The City and the Pillar* was prime arcanum: The endpapers of the copy in my college library were covered with the graffiti of assignation.

A decade later came William Burroughs's *Naked Lunch*, a phantasmagoria blending the voice of pulp fiction with sci-fi, the Beat drug hunt with savage social cross sections of the American class system, the McCarthy era gay's terror of authority with earthily ecstatic gay encounters—the Meet Café, the Dream Police, the Paregoric Kid, Freeland, "and always cops." Burroughs's gay is The Scene before there *was* a gay scene: blue movies, tea rooms, hustling, pickup fantasies. The homosexuality is but an element in a wigged-out mind-control paranoia trip, but its use is so striking as to seem primary, perhaps terminal. Burroughs's atmosphere is that of an end-of-the-world carnival midway where everything goes, and his characters are either idiot polyester squares or sensualistic street kids who make war on the squares. (Women serve intermittently as minor villains.) Burroughs's dream of true love is one teenage boy hanging another; he catches what men most fear and phrases it the way men tend to speak, and the combination is devastating. Still, what could follow *Naked Lunch* except comparable books by the same author?

If Vidal was a clear-eyed naturalist and Burroughs a fantasist, Patrick Dennis was the camp jester, mixing a fascination for high socì with a closeted crush on the available hunk. Dennis was celebrated for *Auntie Mame*, in the mid-1950s, but he broke through his closet with *Little Me*, in 1961, the book that introduced camp to straights—satirizing the laws of gender, preening in bent glamour, ridiculing women, and adoring yet despising the hustler. Dennis was a pioneer in camp, in fact: Carmen Miranda may have invented it, but it was Dennis who noticed it. All his novels depend on it to some extent, but *Little Me* is made of it, as the ridiculously unwitting memoirs of Belle Poitrine, a woman yet the first of the "actor-models." Innovatively, the book came out with photographs in the same spoofing tone as the text (Dennis himself plays one of Belle's husbands), and near-naked shots of the book's major hustler, one Letch Feeley, came off as one of gay's first acts of public mischief. Vidal was temperate, descriptive. Burroughs lived on a planet in another galaxy. Dennis was *impudent*. One caption reads, "Luncheoning with 'Roz' "; but the picture is a film still of Rosalind Russell at dinner, with a separate shot of our Belle, separately tabled, pasted in. The ribaldry, the hip put-down, and the emphasis upon showbiz as the essential American vanity addressed many a gay youngster, told him he was not alone. The very existence of such a book suggested that an entire gay world lay behind it: *Little Me* was a promise of Coming Out.

If *The City and the Pillar* was a speculation on the kind of life a gay man might lead, if *Naked Lunch* comprised a gay writer's hallucinations on a bundle of topics, and if *Little Me* was a straight story told in a wicked gay style, John Rechy's *City of Night* was something new—a look at the gay subculture by an inhabitant. Excerpted in the early 1960s and published complete in 1963, *City of Night* tells of the underworld of queens, johns, trade, and cops, where love is money and "youngman" a notion so fundamental that the two words agglutinate, as if groping each other. Rechy serves as his own protagonist, in the first person: a sensitive, intelligent, and educated man who drifts through the ghettos of New York, Los Angeles, San Francisco, and New Orleans, as often taking part as observing. It's a powerful performance, more impressively felt than Vidal and more coherent than Burroughs; but then, it's almost absurd to compare these four classic pre-Stonewall titles, for each is unique, beyond genre rather than defining genre—and thus could not furnish a model for the next generation. In the early 1970s, gay fiction was virtually on hold, and the writer who would become famous as Andrew Holleran asked me, "But what would a gay book even *be?*"

Yet Holleran was to be a founding uncle of Stonewall

lit, as a member—along with Robert Ferro, Michael
Grumley, Larry Kramer, Felice Picano, Edmund White,
and George Whitmore—of an informal writers' workshop
that called itself Violet Quill, formed precisely to learn
what gay fiction might be. Kramer had written the
screenplay of the noted Ken Russell film based on D. H.
Lawrence's *Women in Love,* and Picano was a successful author of (straight) pulp thrillers, but White was
the group's apparent heavyweight, having published, in
1973, a novel praised by Vladimir Nabokov, *Forgetting
Elena.*

In brief: An amnesiac awakens in a beach house in a
community so ritualized that he has only to ape his
housemates and he will be accepted. Decoded, this is Fire
Island Pines—or, more generally, early Stonewall life,
with its strictly disciplined body language and uniforms.
The man has an implausible romance with a woman and
the plot evaporates like the man's memory. Still, a model
for a kind of gay fiction had been erected: ultra-high-style
narrative voice, high-tech sensibility, an awareness of the
decor of culture—fashion, the names of obscure writers
and artists—that some might call precious, and echoes of
other high-style authors, not only Nabokov but Henry
James and Marcel Proust. This was, perhaps, fancy writing that gets a lot of respect. How else shall the straights
be able to hail us than for our ambitious poetry?

However, much of what came out of Violet Quill was,
like *Forgetting Elena,* more clever than wise, and self-
regarding rather than perceptive. At least now the books
were openly gay. The year 1978 was when Stonewall lit
seemed to open its era: White's *Nocturnes for the King of
Naples* appeared in the spring, followed in the autumn
by Kramer's *Faggots* and Holleran's *Dancer from the
Dance.* The three books made a certain history in that,
unlike their predecessors, they documented the fearlessly

uncloseted gay life of Stonewall; and *Nocturnes* claims a place in the indexes for an amusing anecdote that finds the St. Martin's Press editor Michael Denneny attending the house's Wednesday morning editorial conference drowsy and unshaven to announce that he has been up all night reading White's manuscript, and that he has decided that St. Martin's will publish the book or Denneny will seek work elsewhere; then he splits to get some sleep.

Of such bold moves was Stonewall lit created, for many a writer and editor can tell of friends urging him or her not to confound the received cautions, not to insist upon making this invisible world a public matter. Still, there was a limit to how much *Nocturnes*, *Faggots*, and *Dancer* could tell either a straight or a gay readership about gay life. *Nocturnes* is a series of wistful friezes, heavy with wordplay and high-culture references:

> When I was a teenager—oh my love, don't fear, I won't read off a Leporello's list of infant conquests, the constant inquests of evenings, troubled nights, the wan dawns of Don Juans.

Faggots is apparently meant as a revival of Restoration drollery, with its huge cast and parodistic observation of the Unities; but with characters named Randy Dildough and Dordogna del Dongo, and with a narrative that is too absurd to be real yet too realistic to be absurdist, this is but the forgeries of wit. *Dancer* is by far the least exasperating of the three in its attempt to forge a mythology out of the icons and ceremonies of gay culture. Its hero, Malone, undergoes an archetypal voyage from middle-class America into a gay paradise in which he grows from adherent into deity, passing on into legend so thoroughly that he no longer needs to exist corporeally and thus vanishes. Holleran times Malone's disappearance to the fire at the Everard bathhouse in 1977, as if marking an end to the first era of gay liberation. Malone is last seen plunging into the bay that separates the Pines from Long Island—the gay world, so to say, from "true life." Did he drown in the bay? Die in the fire? Abandon gay life? *Dancer from the Dance* is on one level an epitaph (Samuel Beckett: *Malone Dies*), on another a hymn to the deathless vigor and appetites of gay life.

Unfortunately, the writing is at times sloppy. Images that might have caught a movement in a phrase are constantly repeated; Holleran uses "painter's jeans" and "T-shirts" as if they were summoning terms of a ferocious power. The inevitable sarcastic queen figure, Sutherland, is a caricature, one of those inventions that seem based more on Eve Arden than on anyone in real life. *City of Night* had its share of drag queens—Miss Destiny, Darling Dolly Dane—but they are uniquely tilted, persuasive characters. Holleran's drag queen is a gadget. There are cultural gaffes, as well—the confusing of John Quincy Adams with his father, John Adams, or the spelling of the name of the singer Patti Jo as "Patty Joe." Violet Quill plumed itself on its polymath command of *belles lettres*, but Holleran's *Christopher Street* magazine columns—the "New York Notebook"—are similarly loaded with the overachiever's errors. We read countless misstated references—to one of the most famous lines in *King Lear*, "As flies to wanton boys are we to the gods; / They kill us for their sport," which in Holleran's misquotation turns into a drivel about "wanton *flies*"; or to Harriet Beecher Stowe's Little Eva "alone on a small floe," though it's the runaway slave Eliza who crosses the ice—Little Eva never leaves the plantation; or to the "Mounties in *Rosalie*," though it's *Rose-Marie* that has the Mounties—*Rosalie* has West Point cadets: and why cite a hopelessly obscure operetta in the first place? Holleran even offends one of his gang's major gods, describing Henry James's *The*

Golden Bowl as being "about death: the untimely death of someone young and fortunate"—but no one dies in *The Golden Bowl.* Holleran might be thinking of *The Wings of the Dove* or *Daisy Miller.*

There was something precious about Violet Quill in general. They would have been smarter to use Tolstoy, Dickens, or Joyce as their archons—not so exquisite but more vital. John Weir hit the nail on the ace in describing Edmund White as

> the High Gay God of Old World niceties and straining American modernism, with aesthetic proclivities that tend to focus on Greek art, British table manners, French literature, North African excursions and dark-skinned boys who will do anything for Western European money.

In short, Violet Quill seemed more like the last era of Old Gay Lit rather than the beginning of New Gay Lit—all that faded European prestige. It's not that the beautiful books were empty, exactly, but that they were too often egotistical. Violet Quill's ultimate moment was the notorious grammatical error that glares out of the opening sentence of Robert Ferro's story in the first of the *Men on Men* anthologies, edited by George Stambolian, a devotee of Violet Quill. Ferro had written, "After some time he realized the house was speaking to whomever might be listening: this was Mark." No, the relative pronoun is the subject of the verb, not the object of the preposition. When Stambolian pointed out the gaffe, Ferro insisted—as he always did when an editor tried to coach an improvement—"That's how I wanted it," apparently more threatened by criticism of any kind than by appearing unlettered before his readers. It's a small point, but it typifies a movement that was less about good writing than about vanity.

Ironically, one somewhat forgotten member of this group understood that gay lit must wrestle with earthly matters, with the life as lived. In 1980, George Whitmore brought out *The Confessions of Danny Slocum*, a novel that turned against Violet Quill's affectations with such impressive sociology that the Library of Congress assigned it a nonfiction decimal number, under Homosexuals, Male—New York (City)—Biography. Nevertheless, it *is* fiction, on an intriguing idea: What do you do in a sexually oriented culture if you're sexually handicapped? Danny's problem is a failure to climax—thus his last name. Whitmore details Danny's therapy in a handsome naturalism, finally turning his graduation ceremony into a metaphor for "performance" in a comic nightmare of going onstage unprepared and unsupported. The emphasis on sex—on the need not only to get some but to be good at it—is something that only a gay writer would have built a novel upon, for much of gay culture *is* sex in metaphor. Like the life, the tale is concentrated, ruled, closed. Danny has a "political friend," a "dancing friend," a "feminist friend"—one of each, half an Ark— and a sense of humor. At first, the novel seems limited by such concentration, or perhaps simply by being set, like all Violet Quill novels, in New York. But then, New York is where Stonewall began and where the first styles were set; and Whitmore's New York really serves as a universalized gay locale, the anyplace where one is judged by one's sexual presentation. Alone among his colleagues, Whitmore had touched upon something basic in gay life, something so important that it *had* to be written about, and Whitmore thus marked a breakaway from what I think of as the first wave of Stonewall lit.

The second wave arrived in the early middle 1980s, when a new group of writers apparently decided to inaugurate gay lit all over again. This time there was no clique of decreeing apprentices. But there was something of an alignment in the younger writers' rejection of first-wave principles. David Leavitt's stories and, especially, his first novel, *The Lost Language of Cranes*, in 1986, epitomize the new approach: The narrative style is graceful but direct, the characters are personable rather than glamorous, and the life is real—having a boy friend, coming out to one's parents or one's wife, responding to the electric personality of a friendly but unavailable straight man, being forced out of one's apartment when the building co-ops. Leavitt's focus on the softer-grained gay—collegiate, obliging, harmless—made him the gay novelist of choice among heterosexual critics. His picture of gay life is a bunch of wounded birds clutching each other, and he promises not to put readers through the unnerving clarity of a sex scene. Nevertheless, Leavitt's delineation of middle-class gays amid family and friends popularized a valid format for gay fiction in the middle 1980s—a notion, in fact, of what a gay book might be: the adventures of a gay man, living his life.

Exploring the family-and-friends background is one of the second wave's priorities, as if to socialize the gay image after Vidal's and Rechy's drifters and White's and Holleran's alienated *flâneurs*, rooting their fiction in a reality so engaging that, fifty pages into their novels, one starts casting the film versions. The first wave imitated art; the second wave imitates life. Consider the first paragraph of John Fox's *The Boys on the Rock*, from 1984:

One of Tommy's legs is shorter than the other and thin as a rail. He had polio as a child, although how I know this or how anyone knows it I can't remember because it's something you never heard him talk about and whenever anyone else talked about it they'd whisper as if he was five feet away even when he was nowhere around. He has this very square jaw with muscles on it that he'd flex and lock and unlock when he was embarrassed or angry about his leg, which was quite often, and he'd usually wind up taking it out on Lorraine, who has these huge tits that he's crazy about. She's very large and tall—almost as tall as I am, and whenever she took off her glasses to clean them she looked like she was looking in about five different directions at once—including you—but some people thought she was pretty.

That's Billy Connors talking: a teenage swimming champ just edging into self-awareness as a gay man, away from hetero cover-dating into an affair with a chap who seems like a slightly older version of Billy till he reveals an unwillingness to live as openly, *honestly*, as Billy intends to. However, Fox's treatment of the breakup of Billy's romance is characterological rather than political, for second-wave writers are more concerned with airing their feelings than in exhorting a readership on the Issues. The second wave, above all, deals with "ordinary" people, de-emphasizing the gym-and-disco circuit riders celebrated in first-wave fiction but also catching its characters while they are still struggling to understand what a gay identity means to them as individuals and have yet to relate to the concept of a gay community. Joseph Hansen's plodding insurance investigator, Dave Brandstetter, and Edward Swift's transvestite, Timothy John Coldridge/Miss Jessica Gatewood, of Splendora, Texas, would have to be the protagonists of two very different kinds of fiction, Hansen's methodical whodunit and Swift's southern gothic spoof. Nevertheless, both characters are developed existentially, learning who they are and what they want as they pursue the day-to-day of their lives. We may be unclear on their sexual fantasies or whom they would vote for, but we learn a lot about how they spend their time. Thus, John Fox enhances the growth of his hero's self-realization by showing him slowly pulling away from his straight friends and his parents toward his gay friends and an understanding aunt, finally rejecting the closeted lover "for being such a chickenshit."

Michael Cunningham's story "White Angel," included in this anthology, typifies the extraordinary power of the best second-wave writing. When "White Angel" was first published, in *The New Yorker* in 1988, it attracted a great deal of attention for its nervous, loving, bitter look at the relationship between a nine-year-old and his dazzling older brother, a midwestern contemporary Huck Finn; the piece won the National Magazine Award. It is not an overtly gay story, but the worship of the hip and sexy older male is a recurring theme in gay lit, and—as Cunningham reveals in his novel *A Home at the End of the World*, of which "White Angel" is a part—the younger brother, Bobby, grows up to be gay. Shedding his birthright ties to bond first with his lover's parents, then with his lover and a woman in New York, Bobby travels a road typical of gay life, in search of a non-biological "family" to replace the one whose loyalties didn't take. Jesse Green's "Mirandas" similarly proposes an example of the gay "extended family," though his tale is narrated by a straight woman, awkward in love and work, who builds her nest under the protection of yet another hip and sexy older-brother figure.

Note that, in Green's "family," to both the straight woman and the amiably pathetic gay sidekick who has also taken refuge in this singular household, the dazzler is friendly but ultimately withholding. He "loves" them: but won't give them love. In "White Angel," the cynosure wants to share his power with his amazed younger brother. "Today you are a man," the older brother announces after the younger brother has witnessed him having sex with his girlfriend. "When I saw you out there spying on us I thought to myself, *yes.* Now *I*'m really here." This use of sexuality as a gesture—or, as in Green, a limitation—of friendship is a routine transaction of gay life, one that the second wave was bound to record.

Gay writers also, at times, view sex as a potentially destructive element. In a system in which all men are more or less randy and willing, how does one maintain balance, responsibility, self-respect? "I'm not a twenty-dollar whore," I used to say when turning down writing jobs I felt were beneath me. "I'm a fifty-dollar whore." Joke. But the cop in Rex Knight's "The Number You Have Reached" takes that joke seriously: No one's going to have him as a fantasy. He insists upon being real, a feeling man rather than a sex cartoon. On the other hand, the narrator of Robert Trent's "Hard-Candy Christmas" uses sex to disentangle himself from relationships. Trent's protagonist resents having to show up for a dysfunctional Christmas dinner at the country club when he could spend that time cruising. Yet he fantasizes about an alternative Christmas of depth and reach and true family affections, a Christmas with the resonance of the generations in communion. Sex is a gay language. It is, for good or ill, how we know each other. Knight says, You cannot have sex with me without knowing who I am. Trent says, If you have sex with me, no one will have to know who I am, especially me. While we're constructing the definition of a gay book, we must remember that gay writers have stood among the revolutionaries—for decades—in the war for sexual honesty in lit.

"It's wrong to say that all gay men are obsessed with sex," says the title character in Paul Rudnick's play *Jeffrey*. "All *human beings* are obsessed with sex. All gay men are obsessed with opera."* Gay lit is obsessed with trying to reckon the advantages and disadvantages of a culture apparently dominated by men who are always on the make. Heterosexual critics look askance at all the erotic activity in gay fiction, conveniently forgetting their Henry Millers and Philip Roths. But it seems self-evident that men are sexually more predatory than women, so a community of homosexual males will naturally enjoy a more liberal erotic life than a community of heterosexual males and females will: because the women want to covenant with their partners, while the men say, "Let's do it." At that, the notion that gay lit is a sex carnival in which the reader plays a tourist riding a bus through downtown Gomorrah is misinformed. Far too many gay writers are almost officiously reticent about sex, like a Hollywood movie of the Production Code era. Going back to the six gay novels I mentioned at the start of this piece—chosen at random, by the way—I notice that their authors' emphasis on sex is about that of today's heterosexual authors, with Charles Nelson considerably above the average and James McCourt somewhat below.

Sex intrigues gay writers particularly as a stylistic choice, almost an existential one. With so much Going On along the bar-and-club circuit, how does one stay home, ever? How does one buddy up, even temporarily, when the Perfect Lay could be waiting at the Roxy with your name engraved upon his heart? No fewer than three stories in this collection deal with this question, John Edward Harris's "Cruise Control" making it central in its dialogue between two gay archetypes, the unapologetically promiscuous man and the innocent who seeks a life's mate. Which of the two will be happier? A friend of

*This vastly quoted epigram bears a seldom-repeated but equally quotable capper: "[Sex and opera] are not the same thing. You can have good sex."

mine stares at a prestigious writer and his lover at a party—such a handsome pair, well-dressed professionals, enviable. "Should I be like them?" my friend asks me; but his tone is doubtful, and I know he is already planning the night's post-party cruising schedule.

"Should I be like them?" is another fundamental question of gay life, therefore of gay lit. In an interview in *Lambda Book Report*, the young southern writer Joey Manley described any deviation from big-city sexadisco gallivanting as not being, according to some, "gay enough. As if you led the kind of life Felice Picano led or you weren't gay." Was gay lit fantasizing or describing? How much gay can a gay novel contain? Is monogamy a fairy-tale choice, promiscuity bad advertising? Must everything happen in New York or San Francisco? Aren't there gays who don't brunch or know who Montserrat Caballé is? This went beyond Should I be like them? This was Who else dwells in the gay world, and shouldn't the fiction be finding him?

Accordingly, the second wave's naturalizing effect sought out a wider range of characters, and the prototypes began to dissolve: Each story is different because each person is different. Second-wave characters cruise moderately, don't read French novels, and know women. They may not live in New York. Half the writers in this collection take us to small-town or rural America—not because I instituted a geographical quota but because New York has lost its glamour. Along with San Francisco and Los Angeles, New York has become a City of Death, a setting that almost invariably necessitates discussion of or reflection upon AIDS. Writers who wish to treat homosexuality in a purer state—apolitically, chastely—move to the outback and childhood, as, in this volume, Jim Provenzano and Richard Davis do. Of course, the New York writers of the second wave *have* to deal with AIDS, as Jesse Green places a dying man on an upper floor while he takes a CAT scan of the souls of those belowdecks; or as John Edward Harris alarms us with a character's statement that "I've never had safe sex, never used a condom. I wouldn't know how." Ironically, the sole story in this book that deals with the plague on a virtually line-by-line basis, Abraham Verghese's "Lilacs," brings us out of New York into the heartland, for a last ride with a PWA whose defiance of business-as-usual culture is well-nigh apocalyptic.

AIDS and politics lead us to the third wave, which rolled in during the late 1980s. If the first wave was the wrong people at the right time and the second wave rushed into a needed renaturalization, the third wave is political, archetypal, experimental. This was the generation that grew up when lit by and about gay males had become one of publishing's sub-industries, taking advantage of a national network of gay bookstores, the discretionary income of the upmarket bachelor, and a readership hungry to see its unique styles ratified. As Joey Manley says, "I belong to the first generation of gay writers who had too much to read."

Actually, the third wave is not as different from the second wave as the second is from the first. The second wave rejected the first wave. The third wave builds upon the second wave: intensifies its view of gays as alienated from straight culture while treating the family somewhat comically; graduates the implicit politics of coming out into outright activism; looks for new voices and narrative structures. A typical third-wave novel is Ken Siman's *Pizza Face, or, The Hero of Suburbia*, on the misadventures of Andy, a teenage untouchable, scorned by the girls and bullied by the jocks, forever striving to clear up his disfigured complexion and to develop some heroic undertaking by which to redeem his social status. Nothing works. Worse yet, by the novel's end Andy comes to realize that the politicians, celebrities, and lookers that he has been using for personal inspiration are cast of no finer clay than he—they may even be wholly unworthy of him. This is a truly woeful saga, yet Siman unfolds it in dead-pan style, edging the sorrow into satire and giving Andy's matter-of-fact recitations of his and others' humiliations a wistfully comic voice:

> It was Friday, and through the window Andy could see a lot of his schoolmates at the Pizza Hut, having pitchers of beer with their pizzas. Basically, the Pizza Hut was reserved for popular, athletic people. Unpopular people had to get pizza to go and beer from the convenience store. They'd done away with the salad bar at the Pizza Hut after an unpopular girl lost her eye when somebody threw an olive at her head. She now had to wear an eyepatch for the rest of her life and had a stutter to begin with.

Again, the same story and characters would have been appropriate second-wave material, but by 1991, the year Siman's novel was published, the best gay writers were looking for ways to frame, comment upon, their naturalism in order to underline gay awareness and gay experiences. As a product of southern suburbia, Andy knows nothing of Stonewall city culture; typically, his heroes are not movie stars or porn icons but Jimmy Carter and the first lady of North Carolina, C. C. Cheshire, the governor's wife. As part of a class project in racial harmony, Andy follows her recipe for cheese logs to make a raft upon which he glues figures representing Mark Twain's civil rights pioneers, Huck and Jim, with the predictable results:

> Mrs. Bowell seemed to like the project until she took a bite of the cheese raft and had to run out of the room. She threw up in front of a biology class that was meet-

ing outside to study chlorophyll in plants. Evidently
she had eaten some of the rubber cement.

Andy is doomed to be the class plop whatever class he's
in, yet Siman's uninflected and thus all the more farcical
voice reveals Andy as one whose very isolation will make
him observant and strong. This is gay adolescence seen
within strict realism yet at the same time rising above it,
subverting it—as, in life, gay kids must do to survive.
Andy accepts his attraction to men rather casually; it is
everything else that vexes him. Still, as Siman lays it out,
it is everything else that doesn't matter. Andy's parents
are ridiculous, his coevals are cretins, his role models are
frauds, and even the handsome straight boy who mysteri-
ously befriends him turns out to be gay and a user. This is
the third wave: often comic about serious matters, less
concerned with the family than with the straight world in
general, and less inclined than predecessors were to com-
promise with straight attitudes.

Of course, not all writers observe the rules of the age.
Dennis Cooper, a third-wave talent for his startling S&M
reveries and, when he feels like it, lyrical diction, began
publishing in the middle of the first wave, including the
deviously poetic "A Herd," about a serial killer who preys
on sexy high-school boys. Conversely, Jesse Green's novel,
O Beautiful, came out in 1992, after the third wave had
hit, yet it seems prototypally second-wave in its sharply
observed realism, elegantly humorous narrative style, and
all-basic gay-daydream plot premise of a nice but re-
pressed gay man nursing a crush on a devastating
straight man who, day by day, becomes more and more
available. (Even their names tell us how neatly Green
catches the relationship of the adherent and his idol in
blundering, agonized, middle-class Martin and manipula-
tively pornographic Matt.) At that, while the excerpt I

xxxii / *Waves: An Anthology of New Gay Fiction*

have included from Michael Cunningham's *A Home at the End of the World* reads as a second-wave piece, the novel as a whole is third-wave for its unusual device of letting the major characters take turns narrating the chapters.

Thus, the three eras that I propose as critical structure are meant merely as guidelines to explain how Stonewall lit began, reestablished itself, and developed. Nevertheless, I am struck by how my authors epitomize the conflicting styles of the second and third waves. Had Jim Provenzano written "Forty Wild Crushes" ten years ago, he might well have built up his characters more, expanded the report on his home life, observed his setting in greater detail. But the second wave had already exploited that approach, so Provenzano devised a unique construction—a slim narrative extrapolated by forty whimsical footnotes, one for each of the crushes—that brings out his hero's first sexual stirrings, whether for the surprisingly gym-packed Devil in Walt Disney's *Fantasia* or for the comely dude along your paper route who comes to the door shirtless. Thus the tale is third-wave in its experimental layout but also in the way it dims the sounds of daily life to pump up a young boy's erotic imagination—somewhat comparably to Siman and *Pizza Face*, but this time treating a socially integrated character who balances peer-group command with imitations of Jo Anne Worley.

G. Winston James's "John" also realigns the family-background, social-class, sex-life elements of the second wave, here into a pointed "day in the life"—a miniature, if you will, of Isherwood's *A Single Man*. But where Isherwood hopped himself up on Hindu concepts alien to both gay life and American life, "John" erects its epic upon the echoes of old conversations, bending realism into a subtext that not only frames the tale but explains it. James's New York is anxious, doubtful, demanding. Ontological.

What is the *purpose* of my feelings? The midwestern mall of Scott Heim's "Imagining Linc," conversely, is sunny, lazy, accommodating. Who cares about purpose? One might see Heim's two erotically inventive boys as mischievous, the parents as doting or dim. No. The boys are revolutionaries—casually ready to defy authority to the utmost—and the parents are conservatives without a cause. When Heim's charismatic hero enters his empty bedroom crying, "We're coming in," it is meant as a joke but it sounds almost like a war cry. James and Heim warn us that, from now on, parents will never be so confident. Accidents happen. The second wave describes how it feels to be gay in the "real" straight world. The third wave regards the real world as gay, straights as ridiculous interlopers.

The experimental side of the third wave, toying with format, voice, and subject matter, is represented here by Michael Scalisi's "Three," short pieces that explore the potential of first-person narrative, from the anytime, anywhere fable of the rival brothers through the street encounter taken down verbatim to the European adventure that reads almost as a treatment for a movie in which Antonioni characters behave in a Bertolucci manner. The third wave is knowledgeable but also hip—note the one-size-fits-all ghetto lingo in the second of Scalisi's trio, reflecting the acculturation, among Hispanics and even some white kids, of inner-city black lingo.

Brad Gooch invents his own lingo, that of hip New Yorkers who delight in putting a sleazy spin on their own glamour. The dialogue in "Satan"—set forth neat behind colons, as in play or movie script—has the breathless aggression of sex talk, emphasizing these characters' impulsively domineering approach to human relationships. Who controls whom? is the operating psychology in many a gay story—Weir, Cunningham, Verghese, Knight, James,

Green, Heim, Trent, and Scalisi all deal with it, whether from an emotional, physical, cultural, or political viewpoint. But Richard Davis's "Marty" presents two isolated boys struggling to sustain each other, not for control but for salvation—at that on a frankly biblical level. Gay lit has regarded erotic involvement as simultaneously nourishing and predatory since *The City and the Pillar*—even, if you will, since Ronald Firbank. Third-wavers especially honor this tradition of suspicion and ambivalence in the matter of love, though Gooch absolutely deconstructs the romantic urge while Davis absolutely exalts it.

John Weir's "Homo in Heteroland" opens this collection, partly because I know that Chuck Ortleb will have a heart attack when he sees the word "homo" but mainly because this very third-wave piece essentializes Stonewall lit. It has the high-style voice, the artistry, that the first wave fumbled so badly. It treats its gay hero in the context of family and society, a key connection to the second wave. And it fools you: which is very third-wave, because it reads as fiction but is in fact journalism, John's confidential report on a road trip with his very own straights. Patiently maintaining his contemporary gay honesty even as he performs a highly traditional role as empathic uncle, John catches today's gay man(and woman)hood on the verge of a major historical era, that of the battle for our rights as citizens. We are *of* you, John says, yet we are different—more playful (read Heim), more appetitive (Harris), alienated by hypocritical conventions (Trent, perhaps Verghese), kinkier (Gooch), more intense (James), less intense (Knight).

Gay people often feel like sorcerers in a time when sorcery is forbidden: We wield the wild magic but cannot share its wondrous healing powers. Geoff Ryman, Canadian-born, raised in the United States, and now living in England, describes himself as a fantasy writer who fell in love with realism. Because I am a fantasy writer, I am particularly aware that every work of fiction, however realistic, is a fantasy. It happens in a world that is an alternative to this one.

Ryman writes this at the end of *Was*, a novel of 1992 that brings together the author of *The Wizard of Oz*, L. Frank Baum; a new "real-life" version of Baum's Dorothy; MGM's version, Judy Garland; and a young gay man of today, a PWA whose life—like theirs—is fused with a vision of Utopia. Obviously, the fantasist hunting realism would make a major work of "realizing" Oz—exploring the real lives that may inform the conception of a marvelous fairyland where life is so sacred that (almost) no one ever dies. Ryman's self-description might suit any third-wave writer, even any gay writer. Gays deal in fantasy throughout their most impressionable years, a fantasy of who they might ideally be warring with a fantasy of who they pretend they are. Ironically, gay lit's most invigorating concern is to set down the data on what being gay is *really* like, how it feels from the inside of the world that is an alternative to this one: A gay man, or woman, views life. That, surely, is what a gay book might be, without the slightest apology to the John W. Aldridges. We were not put on earth to dish up a likeness of hetero lit with two pairs of pants. "Zeda Earl thinks she has to imitate everybody she sees," runs a passage from *Splendora*. "Suppose I'd better tell her she must learn to imitate herself for a change."

WAVES

An

Anthology of

New Gay Fiction

HOMO IN HETEROLAND

John Weir

My nephew John is six years old and looks like Florence Henderson. Blond and bossy, with relentless optimism and a bright soprano voice, he likes pancakes, swimming pools, cartoons, television, and weapons and destroyers of all descriptions—guns, bats, bombs, swords, and toy soldiers, which he calls Ninjas. He is the oldest of three boys; I am the younger of two. During the time I spent with my nephews this summer, on vacation in Atlanta, I fell into ancient, regressive younger-brotherly patterns, not only with him, but with my own brother (who is, after all, older), and with my sister-in-law (the oldest of four). For a week and a half, I was everybody's little brother—not just the House Homo, not just the Art Fag from New

York, but the lagging, lisping, and reluctant youngest member of the whole American family.

We were going to Atlanta to look for a house for my brother, who was finally weary of Westchester. He even bought a heteromobile just for the trip. It was a big, blue bubble of a car, a Chrysler van with fake wood siding, a romper-room interior, and wholly automated acces-sories—from cruise control to power door locks and a digital odometer-clock-and-compass combo, to which my brother pointed impatiently whenever I asked which di-rection we were headed in. "Read the compass," he would say, exasperated, as my nephews giggled delightedly into their palms. We were all accustomed to my absentmind-edness, developed during my childhood as a defense against the precise and organized big brothers of the world, and which I have relied on ever since.

One of my favorite strategies for survival with my brother is to play like Miss Caswell in *All About Eve*, the Marilyn Monroe part, helpless and dumb but with a certain wacky wisdom. Driving to Atlanta, it felt safer, and poetically apt, to obscure my intelligence in this slightly campy, classically homo-underground fashion. After all, I was traveling with a family that had recently cheered the Boy Scouts of America at a Fireman's Carni-val Parade in my brother's and my hometown in rural, northwestern New Jersey. We stood at the corner of Hal-stead Street, in Clinton, on a gray June day, and shouted, "Hip, hip, hooray," as the little boys in blue marched homophobically by. My heedless nephews were going to grow into Boy Scouts, and be taught to hate queers. It seemed unlikely that anyone in my brother's family, including me, would correct their misapprehen-sions.

For I was a homo in heteroland, and all my brave po-litical opinions, my aggressive outness, my pinkness, faded away. By the end of the vacation, I was an off shade of peach, a bumbling, obsequious beige. It's easy to be a card-carrying queer on Avenue A, or a brave young fag at some suburban shopping mall, with comrades in tow. But to burn the torch of gay identity in a blue Chrysler van, and keep it lit for sixteen hours straight, from the Tappan Zee Bridge to the Peachtree Center, through diaper changes and bottle feedings and yet another reading of *Where's Waldo*, was more than I could manage. The secret weapon of heterosexuality is children. Their needs consume all resources, conversational topics, and attention spans. We couldn't talk about gender issues. We couldn't even play a game of Twenty Questions with any assurance. It's hard to talk political agenda when your primary focus is a two-year-old child choking on a Ninja in the way-backseat.

In the scenario my brother and sister-in-law have written for their children in order to tell them apart, John is a stoic—self-sufficient and responsible, while Matthew, the baby, is a saint. And James is a juggernaut—a holy terror, an irresistible force. Blond like his brothers, with the same damp touch of entreaty and attitude of childhood tenacity, he has blue eyes that are hot smudges, like thumbprint impressions burned into his brow by the lingering hands of the Creator. Because he was born with twisted ankles and spent his first year in casts (to straighten his bones), he runs with a crazy, bowlegged gait, as if he had a singular sense of balance. He is selfish, loud, complaining, inconsiderate, unappeasable, nonstop, exquisitely beautiful, a total pain in the ass, and a thorough delight. I have a big crush on him. (Why not admit it? Al Gore tenderly dandled his towheaded son on his knee at the Democratic National Convention, and no one accused *him* of being a member of NAMBLA.)

For much of the vacation, James had a digestive problem: He couldn't take a shit. At first I didn't realize what his periodic bouts of intense grunting signified. Still in diapers, he goes to the bathroom whenever he pleases—on walks in the woods, stopping to read a historical marker memorializing Sherman's March to the Sea, on a ride at Six Flags Over Georgia, or at breakfast at a Waffle House on the ring road into Atlanta. A couple of days into our vacation, though, he started holding on to his shit. Once every few hours, he stopped still in his tracks (in itself an accomplishment), contorted his face, and groaned. "Unh," he said emphatically, for about a minute. It looked like he was practicing breathing techniques for Lamaze. Then he relaxed, going back to his two-year-old mission of search and destroy.

The first time this happened, I was alone for the day with John and James while my brother and his wife took the baby and went house-hunting. The rest of us were left at our motel, twenty miles outside downtown Atlanta, without a car or very much cash. (Part of my little-brotherly behavior included my running out of money after a day and a half, so I baby-sat for my meals.) It rained all morning, and we watched *The Brady Bunch*. The real-life Greg Brady had just come out with the book about his crush on his TV mom, and my nephews and I were equally absorbed by the show (for different reasons). When the rain let up, we walked across the highway to a scummy pond where dirty ducks swam up to us expectantly. We had to disappoint the ducks: We had already eaten the Milky Way bars I used to bribe my nephews to put on their shoes in a hurry.

The pond was at the bottom of a long hill, at the crest of which an Exxon sign glimmered in the midday sun. The clouds had blown away completely, but the air was still wet from the rain, and the sunlight seeping into the asphalt and reflecting off shiny metal surfaces wasn't intense enough to burn the backs of our necks. This was supposed to be the sun-scarred, sweat-drenched South, but it felt like Massachusetts or Wisconsin, or anywhere else on a breezy day after a rainfall in the middle of a highway intersection miles from the center of town. Cars drove by in all directions, and a water tower painted like a big peach, with the legend "Hot-lanta" inscribed upon it, loomed over our motel. It was our marker, signifying home as we climbed the hill toward the Exxon sign.

Atlanta is a city-in-the-making, surrounded on all sides by instant suburbs, neighborhoods that didn't exist a year (or even a couple of months) ago. Drive in any direction away from the city and eventually the sprawl runs out, ending not abruptly like a blooming western city in miles of desert, but gently and apologetically in undeveloped acres of farmland, and green rolling hills. At the edge of suburbia, just before the landscape turns completely pastoral, freshly laid strips of concrete sidewalk line unexcavated fields where new communities are planned. Reaching the Exxon station at the top of the hill, we stared across the highway at a ribbon of sidewalk stretched irrelevantly alongside a field-in-waiting for some new housing development.

Expecting houses, my nephews and I saw, instead, a pile of straw, bale stacked on bale, in the middle of a muddy clay clearing littered with sticks of wood. We ran across the highway holding hands. The straw was damp but not soaking, and John immediately started building a fort. The sticks of wood were the walls, pressed against the straw, and they were also bombs, which John and James hurled at me when I lumbered out of the woods pretending to be someone big and scary. My fourth time out of the woods, I captured James and carried him off to my lair, while John danced delightedly around my feet, aiming bombs at my toes. He had good aim, and he didn't care if he wounded me, and he soon rescued his brother. I limped back to my sanctuary, defeated. We played this game for an hour, until I got them to abandon their fort by reminding them that they had parents, whom they presumably missed, and who would be waiting for us when we returned to the motel.

We headed back down the hill, the soft clay sticking to our shoes, drying against the cuffs of our trousers. I bought them juice at the Exxon station. On the way home, sipping his Donald Duck orange juice contemplatively, John began discussing marriage.

"When I grow up," he said, "I'm marrying Abby."

"Who's Abby?"

"Abby is my best friend," he said, "and I'm marrying her when I grow up. You know Abby."

"I don't remember Abby."

"She was at my birthday party. She had the red hat. She was wearing a red hat, and holding my Ninja Turtle."

James, who was clutching a bottle of grape juice, was staring longingly at John's orange juice. James is never fully satisfied until he has in his possession everything belonging to his older brother. I knew if I made them trade juices, James would want the grape juice; if I made them trade again, he would want Donald Duck. James's goal in life is simple: He wants his brother to be left with nothing. Failing that, he will settle for copying his brother in every particular.

"Me, too," James said, spilling grape juice on his shorts.

"You, too, what?" I said.

"I'm getting married, too."

"Who are you marrying, James?"

James said, "Ethan."

John began to giggle.

"Who's Ethan?" I said.

"Ethan's Abby's brother," John answered, laughing in delight. "James, you can't marry Ethan."

"I like Ethan," James said.

"He's your best friend?"

"Uh-huh."

"He's Abby's brother?"

"Uh-huh."

John raced out in front of me, pointing excitedly.

"James can't marry Ethan," he repeated.

Here was my homosexual moment: I couldn't let it elude me. Feeling somehow like a character in a Certs commercial, I said, "Boys can marry boys. And girls can marry girls. It happens all the time. Sometimes boys marry girls and girls marry boys, and sometimes boys marry boys, and girls girls. I was married to a boy, once," I concluded, reminiscently, Mr. Rogers crossed with Blanche DuBois.

Then James tried to shit. Or tried not to shit, I couldn't be sure. He dropped his grape juice in the grass by the side of the road, and started moaning. His face was pink, and his features were tied in a knot.

"Unh," he said. "Unh."

"James is trying not to go to the bathroom," John said happily, informatively. John is an empiricist, with a slightly malevolent edge. "He doesn't like to go. That's what Daddy said. He doesn't like to go." He walked around us in a circle, repeating himself. "He doesn't like to go."

"All right," I said, "Relax. He doesn't have to if he doesn't want to."

John said, "He's holding it back."

"Well, maybe that's the right thing for your brother, at the moment," I said, hating myself for sounding like a twelve-step program. My New York conditioning: If they were my children, their first words would be "clarity" and "serenity." They'd "put things out there," or else they'd pay attention to "what came up." Luckily for them, I'm childless, and queer.

James stopped groaning. He reached for his brother's juice.

"Want it," he said, as if his trauma had never occurred. He seemed relaxed.

But John wasn't over James's crisis yet. "He's holding on to things," he said with alarming wisdom.

"Well," I said, "aren't we all."

"Want it," James repeated. His brother, in a rare display of generosity, handed him his bottle. A few minutes later we got back to the motel, where we tracked dried clay all over the carpet.

James did finally go to the bathroom. I wish I could say it happened at an appropriate moment, underscoring some release of tension in the atmosphere, a family catharsis—but life is not as neat as fiction, and I don't remember the point after which James had ceased to interrupt our family activities with his constipated moans. In any case, there wasn't any tension to dispel. We did everything on our vacation that families normally do. We ate a lot of bad food at tacky restaurants. We sat in the sun in suburban Marietta next to the railroad tracks and watched the train go by at regular intervals. We wrote postcards to our grandparents.

On our last day, we took a tram up the side of Stone Mountain, a Mt. Rushmore–like amusement across the face of which three Confederate heroes on horseback (Stonewall Jackson, Jefferson Davis, and Robert E. Lee) are carved in the rock. It was appalling. But a group of women dressed for church, in flower prints and Sunday shoes, stood in a circle at the top, and sang a defiant and affirming hymn. They were triumphant women of color. The sunset light was orange-yellow and caressing as the shadows lengthened over the stone, and the breeze blew their dresses, carrying their music away. I envied them; they seemed to know how to live in a treacherous landscape.

We left Atlanta the following morning. Our journey home in the hetero-van was uneventful. More bottle feedings, more greasy french fries, more *Waldo*. My brother and sister-in-law and I traded driving; in the back, the boys went to sleep after it got dark. An hour from New York, James, who was strapped in by himself, woke from a few hours' sleep and started to cry. He was soaked through with urine. We had used all the diapers—and, anyway, we were just about home—but James wouldn't stop crying. I crawled into the back with him, freed him from his seat belts, and rolled him onto my chest. He reeked of urine, and his body was warm and wet. He put his head against my chest and let my heartbeat lull him to sleep. I felt his breath at the base of my neck, and his blond hair brushed my chin.

So many things are irreplaceable, I wouldn't know how to begin to compile a list. James couldn't shit. But I remember my friend Bruce, in 1984, sitting on a toilet in his apartment on the Upper East Side, also trying to shit. I stood in the hallway, by the bathroom. The door was open a crack, and I could see Bruce's hands gripping the towels that hung from the rack in front of him, and I could hear him scream. He had tumors in his asshole, lesions, God knows what, and I could hear him saying, "God help me, God stave me. Help me. God stave me," over and over again, like a chant, broken by screams. He sat there a long time. I kept saying, "Bruce," and he kept saying, "Leave me alone." It's worse when people can

easily speak, or even understand; their words are harder
to hear when they know why they're in pain. I stared at
my palms. I stared at the molding. I didn't know what to
do. Bruce screamed for about an hour, and then he gave
up. His knuckles were red from clutching the towels, and
I can still see his sinewy fingers, brittle with what would
shortly be his death.

Now, my nephew doesn't have a terminal disease. My
nephew is two and a half. He's having his anal phase, or
something Freudian like that. Little boys don't die from
taking a shit, but neither do men and women in their
twenties and thirties. And I had an odd revelation, in the
back of the car, with James breathing steady and slow
against my chest. The chasm separating me from my
brother and sister-in-law: I know what death feels like. I
know its monotony, its repetitiveness, the slow accretion
of losses, until there's nothing to let go of but the foolish
American faith that nobody dies. Cradling my nephew in
the way-backseat, I found it peculiar—not bitter, but
odd—that I should clutch him so protectively, as if the
perils to which he might be subject had been kept, sub-
limely, from his parents, and confided only to me. In some
(Republican, fundamentalist) versions of our family, I
was the evil outside. But driving back to New York I knew
that only I could be trusted, to pray for him, to hold him
to my heart, and to tell him the truth when it seemed time
for him to have it.

WHITE ANGEL

Michael Cunningham

We lived then in Cleveland, in the middle of everything. It was the sixties—our radios sang out love all day long. This of course is history. It happened before the city of Cleveland went broke, before its river caught fire. We were four. My mother and father, Carlton, and me. Carlton turned sixteen the year I turned nine. Between us were several brothers and sisters, weak flames quenched in our mother's womb. We are not a fruitful or many-branched line. Our family name is Morrow.

Our father was a high school music teacher. Our mother taught children called "exceptional," which meant that some could name the day Christmas would fall in the year 2000 but couldn't remember to drop their pants when

they peed. We lived in a tract called Woodlawn—neat one-
and two-story houses painted optimistic colors. Our tract
bordered a cemetery. Behind our backyard was a gully
choked with brush, and beyond that, the field of smooth,
polished stones. I grew up with the cemetery, and didn't
mind it. It could be beautiful. A single stone angel, small-
breasted and determined, rose amid the more conservative
markers close to our house. Farther away, in a richer sec-
tion, miniature mosques and Parthenons spoke silently to
Cleveland of man's enduring accomplishments. Carlton
and I played in the cemetery as children and, with a little
more age, smoked joints and drank Southern Comfort
there. I was, thanks to Carlton, the most criminally ad-
vanced nine-year-old in my fourth-grade class. I was
going places. I made no move without his counsel.

Here is Carlton several months before his death, in an
hour so alive with snow that earth and sky are identically
white. He labors among the markers and I run after,
stung by snow, following the light of his red knitted cap.
Carlton's hair is pulled back into a ponytail, neat and
economical, a perfect pinecone of hair. He is thrifty, in his
way.

We have taken hits of acid with our breakfast juice. Or
rather, Carlton has taken a hit and I, considering my
youth, have been allowed half. This acid is called win-
dowpane. It is for clarity of vision, as Vicks is for decon-
gestion of the nose. Our parents are at work, earning the
daily bread. We have come out into the cold so that the
house, when we reenter it, will shock us with its warmth
and righteousness. Carlton believes in shocks.

"I think I'm coming on to it," I call out. Carlton has on
his buckskin jacket, which is worn down to the shine. On
the back, across his shoulder blades, his girlfriend has
stitched an electric-blue eye. As we walk I speak into the
eye. "I think I feel something," I say.

"Too soon," Carlton calls back. "Stay loose, Frisco. You'll know when the time comes."

I am excited and terrified. We are into serious stuff. Carlton has done acid half a dozen times before, but I am new at it. We slipped the tabs into our mouths at breakfast, while our mother paused over the bacon. Carlton likes taking risks.

Snow collects in the engraved letters on the headstones. I lean into the wind, trying to decide whether everything around me seems strange because of the drug, or just because everything truly is strange. Three weeks earlier, a family across town had been sitting at home, watching television, when a single-engine plane fell on them. Snow swirls around us, seeming to fall up as well as down.

Carlton leads the way to our spot, the pillared entrance to a society tomb. This tomb is a palace. Stone cupids cluster on the peaked roof, with stunted, frozen wings and matrons' faces. Under the roof is a veranda, backed by cast-iron doors that lead to the house of the dead proper. In summer this veranda is cool. In winter it blocks the wind. We keep a bottle of Southern Comfort there.

Carlton finds the bottle, unscrews the cap, and takes a good, long draw. He is studded with snowflakes. He hands me the bottle and I take a more conservative drink. Even in winter, the tomb smells mossy as a well. Dead leaves and a yellow M&M's wrapper, worried by the wind, scrape on the marble floor.

"Are you scared?" Carlton asks me.

I nod. I never think of lying to him.

"Don't be, man," he says. "Fear will screw you right up. Drugs can't hurt you if you feel no fear."

I nod. We stand sheltered, passing the bottle. I lean into Carlton's certainty as if it gave off heat.

"We can do acid all the time at Woodstock," I say.

"Right on. Woodstock Nation. Yow."

"Do people really *live* there?" I ask.

"Man, you've got to stop asking that. The concert's over, but people are still there. It's the new nation. Have faith."

I nod again, satisfied. There is a different country for us to live in. I am already a new person, renamed Frisco. My old name was Robert.

"We'll do acid all the time," I say.

"You better believe we will." Carlton's face, surrounded by snow and marble, is lit. His eyes are bright as neon. Something in them tells me he can see the future, a ghost that hovers over everybody's head. In Carlton's future we all get released from our jobs and schooling. Awaiting us all, and soon, is a bright, perfect simplicity. A life among the trees by the river.

"How are you feeling, man?" he asks me.

"Great," I tell him, and it is purely the truth. Doves clatter up out of a bare tree and turn at the same instant, transforming themselves from steel to silver in the snow-blown light. I know at that moment that the drug is working. Everything before me has become suddenly, radiantly itself. How could Carlton have known this was about to happen? "Oh," I whisper. His hand settles on my shoulder.

"Stay loose, Frisco," he says. "There's not a thing in this pretty world to be afraid of. I'm here."

I am not afraid. I am astonished. I had not realized until this moment how real everything is. A twig lies on the marble at my feet, bearing a cluster of hard brown berries. The broken-off end is raw, white, fleshy. Trees are alive.

"I'm here," Carlton says again, and he is.

Hours later, we are sprawled on the sofa in front of the television, ordinary as Wally and the Beav. Our mother makes dinner in the kitchen. A pot lid clangs. We are undercover agents. I am trying to conceal my amazement.

Our father is building a grandfather clock from a kit. He wants to have something to leave us, something for us to pass along. We can hear him in the basement, sawing and pounding. I know what is laid out on his sawhorses— a long raw wooden box, onto which he glues fancy moldings. A single pearl of sweat meanders down his forehead as he works. Tonight I have discovered my ability to see every room of the house at once, to know every single thing that goes on. A mouse nibbles inside the wall. Electrical wires curl behind the plaster, hidden and patient as snakes.

"Shhh," I say to Carlton, who has not said anything. He is watching television through his splayed fingers. Gunshots ping. Bullets raise chalk dust on a concrete wall. I have no idea what we are watching.

"Boys?" our mother calls from the kitchen. I can, with my new ears, hear her slap hamburgers into patties. "Set the table like good citizens," she calls.

"Okay, Ma," Carlton replies, in a gorgeous imitation of normality. Our father hammers in the basement. I can feel Carlton's heart ticking. He pats my hand, to assure me that everything's perfect.

We set the table, spoon fork knife, paper napkins triangled to one side. We know the moves cold. After we are done I pause to notice the dining-room wallpaper: a golden farm, backed by mountains. Cows graze, autumn trees cast golden shade. This scene repeats itself three times, on three walls.

"Zap," Carlton whispers. "Zzzzzoom."

"Did we do it right?" I ask him.

"We did everything perfect, little son. How are you doing in there, anyway?" He raps lightly on my head.

"Perfect, I guess." I am staring at the wallpaper as if I were thinking of stepping into it.

"You guess. You guess? You and I are going to other planets, man. Come over here."

"Where?"

"Here. Come here." He leads me to the window. Outside, the snow skitters, nervous and silver, under streetlamps. Ranch-style houses hoard their warmth, bleed light into the gathering snow. It is a street in Cleveland. It is our street.

"You and I are going to fly, man," Carlton whispers, close to my ear. He opens the window. Snow blows in, sparking on the carpet. "Fly," he says, and we do. For a moment we strain up and out, the black night wind blowing in our faces—we raise ourselves up off the cocoa-colored deep-pile wool-and-polyester carpet by a sliver of an inch. Sweet glory. The secret of flight is this—you have to do it immediately, before your body realizes it is defying the laws. I swear it to this day.

We both know we have taken momentary leave of the earth. It does not strike either of us as remarkable, any more than does the fact that airplanes sometimes fall from the sky, or that we have always lived in these rooms and will soon leave them. We settle back down. Carlton touches my shoulder.

"You wait, Frisco," he says. "Miracles are happening. Fucking miracles."

I nod. He pulls down the window, which reseals itself with a sucking sound. Our own faces look back at us from the cold, dark glass. Behind us, our mother drops the hamburgers sizzling into the skillet. Our father bends to his work under a hooded lightbulb, preparing the long box into which he will lay clockworks, pendulum, a face. A plane drones by overhead, invisible in the clouds. I

glance nervously at Carlton. He smiles his assurance and
squeezes the back of my neck.

March. After the thaw. I am walking through the cemetery, thinking about my endless life. One of the beauties
of living in Cleveland is that any direction feels like
progress. I've memorized the map. We are by my calcula-
tions three hundred and fifty miles shy of Woodstock,
New York. On this raw new day I am walking east, to the
place where Carlton and I keep our bottle. I am going to
have an early nip, to celebrate my bright future.

When I get to our spot I hear low moans coming from
behind the tomb. I freeze, considering my choices. The
sound is a long-drawn-out agony with a whip at the end,
a final high C, something like "ooooooOw." A wolf's cry
run backward. What decides me on investigation rather
than flight is the need to make a story. In the stories my
brother likes best, people always do the foolish, risky
thing. I find I can reach decisions this way, by thinking of
myself as a character in a story told by Carlton.

I creep around the side of the monument, cautious as a
badger, pressed up close to the marble. I peer over a
cherub's girlish shoulder. What I find is Carlton on the
ground with his girlfriend, in an uncertain jumble of
clothes and bare flesh. Carlton's jacket, the one with the
embroidered eye, is draped over the stone, keeping watch.

I hunch behind the statue. I can see the girl's naked
arms, and the familiar bones of Carlton's spine. The two
of them moan together in the dry winter grass. Though I
can't make out the girl's expression, Carlton's face is
twisted and grimacing, the cords of his neck pulled tight.
I had never thought the experience might be painful. I
watch, trying to learn. I hold on to the cherub's cold
wings.

It isn't long before Carlton catches sight of me. His eyes rove briefly, ecstatically skyward, and what do they light on but his brother's small head, sticking up next to a cherub's. We lock eyes and spend a moment in mutual decision. The girl keeps on clutching at Carlton's skinny back. He decides to smile at me. He decides to wink.

I am out of there so fast I tear up divots. I dodge among the stones, jump the gully, clear the fence into the swing-set-and-picnic-table sanctity of the backyard. Something about that wink. My heart beats fast as a sparrow's.

I go into the kitchen and find our mother washing fruit. She asks what's going on. I tell her nothing is. Nothing at all.

She sighs over an apple's imperfection. The curtains sport blue teapots. Our mother works the apple with a scrub brush. She believes they come coated with poison.

"Where's Carlton?" she asks.

"Don't know," I tell her.

"Bobby?"

"Huh?"

"What exactly is going on?"

"Nothing," I say. My heart works itself up to a hummingbird's rate, more buzz than beat.

"I think something is. Will you answer a question?"

"Okay."

"Is your brother taking drugs?"

I relax a bit. It is only drugs. I know why she's asking. Lately police cars have been browsing our house like sharks. They pause, take note, glide on. Some neighborhood crackdown. Carlton is famous in these parts.

"No," I tell her.

She faces me with the brush in one hand, an apple in the other. "You wouldn't lie to me, would you?" She knows something is up. Her nerves run through this house. She can feel dust settling on the tabletops, milk starting to turn in the refrigerator.

"No," I say.

"Something's going on," she sighs. She is a small, efficient woman who looks at things as if they give off a painful light. She grew up on a farm in Wisconsin and spent her girlhood tying up bean rows, worrying over the sun and rain. She is still trying to overcome her habit of modest expectations.

I leave the kitchen, pretending sudden interest in the cat. Our mother follows, holding her brush. She means to scrub the truth out of me. I follow the cat, his erect black tail and pink anus.

"Don't walk away when I'm talking to you," our mother says.

I keep walking, to see how far I'll get, calling, "Kittykittykitty." In the front hall, our father's homemade clock chimes the half hour. I make for the clock. I get as far as the rubber plant before she collars me.

"I told you not to walk away," she says, and cuffs me a good one with the brush. She catches me on the ear and sets it ringing. The cat is out of there quick as a quarter note.

I stand for a minute, to let her know I've received the message. Then I resume walking. She hits me again, this time on the back of the head, hard enough to make me see colors. "Will you *stop*?" she screams. Still, I keep walking. Our house runs west to east. With every step I get closer to Yasgur's farm.

Carlton comes home whistling. Our mother treats him like a guest who's overstayed. He doesn't care. He is lost in optimism. He pats her cheek and calls her "Professor." He treats her as if she were harmless, and so she is.

She never hits Carlton. She suffers him the way farm girls suffer a thieving crow, with a grudge so old and endless it borders on reverence. She gives him a scrubbed apple, and tells him what she'll do if he tracks mud on the carpet.

I am waiting in our room. He brings the smell of the cemetery with him, its old snow and wet pine needles. He rolls his eyes at me, takes a crunch of his apple. "What's happening, Frisco?" he says.

I have arranged myself loosely on my bed, trying to pull a Dylan riff out of my harmonica. I have always figured I can bluff my way into wisdom. I offer Carlton a dignified nod.

He drops onto his own bed. I can see a crushed crocus, the first of the year, stuck to the black rubber sole of his boot.

"Well, Frisco," he says. "Today you are a man."

I nod again. Is that all there is to it?

"*Yow*," Carlton says. He laughs, pleased with himself and the world. "That was so perfect."

I pick out what I can of "Blowin' in the Wind."

Carlton says, "Man, when I saw you out there spying on us I thought to myself, *yes*. Now *I'm* really here. You know what I'm saying?" He waves his apple core.

"Uh-huh," I say.

"Frisco, that was the first time her and I ever did it. I mean, we'd talked. But when we finally got down to it, there you were. My brother. Like you *knew*."

I nod, and this time for real. What happened was an adventure we had together. All right. The story is beginning to make sense.

"Aw, Frisco," Carlton says. "I'm gonna find you a girl, too. You're nine. You been a virgin too long."

"Really?" I say.

"*Man*. We'll find you a woman from the sixth grade,

somebody with a little experience. We'll get stoned and all make out under the trees in the boneyard. I want to be present at your deflowering, man. You're gonna need a brother there."

I am about to ask, as casually as I can manage, about the relationship between love and bodily pain, when our mother's voice cuts into the room. "You did it," she screams. "You tracked mud all over the rug."

A family entanglement follows. Our mother brings our father, who comes and stands in the doorway with her, taking in evidence. He is a formerly handsome man. His face has been worn down by too much patience. He has lately taken up some sporty touches—a goatee, a pair of calfskin boots.

Our mother points out the trail of muddy half-moons that lead from the door to Carlton's bed. Dangling over the foot of the bed are the culprits themselves, voluptuously muddy, with Carlton's criminal feet still in them.

"You see?" she says. "You see what he thinks of me?"

Our father, a reasonable man, suggests that Carlton clean it up. Our mother finds that too small a gesture. She wants Carlton not to have done it in the first place. "I don't ask for much," she says. "I don't ask where he goes. I don't ask why the police are suddenly so interested in our house. I ask that he not track mud all over the floor. That's all." She squints in the glare of her own outrage.

"Better clean it right up," our father says to Carlton.

"And that's it?" our mother says. "He cleans up the mess, and all's forgiven?"

"Well, what do you want him to do? Lick it up?"

"I want some consideration," she says, turning helplessly to me. "That's what I want."

I shrug, at a loss. I sympathize with our mother, but am not on her team.

"All right," she says. "I just won't bother cleaning the

house anymore. I'll let you men handle it. I'll sit and watch television and throw my candy wrappers on the floor."

She starts out, cutting the air like a blade. On her way she picks up a jar of pencils, looks at it, and tosses the pencils on the floor. They fall like fortune-telling sticks, in pairs and crisscrosses.

Our father goes after her, calling her name. Her name is Isabel. We can hear them making their way across the house, our father calling, "Isabel, Isabel, Isabel," while our mother, pleased with the way the pencils had looked, dumps more things onto the floor.

"I hope she doesn't break the TV," I say.

"She'll do what she needs to do," Carlton tells me.

"I hate her," I say. I am not certain about that. I want to test the sound of it, to see if it's true.

"She's got more balls than any of us, Frisco," he says. "Better watch what you say about her."

I keep quiet. Soon I get up and start gathering pencils, because I prefer that to lying around trying to follow the shifting lines of allegiance. Carlton goes for a sponge and starts in on the mud.

"You get shit on the carpet, you clean it up," he says. "Simple."

The time for all my questions about love has passed, and I am not so unhip as to force a subject. I know it will come up again. I make a neat bouquet of pencils. Our mother rages through the house.

Later, after she has thrown enough and we three have picked it all up, I lie on my bed thinking things over. Carlton is on the phone to his girlfriend, talking low. Our mother, becalmed but still dangerous, cooks dinner. She sings as she cooks, some slow forties number that must have been all over the jukes when her first husband's plane went down in the Pacific. Our father plays his clarinet in the basement. That is where he goes to practice, down among his woodworking tools, the neatly hung hammers and awls that throw oversized shadows in the light of the single bulb. If I put my ear to the floor I can hear him, pulling a long low tomcat moan out of that horn. There is some strange comfort in pressing my ear to the carpet and hearing our father's music leaking up through the floorboards. Lying down, with my ear to the floor, I join in on my harmonica.

That spring our parents have a party to celebrate the sun's return. It has been a long, bitter winter and now the first wild daisies are poking up on the lawns and among the graves.

Our parents' parties are mannerly affairs. Their friends, schoolteachers all, bring wine jugs and guitars. They are Ohio hip. Though they hold jobs and meet mortgages, they think of themselves as independent spirits on a spying mission. They have agreed to impersonate teachers until they write their novels, finish their dissertations, or just save up enough money to set themselves free.

Carlton and I are the lackeys. We take coats, fetch drinks. We have done this at every party since we were small, trading on our precocity, doing a brother act. We know the moves. A big, lipsticked woman who has devoted her maidenhood to ninth-grade math calls me Mr. Right. An assistant vice principal in a Russian fur hat asks us both whether we expect to vote Democratic or Socialist. By sneaking sips I manage to get myself semi-crocked.

The reliability of the evening is derailed halfway through, however, by a half dozen of Carlton's friends. They rap on the door and I go for it, anxious as a carnival sharp to see who will step up next and swallow the illusion that I'm a kindly, sober nine-year-old child. I'm expecting callow adults and who do I find but a pack of young outlaws, big-booted and wild-haired. Carlton's girlfriend stands in front, in an outfit made up almost entirely of fringe.

"Hi, Bobby," she says confidently. She comes from New York, and is more than just locally smart.

"Hi," I say. I let them all in despite a retrograde urge to lock the door and phone the police. Three are girls, four boys. They pass me in a cloud of dope smoke and sly-eyed greeting.

What they do is invade the party. Carlton is standing on the far side of the rumpus room, picking the next album, and his girl cuts straight through the crowd to his side. She has the bones and the loose, liquid moves some people consider beautiful. She walks through that room as if she'd been sent to teach the whole party a lesson.

Carlton's face tips me off that this was planned. Our mother demands to know what's going on here. She is wearing a long dark-red dress that doesn't interfere with her shoulders. When she dresses up you can see what it is about her, or what it was. She is responsible for Carlton's beauty. I have our father's face.

Carlton does some quick talking. Though it's against our mother's better judgment, the invaders are suffered to stay. One of them, an Eddie Haskell for all his leather and hair, tells her she is looking good. She is willing to hear it.

So the outlaws, house-sanctioned, start to mingle. I work my way over to Carlton's side, the side unoccupied by his girlfriend. I would like to say something ironic and wised-up, something that will band Carlton and me against every other person in the room. I can feel the shape of the comment I have in mind but, being a tipsy nine-year-old, can't get my mouth around it. What I say is, "Shit, man."

Carlton's girl laughs at me. She considers it amusing

that a little boy says "shit." I would like to tell her what I have figured out about her, but I am nine, and three-quarters gone on Tom Collinses. Even sober, I can only imagine a sharp-tongued wit.

"Hang on, Frisco," Carlton tells me. "This could turn into a real party."

I can see by the light in his eyes what is going down. He has arranged a blind date between our parents' friends and his own. It's a Woodstock move—he is plotting a future in which young and old have business together. I agree to hang on, and go to the kitchen, hoping to sneak a few knocks of gin.

There I find our father leaning up against the refrigerator. A line of butterfly-shaped magnets hovers around his head. "Are you enjoying this party?" he asks, touching his goatee. He is still getting used to being a man with a beard.

"Uh-huh."

"I am, too," he says sadly. He never meant to be a high school music teacher. The money question caught up with him.

"What do you think of this music?" he asks. Carlton has put the Stones on the turntable. Mick Jagger sings "19th Nervous Breakdown." Our father gestures in an openhanded way that takes in the room, the party, the whole house—everything the music touches.

"I like it," I say.

"So do I." He stirs his drink with his finger, and sucks on the finger.

"I *love* it," I say, too loud. Something about our father leads me to raise my voice. I want to grab handfuls of music out of the air and stuff them into my mouth.

"I'm not sure I could say I love it," he says. "I'm not sure if I could say that, no. I would say I'm friendly to its

intentions. I would say that if this is the direction music is
going in, I won't stand in its way."

"Uh-huh," I say. I am already anxious to get back to
the party, but don't want to hurt his feelings. If he senses
he's being avoided he can fall into fits of apology more
terrifying than our mother's rages.

"I think I may have been too rigid with my students,"
our father says. "Maybe over the summer you boys could
teach me a few things about the music people are listening to these days."

"Sure," I say, loudly. We spend a minute waiting for
the next thing to say.

"You boys are happy, aren't you?" he asks. "Are you
enjoying this party?"

"We're having a great time," I say.

"I thought you were. I am, too."

I have by this time gotten myself to within jumping
distance of the door. I call out, "Well, good-bye," and
dive back into the party.

Something has happened in my small absence. The
party has started to roll. Call it an accident of history and
the weather. Carlton's friends are on decent behavior, and
our parents' friends have decided to give up some of their
wine-and-folk-song propriety to see what they can learn.
Carlton is dancing with a vice principal's wife. Carlton's
friend Frank, with his ancient-child face and IQ in the
low sixties, dances with our mother. I see that our father
has followed me out of the kitchen. He positions himself
at the party's edge; I jump into its center. I invite the
fuchsia-lipped math teacher to dance. She is only too
happy. She is big and graceful as a parade float, and I
steer her effortlessly out into the middle of everything. My
mother, who is known around school for Sicilian discipline, dances freely, which is news to everybody. There is
no getting around her beauty.

The night rises higher and higher. A wildness sets in. Carlton throws new music on the turntable—Janis Joplin, the Doors, the Dead. The future shines for everyone, rich with the possibility of more nights exactly like this. Even our father is pressed into dancing, which he does like a flightless bird, all flapping arms and potbelly. Still, he dances. Our mother has a kiss for him.

Finally I nod out on the sofa, blissful under the drinks. I am dreaming of flight when our mother comes and touches my shoulder. I smile up into her flushed, smiling face.

"It's hours past your bedtime," she says, all velvet motherliness. I nod. I can't dispute the fact.

She keeps on nudging my shoulder. I am a moment or two apprehending the fact that she actually wants me to leave the party and go to bed. "No," I tell her.

"Yes," she smiles.

"No," I say cordially, experimentally. This new mother can dance, and flirt. Who knows what else she might allow?

"Yes." The velvet motherliness leaves her voice. She means business, business of the usual kind. I get myself out of there, and no excuses this time. I am exactly nine and running from my bedtime as I'd run from death.

I run to Carlton for protection. He is laughing with his girl, a sweaty question mark of hair plastered to his forehead. I plow into him so hard he nearly goes over.

"Whoa, Frisco," he says. He takes me up under the arms and swings me a half-turn. Our mother plucks me out of his hands and sets me down, with a good farm-style hold on the back of my neck.

"Say good night, Bobby," she says. She adds, for the benefit of Carlton's girl, "He should have been in bed before this party started."

"*No,*" I holler. I try to twist loose, but our mother has a grip that could crack walnuts.

Carlton's girl tosses her hair and says, "Good night, baby." She smiles a victor's smile. She smooths the stray hair off Carlton's forehead.

"*No,*" I scream again. Something about the way she touches his hair. Our mother calls our father, who comes and scoops me up and starts out of the room with me, holding me like the live bomb I am. Before I go I lock eyes with Carlton. He shrugs and says, "Night, man." Our father hustles me out. I do not take it bravely. I leave flailing, too furious to cry, dribbling a slimy thread of horrible-child's spittle.

Later I lie alone on my narrow bed, feeling the music hum in the coiled springs. Life is cracking open right there in our house. People are changing. By tomorrow, no one will be quite the same. How can they let me miss it? I dream up revenge against our parents, and worse for Carlton. He is the one who could have saved me. He could have banded with me against them. What I can't forgive is his shrug, his mild-eyed "Night, man." He has joined the adults. He has made himself bigger, and taken size from me. As the Doors thump "Strange Days," I hope something awful happens to him. I say so to myself.

Around midnight, dim-witted Frank announces he has seen a flying saucer hovering over the backyard. I can hear his deep, excited voice all the way in my room. He says it's like a blinking, luminous cloud. I hear half the party struggling out through the sliding glass door in a disorganized, whooping knot. By that time everyone is so delirious a flying saucer would be just what was expected. That much celebration would logically attract an answering happiness from across the stars.

I get out of bed and sneak down the hall. I will not miss alien visitors for anyone, not even at the cost of our mother's wrath or our father's disappointment. I stop at the end of the hallway, though, embarrassed to be in pajamas. If there really are aliens, they will think I'm the lowest member of the house. While I hesitate over whether to go back to my room to change, people start coming back inside, talking about a trick of the mist and an airplane. People resume their dancing.

Carlton must have jumped the back fence. He must have wanted to be there alone, singular, in case they decided to take somebody with them. A few nights later I will go out and stand where he would have been standing. On the far side of the gully, now a river swollen with melted snow, the cemetery will gleam like a lost city. The moon will be full. I will hang around just as Carlton must have, hypnotized by the silver light on the stones, the white angel raising her arms up across the river.

According to our parents the mystery is why he ran back to the house full tilt. Something in the graveyard must have scared him, he may have needed to break its spell, but I think it's more likely that when he came back to himself he just couldn't wait to get back to the music and the people, the noisy disorder of continuing life.

Somebody has shut the sliding glass door. Carlton's girlfriend looks lazily out, touching base with her own reflection. I look, too. Carlton is running toward the house. I hesitate. Then I figure he can bump his nose. It will be a good joke on him. I let him keep coming. His girlfriend sees him through her own reflection, starts to scream a warning just as Carlton hits the glass.

It is an explosion. Triangles of glass fly brightly through the room. I think for him it must be more surprising than painful, like hitting water from a great height. He stands blinking for a moment. The whole party stops, stares, getting its bearings. Bob Dylan sings "Just Like a Woman." Carlton reaches up curiously to

take out the shard of glass that is stuck in his neck, and
that is when the blood starts. It shoots out of him. Our
mother screams. Carlton steps forward into his girlfriend's arms and the two of them fall together. Our
mother throws herself down on top of him and the girl.
People shout their accident wisdom. Don't lift him. Call
an ambulance. I watch from the hallway. Carlton's blood
spurts, soaking into the carpet, spattering people's
clothes. Our mother and father both try to plug the
wound with their hands, but the blood just shoots between their fingers. Carlton looks more puzzled than anything, as if he can't quite follow this turn of events. "It's
all right," our father tells him, trying to stop the blood.
"It's all right, just don't move, it's all right." Carlton nods,
and holds our father's hand. His eyes take on an astonished light. Our mother screams, "Is anybody *doing* anything?" What comes out of Carlton grows darker, almost
black. I watch. Our father tries to get a hold on Carlton's
neck while Carlton keeps trying to take his hand. Our
mother's hair is matted with blood. It runs down her face.
Carlton's girl holds him to her breasts, touches his hair,
whispers in his ear.

He is gone by the time the ambulance gets there. You
can see the life drain out of him. When his face goes slack
our mother wails. A part of her flies wailing through the
house, where it will wail and rage forever. I feel our
mother pass through me on her way out. She covers Carlton's body with her own.

He is buried in the cemetery out back. Years have passed—
we are living in the future, and it's turned out differently
from what we'd planned. Our mother has established her
life of separateness behind the guest-room door. Our
father mutters his greetings to the door as he passes.

One April night, almost a year to the day after Carlton's accident, I hear cautious footsteps shuffling across the living-room floor after midnight. I run out eagerly, thinking of ghosts, but find only our father in moth-colored pajamas. He looks unsteadily at the dark air in front of him.

"Hi, Dad," I say from the doorway.

He looks in my direction. "Yes?"

"It's me. Bobby."

"Oh, Bobby," he says. "What are you doing up, young man?"

"Nothing," I tell him. "Dad?"

"Yes, son."

"Maybe you better come back to bed. Okay?"

"Maybe I had," he says. "I just came out here for a drink of water, but I seem to have gotten turned around in the darkness. Yes, maybe I better had."

I take his hand and lead him down the hall to his room. The grandfather clock chimes the quarter hour.

"Sorry," our father says.

I get him into bed. "There," I say. "Okay?"

"Perfect. Could not be better."

"Okay. Good night."

"Good night. Bobby?"

"Uh-huh?"

"Why don't you stay a minute?" he says. "We could have ourselves a talk, you and me. How would that be?"

"Okay," I say. I sit on the edge of his mattress. His bedside clock ticks off the minutes.

I can hear the low rasp of his breathing. Around our house, the Ohio night chirps and buzzes. The small gray finger of Carlton's stone pokes up among the others, within sight of the angel's blank white eyes. Above us, airplanes and satellites sparkle. People are flying even now toward New York or California, to take up lives of risk and invention.

I stay until our father has worked his way into a muttering sleep.

Carlton's girlfriend moved to Denver with her family a month before. I never learned what it was she'd whispered to him. Though she'd kept her head admirably during the accident, she lost her head afterward. She cried so hard at the funeral that she had to be taken away by her mother—an older, redder-haired version of her. She started seeing a psychiatrist three times a week. Everyone, including my parents, talked about how hard it was for her, to have held a dying boy in her arms at that age. I'm grateful to her for holding my brother while he died, but I never once heard her mention the fact that though she had been through something terrible, at least she was still alive and going places. At least she had protected herself by trying to warn him. I can appreciate the intricacies of her pain. But as long as she was in Cleveland, I could never look her straight in the face. I couldn't talk about the wounds she suffered. I can't even write her name.

SATAN

Brad Gooch

*E*ddie is a photographer. He is standing in his divided-up-into-rooms loft in a building way west overlooking the sheet-metal Hudson River on a glaring July weekend afternoon.

He has blue eyes with dilated black centers, the centers like cups of coffee resting on light blue saucers. Black wave hair, pale lips, thin bony fingers like ET's fingers a bit. Dressed right now in an eerie fashion: black leather jacket with ridged shoulders that French, not American, motorcyclists wear, stiff blue jeans, dirty, dirty black boots with rounded, not pointed, toes, scuffed into an erased chalky blackboard look. He is a spook today. Black half-moons under both loonglow eyes.

EDDIE: (on phone) It's me. . . . I want you to go to the corner of Madison and 42nd in your soaked trousers and stand there. . . . I want to find out what frightens you and I want to pursue that. . . . There's this guy who comes and sees me right after he sees his shrink. He wants to be deprogrammed and undo all the work he just did. . . . Hail Satan.

When he hangs up the phone he stands for a few minutes next to a nineteenth-century black marble bust of Mephistopheles, the bust's head swerving down into a straight point, the point at the end of Mephistopheles's black (though imagination turns it red) beard, the beard that matches the carved goatee.

He then flicks on the air conditioner. To cool the swampy feeling of being stuck inside his leather jacket. And yet not wanting to take it off. The canned refrigerator air starts to swirl around, like breath exhaled visibly in cold weather.

A loud bzzzzz through an intercom, sounding like a train siren with a bad nasal cold. It's Eddie's assistant, Thom. Eddie likes to work on developing his photographs on Sundays in the summer when the streets are empty and the skies look hot to the touch, like a copper skillet, heated, but still scoured clean, no butter or eggs dropped in yet.

Eddie's assistant makes it up the few flights of splintering wood stairs, broken like the bones of a back cracked in an accident. He pushes through the already opened door. Is black, a few inches over 6 feet, early twenties, broad shoulders, smooth skin, tough boxy face with ungrazed cheeks, a sweet Mike Tyson mien. Is wearing a gray work shirt, black shorts with red Marine logo, white socks pulled up with yellow stripes tingling at the top, cheap light brown suede workboots above ankles, not laced all the way up.

Eddie and Thom lived together last year. Thom was in the Navy. Met Eddie at a bar called Keller's mostly for black men on West Street in the West Village located under the hotel converted into a hospice for AIDS sufferers. (The hospice where every room is a crucifixion scene.) After living for a while on a narrow red rubber mat on the floor in Eddie's room (Eddie has a bed with four gold posts) he went forever AWOL, moved in. His trial is still pending. Then the heat was turned down on the stove of their passion, and Eddie set Thom up in a residence hotel nearby on Washington Street (around the corner from the meat district where cow carcasses hang bloodily all day long looking like so many butchered animals in Soutine paintings), and hired him as his assistant.

The two don't speak on entrance. Instead Thom wheels through the rooms of the loft. Careens. Roves. Walks jauntily. Looking for some scent of anything. Through the living room with its short black candles burning, wounds eating at themselves, bruises deepening from black into purple-blue. Past the bedroom with its fancy Venetian framed paintings of chipped buildings and scattered gondolas. The empty kitchen. The empty bathroom. The busy vista of the photographing room where pictures are stacked against walls. Cocaine in snuff boxes. The room's meditative airiness contributed to by big front windows and by the vibrations of so much work always always going on. Eddie is a spider.

Thom twinges, but doesn't admit it to himself, as he sees a new photograph, big, leaning against a sun-starched white plaster wall. It's platinum-printed, picking up diminutive nuances of gray, white, silver, black. A black-and-white rainbow. Polished grains of photons. It shows a black man's back and ass, shot from behind, as he is sticking his head down into a gleaming white toilet, as he is perched kneeling somehow on its horseshoe of a seat.

THOM: (booming-voiced, as Eddie walks in) Where'd you get the model?

EDDIE: (appraising Thom for the first time today) Does it bother you?

THOM: (his emotions are heavy pebbles) No.

EDDIE: (always a lightning rod) You're screaming inside.

THOM: How'd you get so mean? You sick dildo.

EDDIE: (sitting down grandly in a kind of electrocution chair, metal, picked up at a novelty antique store in East Hampton) I want you to take the pictures from in there (pointing at darkroom) and line them up out here.

THOM: (low laughs) A lineup.

While Thom is lugging out the oversized prints, each a different elegant snapshot, Eddie is walking at acute angles, but forward on the tips of his toes almost, across and back across the wide shooting room. He stops at one tiny pewter bowl to sniff up some white cocaine powder. Makes those whisking sounds (as of a broom across a wood floor). He can't find a comfortable spot. He is nonstop: thinking, feeling, and walking.

EDDIE: (to Thom) Is it bad? Or is it good?

THOM: (his back bent over a cloud-with-a-silver-lining print) The blow?

EDDIE: (down) No. The way I live.

THOM: It's bad. You're gonna kill yourself.

EDDIE: (reverts to stylized coy) That could be all right.

For what seems like five seconds, Eddie actually rests, leans in front of a window, his palms set into the windowsill, his hand bones as fragile as birds' bones seen through their translucent wings. Then he starts up again.

Reviewing the exhibited photos in a line. They are mostly faces of men and women, as pale as porcelain, as statuary in appearance as the toilet in the adjoining shot, but wearing (at least the tops of) evening dresses and evening suits. These human toilets are celebrities. While they last.

EDDIE: (to Thom) Let's go to bed.
THOM: (offended at the role change) We haven't done that in six months. I can't do it.
EDDIE: (limberly pretzeling down cross-legged on the floor in front of Thom and grabbing on to his exposed, thick, legs) I want to now.
THOM: (sincere) Why can't you ever let anybody get any peace?

Eddie likes that. He laughs a cyclonic laugh. Mischievous. And hugs even harder at the tree trunks of legs.

EDDIE: (reversed, his public never seeing this) Pleeease.
THOM: (getting into it, disentangles, leans back against wall with arms folded) Only if you teach me something first. That turns me on. You know that.
EDDIE: (crumpled down on the floor) That's a waste of time.
THOM: For you maybe. But I'm looking for a mentor.
EDDIE: (plea-bargaining) I'll read you one paragraph of Melville. And then you give me what I want.
THOM: What you want nobody can give you.

Eddie glares at him. He's afraid that Thom is going to start his fundamentalist religious rap and ruin everything. So he doesn't say anything else. Scuffs off to find the book.

Thom is edged up against the window, sort of looking out sideways, feeling vaguely that he is in a black box in the middle of a yellow world. Like the tophat of a magician

covered over with a black wonder-working handkerchief.
Thom isn't acclimated enough to feel that it's the frustra-
tion of not spending a weekend at the beach. That's the
way people in the city explain away the pain of the box. His
life in Arkansas, high school crimes, Navy escape, make
him more comfortable in the box. But not completely.

Eddie has a crystal radio for a mind. He wants to get so
used to life in the box that it is more of a release to him
than the illusion of having escaped from the box.

Eddie once said to Rosalina, who will stop by later:
"Only a jack-in-the-box clown pops out of the box."

EDDIE: (walking back in the room) Can't find the book.
THOM: (royally) Then make it up.
EDDIE: (liltingly) If you let me tie a cord around your
    neck and lead you into the bedroom while I recite
    to you.
THOM: (not yet knowing what Eddie means) Deal.

Eddie is now awake again. He stops by an urn and
straws some cocaine into his nostril. Then he scrapes into
his bedroom and returns with a red paisley silk tie that he
ties around Thom's neck as a device to pull him with.

THOM: I need a cigarette.

Pause.
Thom takes a white cigarette from a nearby red pack.
Sticks the stick in his mouth. Feels the smoke making a
cloud in his lungs. Feels the pulsing start in his lower
arms. The worries sprouting in his stomach like lime-
green weeds, ugly and beautiful at the same time. He
waits until he's down to the tan filter. When finished, he
stubs it under his workboot.

EDDIE: Ready?

Thom nods his head down, as if placing it on a block to be axed off, guillotined. Eddie starts leading him by pulling, talking all the while.

EDDIE: (barking) Put your hands in your pockets.

Thom puts his hands in his tight front shorts' (cutoffs', actually) pockets.

EDDIE: (tugging while walking backward, facing Thom) I came out of New Jersey. . . . I wanted to have my own band. . . . I wore a black leather jacket, like this, but with a red bandanna around my neck, and I played a guitar, I played noise. . . . Then I met Blouse. She was from New Jersey too. She was the real thing. When she got up and sang poems at CBGB's there was devils in the house, rising out of the smoke of our cigarettes, making us want blow-jobs, I mean making us want to fuck up the order. . . . You know when people talk about devil worship, they're corny suburban trolls, like swingers in those clubs . . . but with her you didn't know if she was good or evil, she was a devil and an angel at the same time, that's what it's really like. . . . You following me? . . . So I decided to become a pho-tographer. . . . And I went to the Mineshaft a lot, and I wore chains and whips and colored hankies out my back left pocket. . . . I went down the beat-up tunnel where you beat up everyone you meet until you get beat up yourself by a nameless thug and you're left for dead. . . . I used to bring guys home and photograph their scenes. . . . We're here.

Eddie is carried away. It's partly the drugs. He has been practically hopping back a step at a time. Like some

surreal mascot for some surreal high school band. A mar-
tinet. He is now sitting on his bed with Thom standing in
front of him, hands in pockets, halter around tree-stump
neck (18-inch). Thom has a big grin pasted over his face
like a poster. It's a close moment.

THOM: I like you like this, man.
EDDIE: Like me more.
THOM: Can you take it?
EDDIE: I can.

It's like this. What goes around comes around. And then
all of a sudden there's a release, a turn into the great verti-
cality. A roller coaster chugs one last right angle and then
whoosh, it's all downhill. The parishioners face forward to
a mysterious point beyond the checkpoint of the old altar.

THOM: (standing there, all emotional) I feel like when
    you're talking to your friends that I can't talk in. I
    never read any of the books. They know that I
    don't know.
EDDIE: (goosefleshed by this remark) Then don't say a
    word ever again. Live in silence. All shut up.
THOM: (laughing) That'll be the day.
EDDIE: Call me boss.
THOM: (hating to have those two wires crossed) No . . .
    boss.

Eddie now pulls Thom down on top of him on the bed.
When the two fit they both feel a healing pressure, below
from above, and above from below. Eddie undoes Thom's
shorts' zipper and starts to slide them down. Thom takes
the lead and finishes the job. Stands up and strips totally in
the boudoir with its unlikely hanging gold censers and red
velvet drapes. Eddie doesn't undress, leaves on even the

jacket, but does release his spring from its box. Draws Thom back down. Turns him over to stick his latex-covered penis deep in toward Eddie's bowels, the bowl of his bowels. It's the pestle stirring the mortar. Like in the old days when prescription drugs and salves were actually made by hand, like a baker pounding the dough for a pie.

While Eddie is riding Thom he feels that he is on a fling, a crippled god riding Pegasus, the winged horse. Eddie was a pervert early. One of those New Jersey kids who spent his time behind the venetian blinds looking out at the neighborhood go by. Unhealthy. Now he has found power in that old defeat. He is the artist. An artist and a devil are the same. Getting even, hanging chandeliers in Hell to simulate, or surpass, in a sulky way, the natural stimulating light of the sun and the stars.

Thom is oblivious of those old classroom cosmologies. He is feeling the pleasure from giving pleasure. The scraping of the mixing stick in his bowl is not relaxing exactly. It hurts. But his heart is positively crimson from the return to, and of, Eddie. He has been aching and not even knowing it. And now the relief of the ache makes him cry.

It's true. Later, when Eddie is lying back on his back, sticky inside the jacket, looking up at the gilded hump ceiling, its plaster hanging like sliced skin, he hears and feels Thom next to him, face in the pillow, sobbing. Eddie feels like he just won a point, a point in a game of self-satisfaction. Thom feels a release of tears that moisten his porous face. His stubble is moss. And then finally he slows down, and stops.

Eddie rolls over on his side. The copy of Melville is down on the floor by the bed. He had been reading before sleeping last night. The spine is breaking as it's open, pages down. Eddie picks up and reads out loud from "Benito Cereno" while Thom heaves without moving, facedown, spine stiff.

EDDIE: (voice so studiedly hollow it's resonant) "Presently, while standing with his host, looking forward upon the decks below, he was struck by one of those instances of insubordination previously alluded to. Three black boys, with two Spanish boys, were sitting together on the hatches, scraping a rude wooden platter, in which some scanty mess had recently been cooked. Suddenly, one of the black boys, enraged at a word dropped by one of his white companions, seized the knife, and, though called to forebear by one of the oakum-pickers, struck the lad over the head, inflicting a gash from which blood flowed. In amazement, Captain Delano inquired what this meant. To which the pale Don Benito dully muttered, that it was merely the sport of the lad. . . ."

Just as Thom is beginning to hear bees buzzing in his head, a signal of sleep coming on, and as Eddie is slipping increasingly into an arch British narrating tone, like the narrator of a pirate movie, the shrill bzzzz sounds off again.

EDDIE: (slamming hard-backed book shut) Fuckin' A.
THOM: (muffled by pillow) Who's that?
EDDIE: Rosalina.

Thom feels his stomach contract. He makes a noise between a groan and a whine. Eddie slaps him on one rising cheek of his behind.

EDDIE: Get dressed. Or don't get dressed.
THOM: Maybe I won't. To punish her.
EDDIE: Or turn her on.

Rosalina is an Italian woman from Milan married to a banker from Idaho. They live in the residential towers of the Museum of Modern Art. She loves to spend money on art. Eddie is one of her favorites. (Performing monkeys used to wear red velvet uniforms with fezes and they banged cymbals together.)

She's wearing a black oversized shirt flowing out over black tights and black flats. Her earrings are heavy pendulums of light lead. Her face creased and blackened by the sun. Her nails as dazzlingly light blue as the painted grotto skies of a chapel in New Mexico. New Mexico, where she went once to visit the artist Georgia O'Keeffe as part of a tour organized for the trustees of a cultural center. Her hair is black with gray streaks. She drinks water to stay thin. Is in her early forties.

Rosalina and Eddie sit and talk in the main room, he on a black beat-up leather couch, she on a chrome-leather director's chair. Next to the statue of the Cyrano de Bergerac Satan.

EDDIE: (pulling air through his teeth during pauses, legs crossed, face half-lit like the moon, by a beaded Tiffany lamp on the gray metal filing cabinet next to the couch) Oscar came down out of the plane and threw his arms around me.

ROSALINA: That's not the way he treated me. He found me in the swimming pool. I mean he found me and fingered me in the swimming pool.

EDDIE: You're such a tramp. How does your husband keep from hiring a hit man to blow you off?

ROSALINA: (giggling) Cattivo ragazzo.

EDDIE: I want to take your picture as Cleopatra under the shin of a Mark Anthony.

ROSALINA: (whining, pleading) Why don't you stay some weekend with us? In the country?

Meanwhile Thom is stalking again about the room, sitting and standing up, in shorts, no shoes, no shirt. Every

time they speak he feels that he is a garbage bag into
which another wad of paper or empty bottle has just been
stuffed, so that he can't hold anymore, can't breathe.

THOM: (to Eddie) I want to work.
ROSALINA: (looking at a far speck of a fly on an orchid-
painted wall) I'm sure that's the last thing Eddie
would discourage you from. (looks to Thom for his
reaction)

So Thom stands up and walks over to Rosalina's chair
and bends over from the waist to kiss her on her face. As
he does, she automatically reaches for his thighs and
grabs them. Her heart feels like she drank too many cups
of coffee.

ROSALINA: (innocently) What do you want from me?
THOM: I want you to take my picture.
ROSALINA: (standing up stiffly, squeezing by him, angrily walking to a window that looks out on a kind
of metal chimney on the wall of the next building)
Eddie takes the pictures. I admire them.
EDDIE: (nodding with head for Thom to get out, go to the
next room, while talking smoothly to Rosalina's back
as if not so directing) Did you ever see drawings
done by grade school kids in New York? They draw
buildings next to each other with lots of windows. At
least the happy ones. But no trees. No lawns. None of
the clichés of suburban kids' drawings.
ROSALINA: (turning around as if just asked to dance at
an old-fashioned prom) How far out.

Thom by now is standing in the rear photographing
room. He strips out of his shorts so he is standing there as
naked as a persimmon tree. He can't smell the fruity as-

tringent bitter smell that is stinking up the air around him, that is most powerful in and around his armpits, in which hair as bushy as the hair on his head has sponged up the acrid sweat.

Thom fusses for a bit with a Hasselblad camera on its tripod, and with a light on a pole. He makes some connections. Then stands back there, having set the timer, and lets the camera automatically take his picture. It is flashing and flashing. He is against the light and is in the light. The image that is registering on the negatives (unseen by him) is of a threatening ghost come to bring the living nobodies to true feeling and beingness in the land of the dead.

Thom is savoring some attention for a change. He has usurped Eddie's job. He is both the flasher (photographer) and the flasher (exhibitionist).

Meanwhile Eddie and Rosalina are nattering in the next room. They don't know about Thom's self-portraits. She is showing her teeth and talking about her new old Julian Schnabel painting. Eddie is teasing her with the big dick of his comments.

Suddenly the phone rings. It's one of Eddie's anonymous sex calls. He's part of a network. It's a 900 number. They have in common devil worship, or at least the sexual fantasy in their heads of devil worship. And they get each other off by reciting their tape loops to one another all day long, whenever a call is made.

Eddie takes the call in front of Rosalina, no sweat.

EDDIE: (talking now on the phone, standing up) We have a group of guys gets together. . . . You're supposed to recite the Latin Mass backwards. But most of these guys couldn't say their names backwards. So they say anything that comes into their heads. Dirty words. Curses. Spanish. Anything. . . . I know one guy who likes to have Satan worshiped through the medium of his own phallus. . . . You want me to give him your number?

Rosalina is sitting back in her chair. At first she is trying to keep a pleasant something on her face. But as the talk continues she feels an alarm going off all through. She tries not to feel the alarm. She's used to being a personality, not a soul.

ROSALINA: (to Eddie, who's ignoring her, still talking in a voice only half his own, half that of a, a Bruce Springsteen, very New Jersey–sounding) Eddie this is boring. Stop it. It's excruciating to me.

She doesn't know it but when she does finally stop protesting, stops saying words, while Eddie keeps saying more and more words ("cockring," "crack"), her face freezes into a sphinx expression, of the statue of the Black Madonna in Chartres, and it just stays there, more like a photograph than a face.

Now Thom is spent. The film is spent. The lights are all flashed out. He walks back naked into the room. He can hardly move. What is this fatigue? It's as if his soul has been sucked out of his body. As if the Amish fear that photographs steal the soul is true.

THOM: (trying to rub the tiredness off his face with his big palms) I have bugs on my face.
ROSALINA: (spaced, too) You have no clothes on.
THOM: I've been had. (pointing accusingly at Eddie who's cutting his abusive conversation short) He's not happy. He's miserable.

Eddie stands there, even whiter. Doesn't want to look toward Thom.

EDDIE: (to Rosalina) Are you the next to strip down to your skin? Go ahead. I'll do a free Eddie portrait if you do.

THOM: (to Eddie, steadily) You're a dog.

ROSALINA: I'll do that.

Just as Rosalina is ready to make a move, as she kicks off her flats, Thom pounds over and smacks Eddie. It is violence. Smack. Thom's flat pink palm leaves a pink handprint on Eddie's cheek, not clearly delineated, but there, like a crushed pink flower. A pink carnation run over by a car. Smack. Thom bangs the other side.

Eddie just takes it. He has always turned his anger into games with rules. Now he can't get his bones and his muscles and his skin and his head in a line.

EDDIE: (quietly, between smacks) Stop the brutality.

THOM: Ask me again.

Thom pushes Eddie so that he flattens up against a wall.

EDDIE: (screams) You're gonna punch me into the wall-paper. I'll bleed on the wallpaper.

So Rosalina now starts to scream.

ROSALINA: (frantically lost) This is disgusting. It is in-dulgent.

EDDIE: Run Rosalina!

Life is most itself at those rare moments of passion when it is like a bad movie, when poised people say dumb lines they would never otherwise say.

THOM: Take off your clothes Eddie. Or I'll beat you some more.

EDDIE: You take 'em off.

THOM: Say what?

But Thom does. He turns Eddie around, gripping him by the back of his jacket, and pulls it down and off, as if it were a coat he were helping a lady out of. Then he trips Eddie so Eddie falls into a translucent bundle of curves and angles on the floor. Drags him around by two legs, his back scraping, while pulling off boots and chinos. When Eddie tries to undo himself from the tangle, to struggle against gravity, Thom pushes down on one arm with one pressing foot.

Eddie is like a pencil that Thom is scribbling with on the floor.

ROSALINA: (curled hopelessly now in a magenta armchair) What can we do to get you to stop Thom?

THOM: (booming) I want Eddie to renounce the ways of Satan.

Eddie and Rosalina look fast at each other: her eyes a few feet above his. Worry.

EDDIE: If Thom weren't out of control, I'd laugh.

THOM: (pushes Eddie's chin back with his toes) Fast.

ROSALINA: (pleading) Do it.

EDDIE: (flat on floor, as if talking to ceiling, but really to Rosalina) Thom's certifiable. That's why he's not in the Navy anymore. I checked.

THOM: Here's the deal. You gotta break the statue. You gotta cut the phone cord. You gotta sing a hymn. And you gotta take a picture that's nice that ain't evil or death no more.

ROSALINA: (stiff as cardboard) I can't sit still for this.

    She starts to stand up but Thom walks over and wraps his arms around her, his wet body subdues her and she sits back down.

    Eddie does it. As white and bony as a newborn deer. While he walks about performing on his wobbly deer legs Thom turns on an antique transistor radio from the early sixties. It plays two or three AM stations at once, making an annoying white sound. No one seems to notice. Rosalina lights up a long Benson & Hedges menthol and looks confused, stroking her one leg curled up under the other.

    Eddie smashes the Mephistopheles statue. He smashes it with the wooden handle of a broom. The pieces don't splinter sharply, like fireworks. The explosion is mute. The more perceptible explosions are in Eddie's face. He looks teenage again. His black hair innocently greasy. His pale face as simply white as a boy whose voice is changing in a television situation comedy.

    Next Eddie cuts the cord of the phone with long scissors he finds in the closet. They are used to crop pictures somehow. But they look like shears used on tall hedges in the suburbs where Eddie came from to go to art school. He tenses over the line (with resilient metal wires wrapped inside) until the severing is done. He is breathing hard.

ROSALINA: (struggling to change her position in the chair) It's worse and worse in here.
THOM: (checklist-fashion) Now sing the hymn.
EDDIE: (very tough guy) To what?
THOM: To me.
EDDIE: (a new voice, croaking) I can't do anything silly, Thom. This is too serious for me. I'm too into it.

ROSALINA: (standing and drawing in far and long on the nicotine stick, annoyed) I stuck around for all that danger before. I have character. But to see you seriously whimpering—yes Eddie, whimpering. . . . I see something creepy and boring creeping into you. (angrily:) That I can't stomach.

Rosalina walks out the black metal door without looking back. Metal clangs shut. The sound equivalent of an exclamation point. Rosalina is feeling secure in her judgments. Though actually she is navigating by mere distortions of stars, not by real points of longitude and latitude.

Eddie now is sitting on the couch, knees falling way apart, shoulders splayed.

THOM: (relaxed in front of him) You don't have to finish the ceremony, bro.
EDDIE: (a joke between them) Okay homeboy.

Eddie now lies down flat naked on the cool black crinkled couch. He falls into a sleep. The sleep is like a suffocation. Like the gloved hand of an anesthetist pushing down over his face until there is no more living oxygen. He hears the voices of operating nurses and doctors as he goes under. He wakes up many hours later. Calls for Thom but Thom is nowhere. Picks up phone but phone is dead. Stands up from couch. Walks into bedroom. Puts on uncharacteristic pair of white Brooks Brothers boxer shorts. Walks into studio. Sits on wood chair. Legs up on windowsill. Smokes a cigarette that makes his heart hurt every time he breathes in.

There is a melon-colored eighth-of-a-moon in the purple-blue-black sky. Eddie talks to it out loud. While a tape of Mathilde Santing, a Dutch chanteuse who wears men's suits and bleaches her spiked hair white, plays

from the tape player on the floor in the corner. Eddie slid
it on.

EDDIE: (low, since he doesn't really have to be heard, as
low as movie actors can talk, but stage actors never
can) Mom. The floor finally caved in. Thom taught
me a lesson. Thommie. And now I have to take different pictures. I have to take only pictures of people who I need. Or even things who I need. And I
have to put them all together like bread crumbs.
The floor finally caved in Mom. And if I don't take
what I need, soon, I'm gonna be miserable. I
thought it was cool to be miserable. I remember
this girl in high school, Phyllis. She was the kind of
girl who was interested in a guy only until he was
interested in her. And then she got cold as ice. She
ended up alone and miserable. This is me speaking
Mom. Believe it or not.

Eddie stands up. He walks through the cut-up loft
looking for something to photograph. But there's nothing.
Except this white lily flower in a black onyx vase. He
doesn't want to photograph it. Why not? But he breaks
through that feeling and grabs the vase in his hand, feeling as if he's sticking his hand through a plate-glass window. Can't make any phonecalls. The switchboard in his
head has stopped lighting up.
Eddie walks slowly back with the vase into the studio
room. Puts it on a wooden high stool. Takes its picture.
The lily looks cool.

FORTY WILD CRUSHES;

or, Whenever I See a Dachshund I Think of G.I. Joe

Jim Provenzano

The day before it happened was a Friday, the sort of day when kids in the fourth grade feel the growing wave of freedom, and they surf it all the way to the three o'clock bell. Teachers either try to survive it like bent palm trees, stand through it like dumb sunbathers, or get the hell out of the way.

First thing in the morning after the Pledge of Allegiance was Show and Tell, enough to make dopey farm boys like Tony Markley[1] quiver. Someone would have to pick a bit of entertainment for the class. Most forgot and merely chose a poem from the chewed-up books that lay on the back shelf of the classroom.

---

[1] Lanky, large-penised redhead. Later arrested for assault in a bowling alley.

I volunteered on Show and Tell days, and often played albums for the class's enjoyment, from *Dumbo* to *Fantasia*.[2] I even whipped up full-cast restagings of *Wild, Wild West*[3] episodes. It was someone else's turn, today, though. Some girl read a poem so softly it didn't get past the pages.

In History, Mister Watson[4] was talking about Christopher Columbus—a bunch of lies, of course, but that's all that was in the big-lettered book we read. I was already a few chapters ahead, and decided to snap a rubber band at Jim Weirneckie,[5] who sat behind me. Sometimes, when we had free time, Jim would lean back in his chair, a very stupid thing to do. Kids or teachers would jerk the chair out behind you to be cruel or to teach you a lesson. I liked Jim because we shared first names, and when he leaned back I would steal glances at his crotch.

Lee Bacchus[6] was sitting next to me and passed a note. I thought it was for me, but he nearly growled when I

[2] I knew I was in trouble when the Devil in the "Night on Bald Mountain" scene got me excited. He was so huge, so powerful, and the first cartoon muscle hunk I ever saw. Did those Disney people know what they were doing?

[3] Tight-panted, muscular Robert Conrad became a major obsession. In every episode of this oddball adventure series, Conrad's Jim West managed either to get his shirt off or to get tied up in some sadomasochistic manner by a vicious homolust-subverted evil megalomaniac. I often wanted to tie men like him up, although I never tied any boys up, or got tied up, until much later.

[4] Tall, wore glasses, had a wife and kids, but was later divorced and went into real estate. Totally humiliating when, five years later, we tried to sell the house and he took people through it a few times a week. I had to keep my room spotless every day, like in a museum.

[5] Years later, in junior high school, he got me stoned once at a party. Later went to jail for possession.

[6] Blond, bee-stung lips. Later became a Navy SEAL and went prematurely bald.

started to open it. It was for Beth Emery,[7] who sat to my right, a wispy girl who never talked to boys. I was Lee's Cyrano for the moment.

Mister Watson came walking through the aisle, his hips at my eye level. That was nice. He was a large muscular man who also did some coaching. I pretended to have a question. He leaned in close so I could smell his after-shave. His hands were huge.

Unable to concentrate, I looked up at the wall at the posters of the Apollo moon landing and the picture of Buzz Aldrin.[8] I'd been fascinated with astronauts since second grade, when we were forced to watch the moon landings. Most kids fell asleep in the dark classroom watching the black-and-white monitor, like Joey Vercillo,[9] who invited me over for dinner once with his family. We had Salisbury steak. Before then I didn't think anybody ate that outside a school cafe-teria.

Mister Watson talked some more up at the blackboard. I looked in my school box under my desk and secretly fin-gered the monogrammed pencil I'd stolen from Steve Ely[10] a month before. The bell for lunch period was about to release us. All eyes went to the electric clock on the ce-ment wall.

Hurled into eager lines, we each checked who had milk money, who packed, and who had a lunch ticket. I

[7]Thin, blue-eyed. Became a state tennis champion in college. I had a crush on her. Yes, she was a girl—so what?

[8]Astronaut with a terrific haircut.

[9]A boy who featured in my first sexual dream, in which we floated about in space holding hands.

[10]Unspeakably beautiful boy with eyes like buttons. Would get a concussion on a Cub Scout sled-riding trip at the country club. My mom took him to the hospital in our car. I wiped up his blood and se-cretly tasted it. They moved away when his parents got divorced.

brought my Atom Ant[11] lunch box, but stood in line with
Mitch Waller[12] and Gary Wharton,[13] my lunch friends,
because I would never sit alone waiting for someone to
come by. Mom had bought me the metal box after Jackie
McBeth sat on my brown-bag lunch the day I kicked her
in the butt.

Sitting down, Gary opened his *New Zoo Revue*[14]
lunch box and floated his Hostess Cupcakes by me.
Since I had a Twinkie for dessert, I didn't care. Gary's
gums turned black after eating his devil's-food desserts.
Mitch ate his school lunch: macaroni and cheese. Gary
told a fart joke and Mitch laughed milk out through his
nose.

Before leaving the cafeteria, Mitch and Gary argued
about who would win, Muhammad Ali[15] or the other
guy, while I snuck my Ritalin, which my mother kept
wrapped in a napkin and a rubber band in my lunch
box. I swallowed it at the drinking fountain. I was hyper-
active and the pills kept me from climbing the walls. Gary
and I put our lunch boxes in the line by the playground
doors with dozens of others: Peanuts,[16] the Flintstones,[17]

[11]Atomically powerful cartoon insect.

[12]Mitch was queer, I knew it. He knew it about me, but he wasn't as
handsome as his older brother, Ben, a natural athlete who often pa-
raded around in his underwear at their home when I visited. Mitch
died of AIDS last year.

[13]I usually did not have crushes on my friends, only boys I couldn't
speak to, men, or TV characters. Gary now lives in Florida and owns a
furniture store.

[14]Stupid tree-house show with people wearing costumes like a
hippo, a frog, and an owl. The guy on the show sang songs, wore
glasses, had a mustache, and was attractive in a dorky way.

[15]Beautiful black boxer. You know the rest.

[16]I often impersonated Linus.

[17]Barney Rubble was sexy.

the Jetsons, the Monkees,[18] and the Banana Splits.[19]

Once outside, clans re-formed. I stood under the elm trees and watched Brian Harlan[20] manipulate a magnifying glass. He burned a hole in a leaf. I skipped rope with some of the girls, oblivious at the time of how obviously girlish I was. Most of the boys were playing out in the field, some game with a ball. I had no idea what it was, just that they all usually came back to class flushed and wet.

I went over to the seesaws and jumped up on the middle, riding between Lorna Beck and Missy Gosnell, two girls I could hurl into convulsive laughter merely by saying "Donny Osmond."[21] I even wore purple socks once to make them laugh.

Beth Emery's hair was white-blond. I really noticed her hair that day, when she fell and broke her arm. She and another girl went on a dare and teased a dog that was tied to a rope in the yard next to the playground. The dog leaped at them. They tore off running, and Beth tripped just as she reached the asphalt. A crowd of kids formed around her screams. She had broken her arm, and I became a sort of nursemaid until the principal took her away to the hospital. She was quite beautiful as they led her off the playground, a wounded princess after the

[18]So were all the Monkees, except Mickey Dolenz.

[19]Hanna-Barbera cartoon show with three costumed creatures: a monkey, an elephant, and a beagle. They joked around on a trippy set that looked a lot like *Laugh-In.* One of them would shout, "Uh-oh, Chongo!" and they'd cut to a live filmed continuing adventure story set on a desert island, which featured a very young Jan-Michael Vincent. He often got in fights and ran around in wet jeans, without a shirt.

[20]Buck-toothed neighbor. Once I got so mad at him, he was so cute, I threw his glasses and broke them. He got in a freak accident in college and is now a paraplegic.

[21]Goofy Mormon pop star. Recently attempted a comeback.

hunt. The dog kept barking, until an old lady came out of the house, swearing at us.

In the hallway between classes, I saw Steve Johnson,[22] whom I loved. He lived in my neighborhood, but since he was in sixth grade, and I was in fourth, speaking to each other in school was sacrilege. We shared secrets at home. He had a short crew cut and wanted to go into the Army when he grew up. His dad had been in the Army. Mister Johnson[23] looked a lot like Steve, only bigger. He reminded me of Dennis Weaver.[24] I was to see *Ultraman*[25] with Steve on Saturday afternoon, since they had a bigger TV set and our moms went to some club together. I sometimes tried to get Steve to come over to my house, since at his we had to play with Peppy, his dachshund. I hated Peppy and she knew it.

"I'm going to Steve's tomorrow," I bragged to Gary.

"So marry him."

I shoved him, but we wouldn't fight.

The brisk wind that day, hot and thick with the ensuing summer, wafted into the classroom windows. Everyone was all excited about Beth Emery going to the hospital. Back at our desks, Lee Bacchus didn't seem to notice her absence.

[22]Wiry, handsome, tough, cool yet tender buddy who lived down the street. It's all his fault.

[23]State patrolman, now growing old gracefully with his wife, who occasionally overindulged in QT tanning lotion.

[24]Television and film actor, most notable role as *McCloud*, an urban cowboy detective. Also the underappreciated star of Steven Spielberg's *Duel*, as the trucker-hounded driver. But his first starring TV role was as the father ranger in *Gentle Ben*, the story of a young boy with funny ears who owned a huge black bear as a pet. Just thinking how grand it must have felt to sit on a pontoon racer with your father at the helm, the acrid smell of the Everglades blasting by, gave me a warm rush.

[25]Japanese superhero in a fabulous red-and-silver jumpsuit with a zipper up the back and eyes like a hornet.

The day ended with us walking home, Gary and Mitch off in their direction, me going down Claremont Avenue past the tall sixth-grader Safety Patrol. Craig LeFever[26] held us back till the coast was clear. I admired his white straps over his paisley shirt. His hair was like coal wire. I'd once seen my sister's Patrol belt wrapped up in her room, tried it on, but couldn't figure out how to wrap it up again. She got mad. Guys would wrap it through their belt loops, showing them off all day. Girls kept them in their purses.

Home in time to watch *Dark Shadows*,[27] I ignored the pile of newspapers on our front porch. I was a paperboy for the *Star Ledger*. I hated it mostly, but it made money. Mom nagged me to get started on my route, or I'd miss pizza for dinner.

Every fifth house had a dog. Nasty ones. They jumped up in my face and knocked me down. They stunk like old sofas. Dogs scared me. So did the owners—crabby old ladies with drop-kick dogs who insisted I leave the paper in their mailboxes, like it would kill them to walk a few feet. There were worse houses, German shepherd houses, where I just threw the papers and forgot to collect subscription bills. I had one favorite stop, at the home of a college Communications instructor,[28] who came to the door with his shirt off, but he only did that once. He didn't have a dog.

Once my bags were empty, I rode to the A & P to get

---

[26]Freckled student-council type. Dated my sister a few times. Grew up to be a cop in Lorain.

[27]Vampire soap opera. Quentin, the sultry, sideburned, wide-eyed youth played by David Selby, wove into my fantasies, but Barnabas Collins (Jonathan Frid) truly scared me, especially when we went to see the movie version, where there was a lot more blood.

[28]Thickly built, with jet-black hair and a ruthless mustache.

the new *Tiger Beat* magazine, with David Cassidy[29] on the cover. Shaun Cassidy,[30] the two twins on the live-action/animated *Huckleberry Finn* show,[31] and many other guys were shown inside, too, but what made me buy it was the foldout poster of Bobby Sherman.[32] I paid $1.50. "Bobby Sherman, Bobby Sherman," I sang as I rode home on my emerald-green banana-seated Schwinn, having spent half of my week's tips on the magazine. Bobby Sherman, Bobby Sherman, like a cute haircut or a sweet dessert. Inside the center was a Bobby Sherman photograph from his head to just above his thighs. The pants were striped almost as wildly as my bedroom wallpaper, the shirt open to the middle of his hairless chest. I was going to put him on my bedroom wall. The belt, wide as the love of the sixties. The belt buckle, huge, a crown for the mysterious bulge that lay waiting underneath. I knew what lay under the belt buckles of all boys, but Bobby Sherman's belt buckle was different. Boys I knew didn't have Bobby Sherman's magic. His teeth and dimples said that he was nice, but what lay under the belt buckle, the groovy belt buckle, said that he could take you someplace you'd never been, a place bad heroes go. Gary said that the Bobby Sherman record his sister bought had an even better picture of him, but I didn't have enough money for that.

[29]Ambisexual pop star of *The Partridge Family*. Recently attempted a comeback.

[30]His brother.

[31]Their names escape me, but they once posed shirtless together.

[32]Equally successful pop star, often a guest on *The Partridge Family*. Costar of *Here Come the Brides*, as the tender stuttering younger brother, with David Soul as his handsome blond brother, and a big rugged guy as the oldest brother. Don't tell me there wasn't some kind of fun going on in that cabin while they were waiting for those brides.

Homework was out of the question, since it was Friday, and Mom took the day off, too. We ate fast food, usually Dorlo Pizza, our favorite, with diamond-cut little pieces. Red Barn was okay, and Dairy Dolly made great onion cheeseburgers, but Dorlo's was the best, plus the delivery guy[33] was handsome. I asked to take the money to the door.

While we munched, the pizza box laid out carefully over newspapers on the coffee table, I told Mom and Dad and my sister about Beth Emery's broken arm and Brian Harlan burning leaves, but not the other stuff, the secret stuff.

I hid down in the basement den for two hours watching reruns of *The Brady Bunch*,[34] *Gilligan's Island*,[35] *Hogan's Heroes*,[36] and *The Wild, Wild West*[37] on WUAB43. They also showed *Ultraman* and *Johnny Socko with Giant Robot*, but that wasn't until Saturday.

Steve Johnson day.

I did some other stuff. There must have been a movie on, or *Laugh-In*[38] or something. I went to my room. Outside, the neighbors' dog went into a barking fit.

[33]The Pizza Boy. Came to be an icon for others as well.

[34]Greg Brady was quite a dude, especially when he grew sideburns and got his own room. Peter Brady would have done well in a pinch. Never liked the dad, actor Robert Reed, who turned out to be gay. Always barking up the wrong tree.

[35]The professor was sexy, but Ginger taught me glamour.

[36]Men in close quarters wearing leather jackets, caps, freezing all the time, having to keep warm. They served amazing French dinners and dug tunnels to tree-stump escape hatches. Wasn't there a war going on?

[37]See number three. Yes, Robert Conrad deserves two footnotes.

[38]Alan Sues, raging queen of the groovy party TV show, was a secret hero. We once made cutout windows—like those in the show when the credits rolled—in our backyard fort and painted it wild colors. I insisted on playing Alan Sues, and sometimes Jo Anne Worley, because I knew all the chicken jokes.

Before bed, with my new Bobby Sherman poster on my wall, I did some drawings like Jonny Quest. Jonny Quest's dad had a friend, Race Bannon,[39] who was always with them and doing very brave things. It wasn't until recently that I realized Race Bannon was Jonny Quest's dad's best friend. This was a cartoon. Race Bannon was a cartoon. It's not odd to fall in love with a cartoon; people do it all the time.

One particularly memorable episode involved Race Bannon's having to disguise himself in the jungle. He stripped nude and covered his skin with purple berry juice, the cartoon leaves discreetly hiding what I (and Steve Johnson, I prayed) desperately craved to view. Steve had seen the episode too, and hinted about experimenting with a nude juice camouflage himself. I lay in bed, hoping he would.

When I got to Steve's house the next day, I went to their side door, through the garage. Their dachshund, Peppy, sat in the middle of the garage, where Mrs. Johnson's car usually was. I sat down to pet the little black dog, as if to offer a truce.

That's when it happened.

Not knowing that she had just had rabies shots in her ear, I touched her exactly on her sore spot. My face was instantly covered with dog. Her teeth gnarled into my upper lip, got stuck there for a moment as she growled and drooled all over me, and then she snapped free, shredding my lip in the process. I think I must have writhed around on the gasoline-covered garage floor for a while. The cement was very cool, although it was hot outside.

Mister Johnson came running out the screen door from the house, sopping wet with a white towel wrapped

[39]Cartoon hero, two-dimensionally butch. Perfectly military-cut, white-blond hair, voice like gravel, pecs like plates of milk.

around his waist. He must have been the only one home and I must have screamed pretty loud to be heard from the shower at the other end of their house. Funny, you don't remember the pain. I'm surprised I remember this much. Maybe I don't remember this at all, just the stories other people told me.

In the midst of my screaming on the cement garage floor, with Peppy snarling in the corner, next to the lawn mower, Mister Johnson rushed over to me and knelt down. He stripped off his white towel and wrapped it around my face. For a brief moment, I saw his body, wet and quite handsome. I do remember Mister Johnson looked good in a uniform, but at that moment he looked even better—tall, wet, hairy, naked, and nervous: my savior.

His towel covered my face like a barber's steam treatment. My blood soaked it a dull red. I think Mister Johnson held me for quite a while. I think it was very comforting.

I was lucky to have a surgeon fix up my lip quite nicely so I wouldn't look like a chipmunk or talk funny. I just have a thin scar in the shape of a lambda or an upside-down Y.

After the operation, with my stitches blue and sharp and my lip bloated like a fish, Dad[40] took me to the Giant Store to get any toy I wanted. To revenge myself against the dachshund I could have gotten a bike to run her over with, but I already had one. Instead I got a doll. A man doll with blond plastic hair sculpted onto his head like Race Bannon's, with a flexible muscular body and an entire Apollo moon capsule and a silver suit with boots and gloves and a helmet just like Buzz Aldrin's. He was the most handsome man in the store and

[40]My father. I suppose he should be footnote number one, but things don't always turn out like you expect.

he fit in my little hands like a piece of love. He had a scar on his face, just like me, and his name was G.I. Joe.

We returned home—me, Dad, G.I. Joe, and my fourteen freshly sewn stitches. I was the hit of the neighborhood and considered charging admission to let kids touch my scars. Mister Johnson came by to check up on me. Steve did, too, but he seemed a bit ticked off about all the attention I was getting, especially from his father, who put his hands on my shoulders and offered to take me out in his patrol car "just as soon as yer feelin' better." I learned how fear and terror can be so easily vanquished with the touch of a man's big hands. And when that wasn't available, there was always shopping.

After everybody left and all the excitement died down, I was alone. I looked around at the pink, blue, and white vertically striped wallpaper in my bedroom in our house. The Bobby Sherman poster looked suddenly silly, like too much candy, so I took it down.

My upper lip puffing up grotesquely, greasy with ointment, prickled with blue stiches, I stared at myself in the mirror, wondering if I would always be this ugly. Picking up my new yet scarred G.I. Joe, it didn't seem like such a problem. I thought of calling Steve, but knew that I really wanted to see his dad.

I looked around my room and began to think about getting more things. Not toys, trucks, or baseball bats. I would fill my room with things that mattered, things that would hurt me, love me, and leave me wanting more. I would fill my room with men.

CRUISE CONTROL

John Edward Harris

Union Square

ou can't tell me that between 1970 and 1980 you slept with over a thousand men—it doesn't compute."

"Take three a week . . ."

"You had slow weeks, right? I mean, this is ten years."

"Three's average. Rounded down. Three times fifty-two times ten equals 1,560. Even if you say 2.5 . . ."

Bob sucked and fucked his way through the seventies. I know that. I held my own through the eighties, treating my tubes as if they were like the temple of an unusually reticent god who feared human contact. I was content,

secure in my belief that sex without commitment was
self-destructive. As much as I would like to think that a
decade of promiscuity destroyed his soul, I'm stuck with
the facts: Bob's the happiest man I know.

"Oof. Did you see that?" Bob asks.

"What?"

"The messenger."

"Where?"

"On the ten-speed."

Bob points him out and I have to admit it's a nice ass,
but that's not enough.

"The way he bounces on that seat you'd think it's a—"

"Don't say it."

"Dildo."

"This isn't a conversation, it's a hand job."

Bob and I met at the office, in the elevator. He said
something inane about how humid it was; I said, "Sure
hope it doesn't get as hot as last summer," and headed
for the R train at 14th Street. When I realized that's
where he was going, I decided to walk. Bob asked if he
could join me. Given my midwestern manners, how could
I say no?

Now I get a daily sermon on the mount—on how to
mount—from the would-be savior of my sex life; I tell
him to shut the fuck up, that it's the nineties and nothing's safe and nobody's free.

The Flatiron District

"Sure, there were slow weeks," Bob tells me. "Dry spells.
Sometimes I'd leave a bar in tears because getting cruised
meant I'm worthwhile, and if that wasn't happening . . . I

mean I'd do everything I could to get noticed—hold my jacket in my hand to make the veins in my arm pop out, look aloof, recite the Greek alphabet. Sometimes someone would look at you all night and never come over and you'd feel like such a fool. But then I'd get on a roll, eight days a week. Get a load of him."

"Where?"

"The Asian guy."

"Missed him."

I used to associate cruising with that hunted-animal-on-the-prowl-for-meat look—a real turnoff. But Bob makes it seem innocent. Like playing doctor with your best friend when you were four.

"Funny thing is," Bob says, "sometimes I'd go out dirty and dressed like shit and set the whole bar on fire. But you've got to understand that back then I had six-teen-inch arms and pecs out to here."

Reality Check I: When I go to a bar, everyone stands around and stares at videos. I think, "Am I attracted to this guy?" I think, "I'll have another drink and, if he's still there when I come back, I'll say hi." I think, "Stop. Remember pickup technique. You haven't made signifi-cant eye contact yet." I think, "I'm bored with this game, it's getting me nowhere." I think, "I'll catch a cab and crawl under the covers."

Madison Square Park

Bob's head pivots. "Wow."

I'm trying to look in the same direction. "Where?"

"Walking the dog. Check out those calves."

"Yeah, but look at that face."

"If you're lucky, you'll be locked between his legs—you'll never look up."

I would like to believe I have higher standards than that, but then I tell myself, Bob's right, don't look at the whole. Focus on a fragment that turns you on and forget the rest. In poetry it's synecdoche, in pornography a fetish.

"You know, Bob, I can't just look at a guy on the street and get hard."

"Maybe he wasn't your type."

"Type? I don't have a type. I deal with people as if they're human."

"Bullshit. You just don't know what you like."

"No, I don't. I'm not that tired. You can still surprise me."

"Would you like me to?"

"I'm probably not your type."

"No, but you're close. Very close. Maybe if you worked out. I like somebody who's bigger than me in some ways and smaller in others."

Bob's tall but overweight—just let his body go. He has lines in his forehead, thinning blond hair. Given our twenty-year age difference, he's old enough to be my father. So none of those things makes him a knockout.

But it's funny. You can look at a man's hands—hairy fingers, bitten nails—and think nothing of them. But then you get to know him, get to know his hands. Soon you're back in the elevator and those hands are gripping your arm and grabbing your hair, groping your butt and grasping your balls. Then you wake up and look at the clock next to your bed. It's just a dream. His hands worked their way into your erotic repertoire—crashed your party and now they're the life of it—and suddenly you're thinking about him in a different way. Maybe that's what happened with me and Bob. Or maybe it's just the fact that he's always in heat and that when we walk home the manholes become man holes and the mailboxes, male boxes.

28th Street

"Would you always meet at bars?" I ask.

"Not always. A couple of guys followed me home off the subway. Or I'd go to the discos"—and he rattles off their names—"the Cockring, the Barefoot Boy, Galaxy 21, Le Jardin, the Firehouse, Crisco Disco, the Anvil. Or someone I didn't know would call up and say that a mutual friend had given him my number. He'd ask if I was free. I'd ask what he looked like. The descriptions were almost always accurate—there were only two times that I didn't want to be with the man once I saw him at my door. Anyway, he'd come over or I'd go to his place. I liked that best. Then I could leave whenever I wanted to. It's not always easy to get rid of a trick . . ."

Reality Check II: Does anybody use the word "trick" anymore? We go on dates. We see movies. We eat at restaurants. We share cabs and kiss good night and say to ourselves, "Sex isn't all there is."

". . . Sometimes I'd get three calls in one day. Three different guys coming over to my apartment. I'm not doing anything but picking up the telephone."

"What would you do when the trick arrived?"

"Say hi, offer him a drink—I was usually nervous, so a drink helped. About half the men I met would be into wrestling. We'd kid around and then get down to business."

"Didn't it make you feel cheap, empty, used?"

"You bet! But we thought of it as sharing."

"Like you share a urinal or maybe a cum towel when you clean up."

"You don't know what you're talking about. Beneath this hard candy shell beats a heart of gold—"

"Lamé."

"Fuck you, it felt great. But it scared me sometimes. It was so easy. The sex was totally uninhibited because you were never going to see each other again. You wouldn't want to see most of them again."

"Didn't you want a boyfriend, someone you could count on?"

"Sure. I mean, if I liked it and he liked it, we'd get together again. That's how I've met each of my boyfriends, by tricking. It's always made more sense to me than dating. If the sex works—and it usually does—and you don't think you want to spend the rest of your lives together—and you usually don't—then at least you've had sex. I've never had safe sex, never used a condom. I wouldn't know how."

Reality Check III: Sex with strangers isn't a goal for me or most of the men I know. Sure, some of us do it out of necessity because we haven't found that lover that boyfriend that fuckbuddy. But after the euphoria comes the fear.

"Did you get fucked?" I ask.

"Only about five times. But that includes the night ten guys screwed me in Montreal. Everyone was high on something. I wasn't even sore the next day."

I've buried my gang-bang desires so deep inside me that I can't even imagine gratifying them in real life. Bob's stories mix me up. I feel horny and impotent at the same time. So I say, "That way of life, I don't want it."

"Everybody wants it. That's why we terrified the rest of the world. We lived every man's fantasy: to have as much sex as you want. Straight men can't get it. They want it, but unless they pay for it, they've got to get involved. Can you imagine the jealousy they felt? No wonder they're trying to kill us off. We've got something that they can't have, and if they join us, it's the end of their world."

"It's not us against them anymore. Gay people want to settle down, have kids, watch TV. . . . I don't want to have sex with someone else every time I sneeze."

"You've never had it, so how would you know?"

"So what do you want? Separation? Queer Nation?"

"Don't call me that. Don't ever call me that. You call me queer and you've got a problem: my fist in your face."

"We're taking that word away from them."

"You can tell them that when they're bashing your head with a baseball bat. You can tell them all about how you reclaimed that word and how they can't hurt you with it anymore. I've spent twenty years getting 'gay' accepted. I even had to practice using it in front of the mirror to get it to feel right. I wasn't nuts about it, but at least it's ours."

Herald Square

"Comin' our way."

"Give it up, Bob."

"He's looking at you. Look back."

"What do you think I'm doing?"

"Look at those pecs." Bob stops and watches the boy hear us. "Let's knock him out, take him home, pinch his tits, and fuck him."

"Shut up, I'm trying to concentrate."

"He's looking at you. Look back. Catch his eye?"

"Yeah."

"Look again."

"He stopped at the corner."

"Well, here we are. Macy's. Perfect place to window-shop. See you later."

"What do I say if he approaches?"

" 'Hi.' "

"Just 'Hi'?"

"Nothing else."

"Then what?"

"It doesn't matter. If he's free and you're free . . ."

"Let's get out of here."

"This is your chance."

I've had enough so I tell Bob to keep moving.

Times Square

As we cruise, I tease Bob, knocking my elbows against him or swinging my arms so my hand slaps his thigh. When we stop at the corner, I feel him next to me and like it. I press my leg against his while innocently examining a theater marquee. By 46th Street, I'm a wreck. Hot, horny, and mad as hell that I missed what should have been the most sex-crazed years of my life. Instead, I spent my twenties falling obsessively in love with men whom for various reasons I could not have.

"But how did you feel before you'd go to the bars?" I ask.

"My heart would be pounding. Maybe I'd get lucky. Maybe I'd find love."

"You mean sex."

"What's the difference?"

"Oh, come on."

"No, tell me. A man shoves his dick down your throat and tells you not to move. That's love. He makes coffee for you the next morning, that's so much velvet."

"But if you stay with him . . ."

"Well, later, sure, you can tell if it's love."

"It's not the same, Bob. It's not that simple anymore."

"Are you kidding? Nothing's changed. You go to the Rambles and there are still two guys fucking and three more in a circle around them whacking off."

Duffy Square

As Bob tells me about the Puerto Rican he fucked in Central Park—the one who bit his tits so hard they bled—it hits me, the meaning of that cliché: Gay people don't get an adolescence. Growing up in the straight world, you spend your teens defining yourself against the culture or, more pathetically, trying to fit in. Then you move out of the house, out of town. It's your twenties and you should be able to go crazy in that little red Corvette you never had in high school, have sex with anything that moves—like Bob—and demystify the whole god-damn experience.

"Woof!" Bob's into it.

"Bow wow." I'm not.

"Look at those lats."

"What?"

"That guy's back. The one in the tank top."

"Oh, him."

"I like lats."

"You could talk about his lats. He could talk about his lats. You could talk about your delts. He could—"

"Who cares? If you started talking opera, with any luck he'd hit you and say, 'Shut up, bitch,' and you'd think to yourself, 'This is love.' "

To punctuate Bob's point, two black teens walk by. One

grabs his crotch, looks me in the eye, and says: "Don't black men have big dicks? Don't they fuck hard?"

Bob says, "Amen."

Reality Check IV: To reach Bob's state of enlightenment, I would have to overcome a major mental block against anonymous sex. But trying to crash through that block, where would it get me? Let's say I find I like having lots of sex with lots of different men. That's dangerous. Let's say that I find I simply don't have it in me. That's no picnic, either.

Columbus Circle

We part after the cruising, the cursing, and the talk that's made one thing clear: Ten years of being good has left me alone after a long hard day at work with nothing long and hard in sight. I feel like fucking for a year just to make up for lost time.

So I say, Do you want to come back to my place for a drink? And he says, I have a lover. And I say, I know. And he says, We've been together for nine years. And I say, Congratulations. And he says, He's the only man I didn't reject after cumming.

Every day Bob looks for sex nonstop, though he doesn't need it, doesn't want it. I do want it, yet I'm afraid to look for it.

Reality Check V: Fuck reality.

So I say, Maybe I'll call you later. And he says, Cheer up, you'll find somebody. And I hate it when he says that because I feel like I already have.

LILACS

Abraham Verghese

*B*obby sits up on the side of the bed. He feels weak, spinny-headed and hollow. In a little while he tugs at the bedspread and wraps it around himself. Using the chest of drawers and the television for handholds, he stumbles to the air-conditioning unit below the window. He leans over the gray box, turning his head away from the cold blast, fumbling till he finds the concealed door to the control panel, and then blindly punches buttons till it turns off.

He draws the curtain back cautiously. He stares out at the motel parking lot for several minutes, focusing on any movement that might suggest he is being watched. Over the high wall behind the parking lot he sees the blue-green span of Tobin Bridge and, beyond that, the Boston skyline. The parking lot has filled up overnight. He sees Massachusetts plates, New Hampshire plates—an Indiana plate on a jeep reads "HOOSIER HOSPITALITY."

"FIRST IN THE WAITING ROOM." That would be on his license plate. If he had a car. When he walked into the motel lobby the previous night, it had smelled of coriander. The manager, an Indian, had stared at him with alarm. "No vehicle?" he said. Behind the counter, a door stood open, revealing a woman's fat leg on a recliner; a silver toe ring looked welded onto her second toe. There were the murmurs of a TV and the shrill voices of children speaking in another language. Bobby peeled three hundred-dollar bills from his roll, and the man's manner softened considerably. "What it is happened to your face?" the man asked, coming close to Bobby. The woman in the recliner stuck her head around to look.

"Oh, I was born this way," Bobby had answered. He had smiled at the fat woman, who quickly retracted her head.

The bathroom is cold. He brushes his teeth with the bedspread still wrapped around him. He tries not to look into the mirror. Why look? Better to remember himself as he used to be. As he is in the photograph in the briefcase—a photograph Primo took. It is from Myrtle Beach, the summer of 1973, when he was twenty-one years old. In the photograph his hair comes down to his shoulders. He is bare-chested, sitting sideways on Primo's '64 Harley, one hand on the tank and the other resting lightly on his thigh—his own thigh. He is smiling—a strong smile, a smile of certainty. Primo had said something to make him smile, something flattering, and his Fu Manchu mustache looks innocent, young. In the background is Primo's airplane, and beyond that, faintly, the sea, though in the photograph it blurs with the blue of the sky. Carolina blue.

In those days, Bobby worked as a manager in the Myr-

tle Mystery Mall, selling tokens for the peephole diora-
mas, supervising the soda and trinket concessions, keeping the lines flowing through the Dinosaur Cyclorama,
shooing out the couples who lingered in the dark recesses
of the Polynesian Fire-Walk of Love. He was ten years old
the first summer his parents brought him to Myrtle
Beach. They drove down from Spartanburg and rented a
"cottage" (in reality, a double-wide trailer) for two weeks
in late July, in what became an annual family ritual.
Bobby, an only child, distracted, suffering again that
summer with bad eczema, spent most of his time and all
of his allowance in the Myrtle Mystery Mall. He thrilled to
its dark, paneled interiors, the dim, red glow of the Chi-
nese lanterns, the labyrinth of doors and corridors leading to exhibits, but most of all he thrilled to being part of
the clique of boys who hung around in their flowery
sports shirts and shades and seemed unofficially to pre-
side over the whole phantasmagoria. They encouraged
him to disobey the "HANDS OFF" sign on the Iron Maiden
in the Gallery of Torture; they laughed when he tested the
blade edge of the guillotine with his tongue; and later, sitting in a prop room, they let him sip from the silver hip
flask that they were passing around—a mark of his acceptance. He much preferred their company to baking on
the beach with his parents or sitting mute in the backseat
while his father, talking nonstop, inched the Buick into
the family cavalcade that went up and down the Strip in
search of a different fast-food joint for the evening.

The year his father died, Bobby dropped out of the English Honors program at Appalachian State and moved to
Myrtle Beach, landing a job in his old hangout. Every
day, Bobby caught triptychs of himself in the Distortion
Gallery; Bobbys were catapulted out of one mirror and
reeled back into another: thin Bobbys, fat Bobbys. In the
evenings, Bobby went to the Connection, and there he

saw himself reflected in the eyes of guys from Johnson City, Fayetteville, Raleigh, wherever. They would cluster around him, buy him drinks, while he looked over the tops of their heads. One night he saw Primo come in, look around, and leave before Bobby could get near him—it was the only time Bobby had seen a better-looking man than himself in the place. Primo had returned in an hour, dressed in leather. This time Bobby walked over, scattering the people around them.

"If I had known," Bobby said, fingering the straps on Primo's shoulders, "I would have worn my skins."

"It's not too late," Primo said. They didn't make it out of the parking lot.

He rinses off the toothbrush. He has no razor, and, in any case, his beard barely grows anymore. He runs a washcloth over his face and works the corners of his eyes. His eyelashes have grown long and translucent and have curled up at the ends—a side effect of AZT, according to Dr. Chatupadia. Of the six doctors in the clinic at Boston Metropolitan, four are from India, one is from Pakistan, and one is a Palestinian. Chatupadia, who has been Bobby's physician ever since Bobby moved to Boston nine years ago, took a photograph of Bobby's closed eyelids with the eyelashes dangling and sent it to *The New England Journal of Medicine*. Chatupadia was disappointed when they sent the photograph back, saying that what it showed was now a well-described side effect of AZT. He showed the letter to Bobby. " 'Well-described,' they are calling it, Bobby!" he said, pronouncing it *Boobee*. "These people," Chatupadia said, and he wagged his head from side to side, letting the silence stand for all the injustice in his life and Bobby's life. Bobby agreed. *These people* . . .

These people had no place for Bobby. These people were waiting for him to die. Even Chatupadia seemed to regard his longevity, his hanging on despite plummeting weight and daily fevers, as an aberration. He was a bird without wings, suspended in midair, defying the ground below. His Social Security supplement, even with Medicaid, could not support him. It didn't cover the medications for the infections—the opportunists—that threatened to kill him before the AIDS virus did. Five days earlier, after waiting for three months, Bobby was turned down from the only multicenter interferon trial in Boston. Because his white-blood-cell count was too low, Chatupadia said.

"But my count is low *because* of the AIDS!"

"So sorry, Boobee. They won't allow it."

The other interferon trial in the United States was in Durham. He didn't have the money to go to Durham, but he called anyway, not telling them his white count. "Sorry, we are fully enrolled," a tired male voice had said. "And the study protocol only allows our own patients—our own AZT failures—to be enrolled."

"What if I came down there and waited on your doorstep?" Bobby asked.

They had a waiting list of three hundred. The doorstep was full.

"Just give me *some* of the drug! You don't understand—I have no more rope to hang on to."

But they couldn't. Protocol.

These people . . . But Bobby cannot give up. He cannot. He will not give them that satisfaction. He will go to the clinic today, as he has done every Wednesday these nine years. He will be first in the waiting room, as always. He will sit there and show everyone that he lacks neither determination nor, as of last night, money. And he will remind them of their impotence.

"We are an army of Boobees, an army with overgrown eyelashes," Bobby says to the shrouded figure in the mirror. His voice echoes in the bathroom, and he speaks even louder: "Across this great country, our army is converging on city hospitals. We will assemble in the waiting rooms. We will wait for the clinics to open. We will be treated—we Americans—by our Indian, our Pakistani, our Filipino, our Palestinian doctors: the drones. Upstairs, the queen bees will be working on the cure, appearing on television, writing for the journals."

Someone bangs on the wall next door. "Fuck you!" Bobby shouts, but he has lost enthusiasm for his speech.

He pulls his T-shirt on, trying not to snag it on his Hickman catheter. The catheter enters above his right nipple and then tunnels under the skin to pierce the large vein beneath his collarbone and extend through it till it reaches the vein just above his heart. For two years the Hickman has been his lifeline. It has spared him countless needles; blood for testing has been drawn out of it, and all his intravenous medicine, at home and in the hospital, administered through it. He has not used the catheter in two days; the solution he injects to keep it open is in the refrigerator in the South End apartment he abandoned in such haste the previous day. The catheter has probably clotted off, he thinks.

He turns on the TV as he dresses. He flips past the local news stations, half expecting to see his mug flash on the screen, and stops at CNN. He presses the "Mute" button as Miss Cheekbones talks. He speaks for her: "An overgrowth of eyelashes is being described among persons infected with the AIDS virus who are on the anti-AIDS drug AZT." Here she flashes her dimples, and Bobby continues. "Concern is being expressed by advocates that this will result in people being identified in their workplace as infected with the AIDS virus. . . ." He remembers his father watching boxing on television with the volume turned off, providing ringside commentary in his loud voice: "Muñoz,

once again pounding the body, coming straight ahead,
hooking to the ribs—Styles make fights, wouldn't you say,
Marv? You couldn't find two more different fighters.
Concinni hasn't stopped moving, dodging, backpedaling,
weaving—Oh! Concinni is tagged with a left! He's in trouble! He's down! Good night, sweet prince!"

He picks up the briefcase. It is burgundy and made of
soft leather; it belonged to Michael. Michael moved into
the apartment soon after Primo moved out. Michael did
research on mice at the Genecor Research Center—mice
with heart disease. He got sick and moved back to Iowa,
leaving everything: his medicine, his furniture, his briefcase.

The bag has handles that slide out. In the outer, zip-
pered pocket is Bobby's birth certificate, his living will,
his prescriptions, a yellow pad, and a pen. Inside the bag
is the gun. And thick wads of hundred-dollar bills. He
takes the gun out—Primo's gun. In his hand it looks ani-
mate and repulsive. He regrets having it; he regrets having needed it. He walks around the room, looking for a
place to hide it. He has a vision of a child discovering the
gun, examining it, playing with it. Reluctantly, he puts it
back in the briefcase.

He leaves the motel after a last look around. He takes a
bus and gets off near M.I.T., near the hospital. A mist is
rising off the river. He walks onto the bridge on Massachusetts Avenue. Halfway across, the muscles of his
calves begin to hurt. These are not my muscles, he thinks
as he reaches down to touch them. This is not my pain.
He leans over the railing and looks down at the water. A
purple reflection of his face flashes at him, and he pulls
away from the railing.

He starts walking again, watching his feet: one boot
with silver chain, the other plain; left, right, left, right.

This is the only way to do it, he thinks—something Primo never understood. He is angry when he thinks of Primo, and Michael. Primo gave up almost at once. Primo had made the move to Boston with Bobby, in search of better AIDS care, but had bolted from the clinic after the first visit, terrified by the sight of a cachectic young man in the waiting room. Primo's only fight—before he was hospitalized—was to take wild risks in his plane. He tried Dead Man's Stalls and Cuban 8s in the Cessna until they took away his license. Later, Bobby heard from others—because they had separated by then; the path Bobby had chosen to deal with the disease made Primo and his fatalism impossible to be around—that Primo began to cruise, spreading it, poisoning as many others as he could, as if it would ease his own pain. This had enraged Bobby so much that he did not attend Primo's funeral. Primo's mother called him afterward, screamed at him, accused him of killing her son. Michael gave up in a different way: He left one morning, saying that the magic of being in Waterloo, Iowa, eating his mama's cooking, going to the high-school ball games, doing whatever one did in Waterloo, Iowa, would somehow save him. It didn't.

Meanwhile, Bobby had tried it all: AZT, then ddI, now ddC. And ganciclovir. And the underground Compound Q. And intravenous protein feeds. And aerosol pentamidine. He had meditated—he still did. He had gone macrobiotic until he could no longer swallow. "Oh, I may die," he shouts at a car that passes by, "but not without a goddam fight!"

Near the Christian Science Building, Bobby jams one toe between the stones of the retaining wall and climbs up to reach some lilacs that hang from a bush. It is more effort than he thought it would be. He gets the flowers, but his shoulder hurts. He hears the woman's voice before he sees her. "Those are pretty flowers. But you should leave them on the tree."

She wears a track suit and tennis shoes; her gray hair peeks out from under a scarf. A handkerchief is tightly wadded in her hand, and she is breathless. Bobby holds the flowers out to her; it freezes whatever else she was going to say, and she breaks into a shy smile. He drops slowly to one knee. He imagines he catches the scent of her perspiration, sees the steam rising off her body. "The official flower of our state, ma'am."

"You shouldn't have done that," she says, her hands reaching for one cluster, "but they are beautiful."

"Aren't you going to ask me what state?"

"Are you all right?"

He gets up and rubs his shoulder. It is on his tongue to say "the State of Immunodeficiency." Instead, he says, "No, I'm not all right."

Her smile melts into an expression of concern. She moves her feet, conscious that she has tarried too long already, but feels obliged to ask: "Can I do anything?"

"Are you a magician?" Bobby asks. "Never mind. No, you can't do anything. Thank you for stopping, though. Thank you."

She waves and walks away briskly, her elbows pumping high, her lockstep gait quickening; she turns when she nears the bridge, and smiles.

Bobby watches her till she is out of sight; he feels the anger return again. It comes in waves and crashes over him. Yesterday, rage at the mindless bills, the dunning letters, and—finally—the cutting off of his telephone and electricity had carried him downtown. He had seen his reflection as he tore into the Bank of Boylston—a whirling dervish in a black coat, with gun drawn. He almost shot

at the reflection. Could a face really be that purple? He
braced himself, expecting to be challenged at any moment. Instead, they pushed money bundles at him, even
gave him a bag to stuff them in. When the bag was full,
he shouted, "What now? What now?" but none of the
prone figures would move. "What now?" he cried to the
camera on the ceiling.

Too late he remembers that he could have given the
woman some of the money.

He rests outside the hospital by the dry fountain that is
full of butts and matchsticks. Then he starts walking
again, against the flow of traffic as the eleven-to-seven
nurses head for the parking lot. He bypasses the main entrance and goes into the tunnel and walks down it to the
Kass Memorial Building and then takes the elevator to the
fifth floor. He walks past patients' rooms smelling of
Lysol and bacon. In the nurses' lounge the coffee is fresh,
and he pours himself a cup, then snaps open drawer after
drawer until he finds some sugar. He empties six packets
into his cup.

Two people in white come in. One male, one female.
One black, one white.

"Who are you?" one asks.

"Who are you?" he replies.

"We work here."

"*We work here*," Bobby says. Such complacency, such
arrogance, he thinks. "And I am a walking skeleton. I'm a
voodoo doll. I own this hospital." They look confused. He
explains: "I'm your three square meals a day."

His hands are full now, what with the lilacs and the coffee and the briefcase. He moves toward the nurses and
they step quickly aside.

Bobby goes down the stairs to the second floor and

then through a long hallway, past dark labs and locked offices, until he reaches the clinic waiting room. Before the first sip of coffee is past his throat, before he can even sit down, he feels his intestines start to writhe, and he hurries for the men's room.

Back in the waiting room, he takes one lilac stalk and leans over the counter, over the patient-register book, and wedges the stalk between the printer stand and the printer. Laurelei will keep it there all day. She says that whenever she thinks of lilacs or smells them she thinks of him.

He tries breathing and meditation. He wants to feel the prana ebb and flow. *Ommmmm.* His mind strays and he brings it back. *Ommmmm.* But there is only anger. *Ommmmm.* He thinks of his job as a short-order cook in Hoboken, ten years ago, while Primo was enrolled in a six-month course for his commercial license. It was fluid motion for Bobby—a moving line walked past him and they called the tune while he danced. He was the ballerina of Niko's in Hoboken, cracking eggs, flipping hotcakes, buttering toast, sliding the dishes down the counter. Oronfrio, the manager, said he didn't know why Bobby bothered with the men when he could have had any of the women. "Because I can have any of the men," Bobby would say, flipping a morsel of scrambled egg into the air and catching it on his tongue, all the while looking into Oronfrio's eyes. *Ommmmm.* He thinks of his mother in Spartanburg and how she must shudder when she thinks of him with Primo. *That's right, Mama. I was his blushing bride. He did to me more or less what Dad did to you.* She will be surprised when she gets the money he sent her. She will draw the shades and walk around the living room talking to herself, tormented by the knowledge of where the money came from and what she ought to do, and by her greed for the money and her wish to burrow in her house and deny his existence. He laughs aloud, and gives up the idea of meditation.

Three guys come in; two of them are a couple he knows from the waiting room. They run a bar in the South End. Bobby remembers buying some dope from one of them a year ago. The third one—the new one—is not quite with them. He signs in and sits two seats away from Bobby while the couple sign in. Bobby smells aftershave on the new guy, but beneath it is a sour, unwashed smell. It is the smell of fear, Bobby thinks; it irritates him. Laurelei arrives behind the desk and turns pale when she sees Bobby. "Thanks," she stammers when the dope dealer comments on the flowers. "Bobby brings them in," she adds, and looks at Bobby fearfully. Bobby waves back and points at the rest of the flowers, which he has arranged in a soda can on the windowsill, but Laurelei runs into the inner office.

"The official AIDS flower," Bobby says to the new guy, pointing to the lilacs. The new guy looks at the lilacs and then at the purple growths on Bobby's face. "Get it?" Bobby asks, touching the biggest growth, over his right eyelid. "Lilacs out of the dead land. Get it?"

The new guy just blinks. The disease is not choosy, Bobby thinks; this kid is dumb as a coal bucket. The new guy tries to ignore Bobby. He shakes out a cigarette with trembling fingers. There is a ring with a turquoise stone on his pinky, and his nails are long. They would be elegant in a different setting from the Metropolitan Hospital clinic. His brown hair is slicked back in a "wet look"—a style that Primo favored years before it became commonplace. Bobby moves over to sit next to him.

"You didn't really have a bath, did you?" Bobby asks.

"Your hair looks like you had a bath, but you didn't. And you hurried with your breakfast—doughnuts on the way? How did I know? The powdered sugar on your mustache. I'm Bobby, by the way." The new guy has the cigarette in one hand and a lighter in the other. "You can't smoke here. You can shake my hand, though. You can't get it by shaking my hand. Besides, you already got it."

The new guy puts the lighter away and Bobby shakes his hand. The hand feels crumbly, fragile, but it is its sweatiness that primes Bobby, forces him to take more interest in this boy.

"You must be Clovis," Bobby says. "I saw the register. 'Clovis: Forty-five.' Forty-five minutes is for new patients. Must be you. Let me guess. You tested positive— what, two years ago? And you were positive before that but didn't want the test. And now you wake up in the night and you feel cold and you put on socks and wrap your head up, and then in an hour you drench the sheets. And then you feel cold again. That's why you didn't shower, right? You were cold when it was time to have the shower. Am I right? You're shit-scared, am I right?"

Clovis tries to get up. "Sit down," Bobby says to him. "You can't afford not to listen to me. You need to listen to me. I'm a survivor—nine years. If you don't want to live, just keep walking. That's better. Let's begin." Bobby puts both his hands round Clovis's forearm and twists the skin in opposite directions; Clovis yelps. "That's called a barber's twist, Clovis. Keep your eyes on the skin." A shower of fine red dots makes a bracelet on Clovis's forearm. "Oh, oh! You know what that means, don't you? Your platelets are low. You're farther along than you thought, Clovis. Good thing you came today." Clovis's face shrivels.

Clovis's acquaintances are getting out. Clovis tries to

rise again. His eyes plead with the couple, who are standing at the door, but Bobby takes the gun out of the briefcase and sets it on the chair. "Clovis is with me," Bobby tells them. "And don't roll your eyes at me, honey. You guys don't look so hot yourselves. You got a way to make him live? I can make him live. What have you got?" The couple hurry out.

Bobby looks at Clovis; he wonders why he is bothering with this kid. Has Clovis become his hostage? In return for what? Bobby gets up and bolts the door. He paces around and then sits down. He has no doubt the police will be here soon. He takes one of Clovis's cigarettes and lights it and hands it to Clovis. "You can smoke now, Clovis. Everything has changed." He sits down and thinks a while and then picks his words carefully.

"You don't know how special I am, Clovis. I am a nine-year survivor. I've beaten the odds; I am way over the median survival. Look it up, if you want. I'm the only nine-year guy in this clinic. And it wasn't luck either, Clovis. I fought for every fucking bit of it; I *scrapped* for it; I *took* all the responsibility."

Clovis is listening; the fear and gloom that were on his face are momentarily erased.

"Level with me, Clovis. What is the scariest thing about this whole business? That you can die from it? Death? Bang, bang? You probably will die from it, right?" Clovis's eyes get big. "And that fear is what kept you from being tested? And that fear is still there—right?" Clovis's eyes get even wider. Bobby takes out his yellow pad and pencil. He pats Clovis's hand. "The only way to beat this is to lose your fear, Clovis," he says kindly. "The fear doesn't do you any good. In fact the fear can kill you before the disease does. It's like most anything else in life: lose your fear and it can't touch you."

Bobby massages Clovis's hand, trying to imagine what it is like to be a Clovis. What does a Clovis really feel? He sees a "LOSER, LOSER, LOSER" sign flash across Clovis's face. Clovis is giving up, retreating again. Clovis is ugly, Bobby thinks. The dimples are really pimples, he has dandruff on his eyelashes, his face is oily. Clovis tries to withdraw his hand. Bobby considers stopping but feels obliged to continue; let the kid have the massage, for what it's worth.

"It's not illegal to hold hands—is it, Clovis? O.K., I'm going to let go of your hand. I want you to answer a series of questions for me. I'll write down your answers on paper, and then you put that paper in your pocket and carry it with you. Then—trust me—you will have conquered death. It worked for me. O.K.? First of all, where do you want to die?"

Clovis's chin is quivering. Bobby makes lines and draws columns on the paper. He is aware of the absolute silence in the building. "I'm asking you where you want to die? In the hospital? At home? On the street? You live with those guys, right? You all came in the same car, right? You work in the bar for them, right? A little dope, a little head—Hey, *I* know. So, you ready to die with them, in their apartment? In the South End? Or you want to die at your own house, in your mama's arms? Or do you want to die with me?" Clovis begins to open his mouth, but no answer seems forthcoming. "With Mama," Bobby whispers for him. He uses a southern accent. Childlike and *very* southern. "With Mama? Let me guess—Alabama? Tennessee? O.K., you want to die with Mama? You need to write that down, Clovis. Get that down on paper. Otherwise they'll dump you in Roxbury Cemetery. O.K., so you want to die at home. Now, what do you want them to do with your body?"

Clovis is weeping now, his face in his hands, and Bobby strokes the ducktail, his fingers coming away greasy. "It boils down to do you want to be cremated or buried?" Bobby busies himself writing on the yellow sheet. He is aware of the sirens approaching the parking lot outside, but he concentrates on the paper:

BODY	Home	x	Away	
DISPOSAL	Bury		Cremate	x
SERVICE	Yes	x	No	
MUSIC				
TOMBSTONE				

"I personally can't stand the thought of waking up one day to find I'm locked in a pine box with rats nibbling at my eye sockets. If I was you I would go for cremation. It's cheaper, easier for your family."

Clovis is sniffling and carrying on. Bobby lets the X remain where it is. Cremation for Clovis.

"Music? I assume you want a service—so, music. See, that's something you can control. Music: What do you want them to play? Come on, Clovis—music?

" 'Rocky Top,' Clovis? 'Rocky Top you'll always be, Home sweet home to me.' " Singing the song makes Bobby laugh. He gets up and tries to clog but can't move his feet quickly enough. "Good choice, Clovis! 'Rocky Top' it shall be." He writes in "Rocky Top." He lets go of the pad to hold Clovis's hand again, because Clovis is trying to get away. Clovis sits down on the floor, his hand in Bobby's grasp.

"The eulogy, Clovis! Don't forget the eulogy. What do you want them to say? O.K., O.K., you can think about that. But the tombstone, the grave marker. That *has* to be your choice. 'Clovis. Our beloved son—' "

Clovis breaks loose. He unbolts the door, pulls it open, and runs around the corner.

"Wait, Clovis! Put this paper in your pocket."

Bobby picks up the gun but then tosses it out the window. He sits on the floor and carefully folds the paper into an airplane. His body is rocking back and forth with concentration. When he is done, he stands up and looks out the window. He is astonished by the crowd below. He sees Chatupadia and waves. He slowly pushes the window wide open and stands on a chair. With a flick of the wrist he sails the plane out. It is a wonderful plane—the best he has ever made. It catches an updraft and rises in a tight spiral. Bobby is drawn to the window: The yellow plane is still climbing. Bobby steps out on the sill and cranes his neck to follow it. Finally, when it can climb no more, it banks into a lazy left turn. He is aware of voices yelling at him, but they are drowned out by the roar of the plane's engine. He imagines himself as the pilot. The plane finds another updraft. Bobby increases the power to full throttle and points the nose straight up. Gravity works against him, and he watches the airspeed indicator drop rapidly. Just before the plane shudders to a stop, he applies full rudder. He has timed it exactly, and his plane makes a perfect Hammerhead turn, rotating on the tip of one wing. Now he points the nose at the crowd below. He sees his airspeed rise again. The wings shudder and the wind whips at his face. He puts his finger on the "Fire" button. "Coming at you!" he shouts.

THE NUMBER YOU HAVE REACHED

Rex Knight

*I*t was 92 in the shade at 9 A.M. The hot, dry Santa Ana winds that gusted into Los Conejos overnight while Jeff was on duty made it a foregone that the mercury would hit at least 100 by noon.

Jeff didn't care. He liked the heat. Last night, while the town slept, Jeff had issued four speeding tickets, arrested three DUIs, and investigated a particularly messy dispute between a Ford Mustang and a concrete bridge abutment. The abutment won.

What Jeff didn't like was working the graveyard shift: no one to play with during the daytime, and trying to stay awake while keeping the deserted streets safe from speeders. But finally, he was home. He left a trail of clothing in his wake as he got ready for bed and a hard night's day.

The gun belt holding the holstered Smith & Wesson .38 was tossed onto the recliner, en route to the bathroom. The boots were shucked off by the sofa. As Jeff peed, he took off his breakaway necktie and his shirt, casually pitching them onto the bathroom floor. The uniform pants went next, in the bedroom doorway. Naked except for his white crew socks, Jeff sat on the bed, dropped the socks onto the floor, pulled the sheet over his head, and immediately fell asleep.

The phone rang. Once. Twice. Three times.

Jeff fumbled for the receiver. "Hello?"

"Hi."

"Hi."

Silence. Jeff looked at his watch: 11:03 A.M. *This better fucking be good.*

"You there?" asked the phone.

"Yeah," mumbled Jeff. "I'm here. Who is this?"

"This is Mark."

"Mark who?"

"Did I wake you up?"

"Yeah."

"Sorry."

The voice was pleasant. Masculine. Soothing. A radio announcer's voice.

" 'S okay."

"Do you have a hard-on?"

"What?" *What?*

"Do you have a hard-on?"

"Uh . . . a hard-on?"

"Yeah."

It clicked. *This is a fucking obscene phone call!* "Listen, dude, I don't know who the fuck you are and I don't care," Jeff stormed. "Go whack off or do whatever it is that you do and leave me the fuck *alone!*"

"Wait—" The tone was urgent.

"*Look—*"

"Listen, I'm *sorry*. I kind of weird out every once in a while, y'know? Go back to sleep. Sorry I bothered you."

"Okay, apology accepted," said Jeff. "G'night."

"Wait. Sir?"

Jeff sighed. "Yeah?"

"Look, I hate to run this into the ground—but *do* you have a hard-on?"

Despite himself, Jeff laughed. "Okay, partner," he said, reaching for a cigarette, "lay it on me."

"Pardon?"

"Look, I've had three hours' sleep. I'm fucking exhausted, but now I'm awake. So it's either watch *Wheel of Fortune* or listen to you. You've got a sexy voice. I've never had an obscene call before. So just make this good, okay?"

A silence followed.

"So how's it goin'?" said the stranger.

"Goin' just fine," said Jeff, exhaling a drag from his Winston. "What did you say your name was?"

"Mark."

"Mark what?"

"Mark'll do for now."

"How'd you get my number, Mark?"

"I just dialed it."

"At random?"

"At random."

Why in the fuck am I talking to this guy? Jesus Christ, there's eighty thousand people in this town, and this wacko's gotta pick me! (So why indeed *are you talking to him? You're a cop. You know how to deal with it—hang up the goddamn phone.)*

"Do you know who I am?" asked Jeff.

"In what context?" replied Mark.

"Damn, *that's* pretty existential."

"I don't know what that means," said Mark.

"I mean, do you know where I live, what I do for a living, who my friends are, my bank balance—y'know, the basics?"

"No. Wish I did, though."

"Why?"

" 'Cause you sound hot."

"Do I?"

"Trust me," replied Mark. "So tell me, what's your name?"

"Jeff." *Jesus, that was swift. Now again, what is it you do for a living, Officer Novak? Why don't you tell him your address while you're at it, so he can come over and butt-fuck you at gunpoint in the middle of the night some time?*

"Look, Jeff," Mark said calmly, with that smooth voice. "I kind of get this feeling that you're . . . resisting this. But just flow with me, okay? Go with it." There was a pause. "Now tell me about that hard-on."

Jeff was surprised to find not only that his penis was rock hard but that his hand was firmly gripping it. He let go of his dick as if it were a cobra.

"Look, I think—"

"I thought so." Mark's voice was calming. "No big deal, okay? It's natural. I've got a *major* hard-on even as we speak."

"Yeah, I'll just bet you do."

"Jeff—can the sarcasm, all right? So, how big's your cock?"

"Big enough."

"Jeff, Jeff, Jeff. What are we going to *do* with you? This is an obscene phone call, remember? You've gotta cooperate."

Jeff was amazed at the caller's sheer balls. "Christ, you're somethin' else. Anyone ever tell you that?"

"Lots of times," replied Mark. "How big's that dick of yours?"

"Honestly, or just to appease an obscene caller?"

"Honestly."

"I guess about seven inches . . . maybe seven and a half." Jeff's hand unconsciously dropped back down to his cock, and he slowly began stroking it. "So how big's yours?"

"Twelve inches."

"Yeah. *Right*."

Silence.

"Jeff?"

"Yeah?"

"It really *is* twelve inches."

"In your dreams."

"Dude, I am not bullshitting you."

"Okay. So what do you do with this twelve-inch dick?"

"I'd like to stick it up your ass."

"I'll just bet you would."

Mark's voice took on a more intense edge. "What's the biggest thing you've ever *had* up your ass?"

"Oh, I dunno," Jeff replied. "A crowbar, maybe. No, wait, I remember. It was a Gallo salami. Dry variety."

Another silence.

"Jeff," said Mark, in a tone that sounded hurt, "if you're not gonna go along with this, I'm gonna hang up."

Jeff laughed. "*What?* You're gonna *hang up*? Jesus H. Christ, now *that's* rich. A fucking obscene caller's gonna hang up on *me*!"

Silence.

"You there?" asked Jeff.

Mark had hung up. Slowly, Jeff replaced the receiver.

Now, that was fucking weird. I didn't think guys *ever got dirty phone calls. Wait a minute—could this be one of the day shift's dumb-ass jokes? Of course! Flynn's still gunning for me because of that gopher snake I put in his locker. Flynn. Yeah. It's gotta be. Just about his speed, too. Not his voice, though.*

Jeff smoked another Winston, then buried his head under the pillow. The heat outside was getting intense, and despite eight years of shift work, Jeff had never gotten used to sleeping in the daytime. The sound of a lawn edger from the yard next door drilled into his brain.

Why do I feel guilty about pissing off a telephone pervert, ferchrissakes? Could it be that maybe there's a little . . . curiosity . . . about the idea of a phone freak? I've never really thought about . . . aural sex. . . . Hey, that's pretty good—

The phone rang and Jeff caught it on the first ring. "Yeah."

"Listen," said Mark. "I'm sorry I hung up on you. I shouldn't be bothering you in the first place. But you talked to me. I don't know what I expected."

"Get lots of hang-ups?" asked Jeff.

"Oh, I guess you could say that," replied Mark. "I don't expect you to believe this, but I don't do this all that often, you know."

Yeah, right. "No?"

"No. I really don't." Mark paused. "You still feel like talkin'?"

"Sure, why not?"

"You sound hot," said Mark. "What do you look like?"

"Well . . . I'm five foot ten; short, dark-brown hair; green eyes; I weigh one sixty-five; umm, I guess I've got a nice build. Got a mustache."

"How old are you?"

"Thirty-two."

"Oh, an *old* guy."

Jeff bristled. "I hadn't exactly thought of thirty-two as being 'an *old* guy.' " He lit another Winston.

Mark was quick to reassure. "Hey, relax. I *like* older guys."

"Yeah? So what're you, twelve?"

"I'm twenty-three."

"And what do *you* look like?"

"Five-eleven, one eighty-five, black hair—I've got a mustache, too—blue eyes. Damn nice body. I work out."

"Yeah?" Jeff's voice dropped an octave. "Black hair and blue eyes?" *Man, someone sure as hell knows what buttons to push. But I guess if I have to have a fetish, I could do worse than that one. Fuck, I'd do Charles Manson if he had black hair and blue eyes. You don't see too many guys with black hair and blue eyes. Like the PacTel guy the other day who came into headquarters to fix the lieutenant's phone. He had black hair and blue—*the fuckin' telephone guy! *Could it be . . . ?*

"Yeah," said Mark. "And hung twelve inches."

"I think we've already established that," said Jeff, exhaling another drag of his cigarette. "Listen, I'm gonna ask you an off-the-wall question here."

"Shoot."

"Do you by any chance work for the phone company?"

Mark laughed. "No, I'm in drywall. Why? Do you *want* me to work for the phone company? I can go along with it, if that's what you're into."

"No," smiled Jeff. "That's okay."

"So, what do *you* do?"

"I'm a—I'm in social work."

"Like for the county?"

"Something like that," said Jeff, putting out his Winston and reaching for another.

Pause.

"So what do you like to do?" asked Mark, his voice almost a whisper.

Jeff was surprised at Mark's intensity. He closed his eyes. "I . . . I kind of like asses," he said.

"How?" asked Mark.

I fucking can't believe I'm having this conversation. Why am I . . . encouraging . . . this? Why don't I hang up? This is getting a little too . . . personal—

"What are *you* into?" Jeff countered.

"I like asses, too," said Mark.

"How does that work with a twelve-inch dick?"

"Not as well as you might think," replied Mark. "We can still talk about it, though."

"Yeah," said Jeff, slowly stroking his cock. "I guess we can."

And they did.

Eleven minutes later, after hanging up the phone, Jeff reached down to the floor for one of his crew socks, wiped the cum off his abdomen, tossed the sock back onto the floor, and fell asleep for the second time that hot July morning.

The calls continued over the summer. They came about once a week, and at all hours: ten at night, four in the morning, one in the afternoon. Jeff wasn't aware exactly when it was that he began looking forward to them.

By early autumn, Jeff and Mark were old friends. Sexually, they knew each other intimately—without ever having laid eyes on each other. Jeff found himself sliding more easily into the sex talk.

"Get that dick good and hard," Mark would whisper. "Then I want you to shove it up my ass."

"Lie on your stomach," Jeff would growl into the phone, as he stroked his cock. "Are you on your stomach? . . . Good. I'm gonna shove it right up there. Great big cock gonna go right up your butt. Hold on, buddy. . . . No, I'm not gonna hurt you, you know I wouldn't do that. . . . Don't worry, I know what I'm doin'. Relax and take it slow. I'm not gonna hurt you, buddy. . . .Yeah. You're gonna fuckin' love it. Easy, easy. . . . Just hang on, okay? Hang on. Yeah, guy, you're doin' great. Damn nice ass, buddy. Damn, partner, I'm about to shoot."

"Go for it, man," Mark would urge.

"Oh yeah, oh yeah, oh *YEAH*!"

The telephone dates that had begun in mid-July continued into early October. It was always Mark who controlled the *après*-sex conversations—talk that never ventured into emotional or sexual territory. The Dodgers, the new Chevys, the latest lineup on the Fox Network—all "safe" subjects—the comfortable colloquy that was no different from that which Jeff enjoyed with his boringly straight fellow officers.

"How long have you been gay?" Jeff once asked.

"I don't want to talk about that," Mark replied.

Mark was equally abrupt one morning when Jeff inquired point-blank why Mark refused to tell anything about his personal life.

"It's none of your business, okay?" Mark had said curtly.

However, over the months, Jeff did manage to glean the information that Mark really did work in drywall construction; that he drove a Ford pickup; that he was originally from Monterey; and that he occasionally smoked pot. He also found out that they'd both attended the same showing of the latest Spielberg movie one night at a neighborhood cineplex. It had been a late showing, and there weren't that many people in the audience. When Mark told him the next day that he'd also been there with his girlfriend (*girlfriend?*), Jeff taxed his brain for hours in an attempt to match the physical description with someone he might have seen. But he never made a match.

Conversely, Mark knew that Jeff did shift work "as a social worker"; that he smoked Winstons (*"Dude, don't you know that those things are gonna kill you?"*); and his address. That had been an accident.

"So what part of town you live in?" Mark had asked one night.

"The west side," Jeff had said, recklessly adding, "right off the end of West Palm Street."

"No shit?" said Mark. "My sister lives on Harbor View."

"Yeah?" said Jeff. "So do I."

"Where?" asked Mark.

"Twenty-twelve."

"My sister's a block away, in the twenty-one-hundred block," said Mark. "Small world, eh?"

The one thing Jeff never got from Mark was his phone number.

"Sorry," Mark replied the first and only time Jeff had asked. "No can do."

"How come?"

"The chick I live with. I don't think she'd understand."

Jeff was annoyed. "Yeah?" he said. "What about me? How do you know I don't live with someone?"

" 'Cause if you did, you would have told me by now," Mark said simply.

Then there was the whole idea of *phone sex*, which kept coming back to gnaw at Jeff like a wolf in the night. *Am I as crazy as he is? Why the hell am I even talking to this pervert?*

Jeff was always careful to tap-dance around the sexual come-ons that are a part of every cop's job. Jeff looked sharp in his blue uniform, and he knew it. So when a speeder or other petty traffic miscreant—of either sex—

would slyly offer to provide a phone number to him, Jeff would smile and politely refuse the offer. No offense. *Other priorities, you know?*

Jeff's former lover, Tom, whom Jeff still considered to be his best friend, couldn't understand why Jeff didn't use "the cop thing" to his advantage.

"You've got guys out there literally throwing themselves at you," Tom told Jeff after dumping him for a doctor at the hospital where he worked as a paramedic. "You're hot-looking to begin with. But in that uniform you're a fuckin' heartbreaker. Jesus Christ, why don't you ever go for it?"

"It's like this," Jeff replied, "the world is divided into two groups: one that hates cops, and one that gets off on cops. I don't have to worry about the first group. But I will be goddamned if I go to bed with someone just *because* I'm a cop. I mean, why not just give 'em the uniform and let 'em fuck *that*, while I go and make some popcorn or something?"

"That's the most stupid thing I've ever heard," said Tom. "Fuckin' a cop is the Great American Gay Fantasy. You're *the real thing*. What the hell's the matter with you?"

"I want a guy to be interested in *me*, not my clothes. I need a guy to want *me*, Tom."

"But think of all the guys you can get!"

"Is that how I got you?" Jeff asked quietly.

Tom said, "I like you because you're a great guy."

To which Jeff replied, "That doesn't answer my question."

Jeff was pissed. He'd waited for the repairman from House of Video for nearly five hours now. The RCA had crapped out entirely, and this was the last day of the World Series. Fortunately, the TV was still under warranty.

The doorbell rang.

About fucking time.

Jeff strode to the front door and opened it.

"Jeff?"

The man standing on the porch was almost six feet tall. He had black hair, a matching mustache, and piercing blue eyes that looked like they'd melt glass.

"Fuck. I can't believe it. Mark?" Jeff grinned broadly.

Mark smiled back. "Hi."

"I thought you were . . . I mean . . . you're not the guy from House of Video, are you?"

"I thought you were into phone linemen."

"No—I . . . Hey, fuck it. Come in, guy."

"Hey," smiled Mark. "You're all right. For an old dude, you're not bad-lookin'."

"Up yours." Jeff couldn't stop grinning.

"I hope you don't mind my dropping in like this."

"Hey, not at all," said Jeff. "You want a Pepsi or something?"

"A beer might be nice."

"You sure you're old enough?"

"Fuck you, oldster."

"You wish," said Jeff. "Budweiser okay?"

"My beer of choice."

"Thanks," said Mark, as Jeff handed him the glass. "So how come you're home this afternoon?"

"I thought you might call."

"Yeah?" Mark sounded pleased.

Jeff nodded toward the RCA. "Actually, the TV's busted," he said. "I'm waiting for the repairman."

The doorbell rang.

This time, it really was the House of Video. As Jeff argued with the repairman, Mark swallowed the last of his beer and stood up to leave.

"Hey, don't go just yet," Jeff told Mark.

"I've gotta pick up my lady at work. I just wanted to check in with you."

"You'll call?" asked Jeff.

"Bet on it, amigo."

Mark was true to his word. Four days later, at 2:40 in the morning, Jeff's phone rang.

"Yeah?" answered Jeff.

"So whatcha think?"

"I like the package."

"So do I."

Long, heavy, deep pause.

"So," said Jeff, clearing his throat. "Moment-of-truth time, eh?"

"I hope so, Jeff."

"Okay," said Jeff. "Let's get down to it. Ya wanna do it?"

"Do it?"

"Yeah."

"You mean, like we've been talking about all this time? Except formal?"

"Yeah, that's what I mean."

Silence.

"Listen, Jeff, have you really thought about this? I mean, talkin' about it's one thing, but to actually—"

"I'm not gonna dignify that," interrupted Jeff.

"You're really serious, then?"

"I'm *fuckin'* serious."

"Okay," said Mark. "I'm gonna lay some shit on you that maybe might scare you off. But I think it's impor-tant. I'm twenty-three years old. I know I'm hot, and I've never actually done it with a guy. See, it took me a long time to accept the fact that I'm gay. You know I live with a lady."

"Uh-huh."

"Well," continued Mark, "I don't know how much

longer that's going to last. The phone thing used to be a . . . a diversion. I can get my rocks off by dialing phone numbers at random and once in a while hitting on some-one like you who'll talk me through it. It's nice and safe that way, you know? I mean, no involvement, nothing. And then I call you. And, like, I *trust* you. Oh, fuck. I guess what I'm saying is that I guess I'm . . . scared. 'Cause I really don't know the moves."

". . . Oh."

"But I'll tell you something else, Jeff."

"Yes?" Jeff's voice was a whisper.

"I think you're a very hot man. I hadn't really expected that. And ever since I saw you, I can't stop thinking about you. You're *fuckin'* hot. And right now, as far as I'm con-cerned, there are only two alternatives. And those are ei-ther never call you again and forget that you ever existed, or go over to your place and fuck your brains out."

Silence.

"Jeff?"

"I'm here, buddy."

"Okay. That's where I'm coming from. Your choice, dude."

"Get your ass over here."

Jeff hung up the phone, got out of bed, and grabbed his yellow terry-cloth bathrobe. He found his cigarettes, lit up, and began pacing. He walked into the kitchen and poured himself half a glassful of Bacardi, which he downed, straight, in one shot.

Fuck. I can't believe this is actually gonna go down.

Jeff poured another shot of Bacardi. His hands were shaking badly. He downed the drink as quickly as he'd drunk the first. He ground out his Winston, then immedi-ately lit another. His dick was rock hard.

He caught a glance at himself in the mirror above the

fireplace. *Jesus—a yellow bathrobe, ferchrissakes!* He dashed into the bedroom and slid open the door of the walk-in closet. Jeff took stock of what was there: six uniform shirts all in a row; four Arrow dress shirts, for court appearances, weddings, and funerals; one leather motorcycle jacket with the Los Conejos P.D. sleeve patch—a remembrance of the days when he rode motors; one leather bomber jacket, for when he rode his own Honda 750.

Going to the dresser, he rummaged through his overflowing T-shirt drawer. Now, this was more like it. He tossed the robe into a corner and pulled on a black-and-white Raiders T-shirt. Hey, very nice! The shirt barely—but not quite—covered his ass. He was aware that when he walked, the lower part of his butt was exposed. Okay, worse things could happen. *I don't think Mark'll mind.*

The doorbell rang. *Okay, guy,* Jeff told himself as he shot a final approving look in the dresser mirror . . . and *there's the pitch.*

Mark was smiling lecherously as Jeff opened the door. The Levi's, workboots, and blue cotton work shirt emblazoned with LOS CONEJOS DRYWALL and Mark's name in red script over the pocket added exactly the right dash of authenticity. *Now I think I see why some people are into uniforms.*

" 'Bout time, partner," Jeff smiled back.

Mark sauntered into the living room in a slightly arrogant, pigeon-toed way Jeff hadn't noticed before—but which he found extremely attractive. "So," said Mark, fixing Jeff with those cobalt-blue eyes. "Whatcha got in mind?"

"I need some drywall done," replied Jeff.

"Up yours."

"Sounds fine to me, guy."

Mark followed Jeff into the bedroom.

"I like your shirt," Mark said softly, reaching up and gently running a hand over Jeff's buttocks, sliding the back of a finger between them on the way down.

"Yeah, I thought you might," said Jeff. "Want a drink?"

"Uh-uh," replied Mark, his voice husky. "I want you."

"Hell," said Jeff as he slid his hand down the front of Mark's work shirt, "I guess we've gone this far."

Jeff watched as Mark unbuttoned the shirt, fascinated with how hairy Mark's chest was—nearly as hairy as his own. Mark's hand went for the belt buckle of his Levi's.

"Don't," said Jeff. "Let me." With trembling fingers, Jeff undid the buckle, then began undoing the buttons on Mark's fly. He gently slid the 501s down Mark's hips.

"Good Christ!" exclaimed Jeff in amazement. "It really *is* twelve inches!"

Mark let the Levi's drop to his ankles. "C'mere," he said, smiling as he pulled Jeff to him. Again, Jeff ran his hand down Mark's chest—only this time he didn't stop. His hand traveled down farther. Slowly, slowly he caressed Mark's belly, marveling at the solidness of it. Then, lower. Then—

Mark moaned.

Ever so slowly, Jeff's hand moved toward Mark's
Good god, I've never seen a cock like that in my life
penis, and then
Never held a dick like that before
there it was
Enough to choke a fuckin'—
And Mark's hand, lightly resting, fingers spread, on Jeff's left buttock, slowly
Feels nice
moved slightly inward and
Oh, yeah
fingers slightly apart
Like velvet

and

What's he doin'?

finger probing, slightly

Hey, I don't DO that

pushing inward

But it feels kinda nice

and farther into

Owww

and

Mark's body stiffened. The hand withdrew. Puzzled, Jeff looked at Mark. Mark was staring past him, and staring hard. Jeff turned around to see what Mark was looking at. Mark was transfixed by the closet. Confused, Jeff took a step backward and looked quizzically at Mark.

"You're a *cop*," Mark spat out, not taking his eyes off Jeff's neatly arranged uniform shirts.

"Oh," said Jeff, relieved, "Is *that* all? Y'know, you had me—"

"You're a fuckin' *cop*!" Mark shouted. The cobalt-blue eyes were glittering ice.

"Yeah, I'm a cop. Big deal. Listen, if you think I'm setting you up or something, you're—"

"You fucking *asshole*!" Mark yelled, grabbing his Levi's and pulling them up.

"*Hey*," said Jeff. "So I'm a cop, so fucking *what*? Cops can be gay too, y'know. It's even in the city charter."

"Fuck *you* . . . cop!" Mark snarled, hitching up his 501s.

Jeff grabbed Mark's shoulder. "Listen—"

Mark tried to wrench free. Jeff gripped harder. Years of experience in subduing recalcitrant "clients" kicked in as he dug his thumb hard into the pressure point below Mark's collarbone, bringing Mark nearly to his knees.

"*Ow*, you're *hurting* me, man!" The infinite anger in his eyes had given way to instant pain.

Jeff immediately released his grip, shocked by his own reaction. "Sorry—I'm really sorry. Mark—"

"I guess we know how you *really* get off—*faggot!*" Mark bolted for the front door, slamming it hard behind him.

"I'm sorry," whispered Jeff.

Jeff was devastated. *Would someone please explain what in the hell just happened?*

Slowly, he walked into the kitchen, where he poured himself another Bacardi.

And another.

And another.

Jeff smoked his way through half a pack of Winstons, and watched the sun come up through his bedroom window. He flashed again and again on the remark he'd made to Tom more than a year ago: *"The world is divided into two groups: one that hates cops, and one that gets off on cops."*

At 6:17, the phone rang. In his haste to grab it, Jeff knocked the overflowing ashtray onto the floor. He didn't care.

"Hello?"

"¿Hola? ¿Donde está Guadalupe?"

"Sorry," said Jeff. "You've got the wrong number." He slowly replaced the receiver.

JOHN

G . Winston James

As usual, the room was dim and I refused to lie down. Would not pretend to be comfortable. I preferred the feel of carpeted floor against my socked feet to the softness of my therapist's couch. Especially when leather sofas reminded me so much of my mother's softness when I was young. The way she would embrace me in her bed just moments after she'd beaten me, all the while asking me why I was crying.

". . . and the mirror cracked!" I yelled.

"But so what? Break through it," my therapist urged.

"My mother would never let me hold a knife in my hand. I lived in a world of spoons. Don't you see?"

"No. I don't," he said, probing.

"She cut up everything that wasn't soup," I cried.

"Everything! Then she would just sit there and watch me."

"Why?"

"Because she thought that evil little boys couldn't be trusted not to hurt other people along with themselves," I whispered.

After a brief silence, my therapist turned on the lights and allowed me a moment to stand there, two steps from the wall—facing it.

"Do you really listen to me when I rattle on?" I asked.

"Of course I do."

"Then why do you let me come back when we never accomplish anything?"

He thought for a moment. "Because I think I can help you. Help you to break through this wall and get at what's really keeping you and any possible life partner apart." He touched my shoulder. "There's something here, John. It's deep, but we can get to it."

"Maybe," I stuttered, "but I can't pay you anymore. I'm broke."

"You're not coming back?"

I laughed—not knowing whether he'd asked a question or made a statement—then slowly put on my coat and left, reminding myself that I had a friend's piano recital to go to. In the mood I was in, though, I felt I needed to stop somewhere else before I could possibly sit down to listen to Bryan render the many moods of Liszt's Transcendental Etudes.

So I walked out of the office and back into the shadows of my life. Heading to where I knew I should not go. To that place where I would be for the next two, three, or four hours—bored, but trapped. Caught by little desires that would hold me like good sleep, while other pitiful men scurried around me like rats. I'd go there all right. To 42nd and 8th. There.

I walked with very deliberate steps. A tall black man with a straight back, regal neck, and a warrior's gait. I exuded so much self-confidence, I think, that I had none left inside. And even now, I'm not really sure where it is most important that it be.

"Clean under there!" my mother screamed. "I'm not touching it."

"It's foreskin, Mother," I said to myself as I walked. I could name it now, but I never knew then.

"You think Janie and the other kids are gonna play with you with that nasty thing?"

"It's a penis, Mother. My penis. But it is dirty, isn't it?"

"Damn disgusting. Just like your father. Thank God his shiftless ass ain't around no more."

"Don't worry, Mama. I won't show it to Janie. I won't show it to anybody that knows me. I ain't gonna embarrass you."

Sidestepping people. That's what I was doing as I walked. If there was someone directly ahead of me, I moved. Someone too close to my shoulder, I turned. Thank God there was always some room at the side, and that most people seemed to decide a block back that they would not walk the same line as I.

But I looked them in the eye. All of them. I took pleasure in intimidating people as a black man. Especially as I walked to my little hell—it was like practice. There you were supposed to look into people's eyes, but only deep enough to discern which perversion had brought them. It was important to be able to distinguish the size queen from the sadist, and the pederast from the simply lonely man.

Everything else in those eyes was ignored, except the unmistakable look of guilt. Guilt at the fact that so many of us were there at the expense of spending quality time with others—our wives and boyfriends and children.

Loved ones who waited, like my boyfriend did as the hours passed and the bed grew cold beside him, where I should have been instead of dropping quarters into the abyss.

For those other men and me, the peep shows were a temptation we could seldom resist. In various ways, we led ourselves to believe that it was only in places like this that we could be true to ourselves—to our sexual natures. Avoiding everyday questions of protocol and morality to be free to explore one another's lust.

"Where you coming from? When did you sneak outta here?"

"Nowhere, Mama. I was just playing around with Bryan."

"At eleven o'clock at night. Boy, there ain't that much playing in the world, especially if you gonna get your knees that dirty."

"We was just—"

"Gimme them keys and shut your mouth."

Sometimes three or more times a week I made this same trip. Driven by a compulsion to see other men's cocks and to see just how far I would go. Walking through the door feels the same every time—that rush of expectation. Maybe I'll see a big dick soon, so I won't have to waste too much time or too many quarters. But it's not often that I leave in under an hour, all the same.

The ground floor was all straight porn. Racks and racks of magazines wiith bulging breasts and blondes' darting tongues. I passed them with hardly a glance as I headed toward the stairs—dim, with little mirrored tiles forming squares on the walls. Posters of naked men hung above, below, and between the tiles, filling the stairwell with reflections of sex, such that by the time you reached the bottom you were resolute in your pursuit of smut. Walking through the lower door and into the men's shop you put aside any lofty thoughts and became someone simply base.

"Get the hell into your room if you gonna cry! Nobody don't wanna look at you!"

"Why'd you hit me then, if you ain't expect me to cry?"

"Shut yo ass, boy, before I take off them clothes and beat the devil out of you! I don't want to hear about your feelings."

The shop was almost empty except for the attendants, who sold quarters and supposedly enforced the store rules against loitering and public sex. Worse still, there was no one attractive who was free. Most of them were hustlers— homeboys dressed in the roughness they knew would sell even if sex appeal failed them.

Every so often as I walked by, one of them would enter a booth and take out his dick for me to see. I would look up into the Hispanic or black face, then down to his trade. And I would smile and just walk on. The fact is, I'm reluctant to pay for sex. There's something about the payment, I think, that reminds me of a contract—of a responsibility I owe to someone in return for his service to me. Like some warped relationship in which giving love is replaced with the exchange of money. I find the idea distasteful.

So for the most part I avoided them for what felt like an hour. I ducked into booths next to the occasional black man, Hispanic, or white, pressed the "Up" button, and waited for the buddy shade between the booths to rise— but, for that, the other man would also have to press the "Up" button in his booth. I wanted to look full-on at my neighbor as I masturbated. I was hoping to see that humongous dick that would make me grab mine harder and jerk it and pull it faster until I came, eyes closed and lips apart.

It didn't happen. The cocks I saw were mediocre at best. At one point, five of us were looking at one another as the entire row of booths had raised its shades. We looked back and forth across the panes as we yanked on our dicks to get them hard, but there were no sculpted monoliths in the lot, not even a muscled body or handsome face. So after half a minute I pressed the "Down" buttons on each side of my booth and left.

"Whas up?" a muscular teenager asked. He was wearing baggy black denims and a tight-fitting shirt that read BOY across his chest. The B and the Y emphasized his nipples as he stroked his stomach with the hand that was not on his crotch.

"Nothing much."

"You wanna watch a movie?"

I ignored him, hoping that he would read my silence as a lack of interest and leave me alone. I wanted to walk away as I had with the others, but his undeniable sexiness held me.

"You got any quarters?"

He was persistent. In spite of myself, I moved the quarters between my fingers—counting. Wondering if I might spend much more on this young man.

Glancing at my watch before looking back at him, I realized that what had felt like an hour had actually been two and that I had missed the first half of Bryan's recital. Panicked, I moved to leave, but then he reached for his crotch. I watched as his hands pressed into the oversized denim and then gathered up the material around his member. He squeezed it gently. I felt it as if he were touching me. His erection reached and stretched. I looked up to find him peering into my eyes with his head tilted slightly to the side. His lips were as wet as his smile.

"So you wanna watch a movie?" he asked me.

"Are you hustling?"

"Nah, man," he said with his hands. "I'm just tryin' to get some money. So I can get somethin' to eat and, you know, the bus back to Jersey. Can you help me out?" His hands landed on his crotch.

"How much would this help run me?"

"Les go watch a movie. I'll show you my thing and you can tell me how much you willin' to pay. Don't worry, it won't be much for all you gonna get."

He stepped into the nearest booth and stood against the far wall. With one hand he rubbed his swollen crotch, and with the other he beckoned me to come in.

"What you and Bryan doin' in that room with the lock on?"

"Nothin', Mama."

"Get the hell out! I don't know what you'd wanna be locked up in some room with some little boy on a hot day in the summer for anyway. Get out!"

"All right, Mama. We'll go to the park."

I closed the door behind me and felt a strange intimacy in the three-by-three booth. It was like being jammed crotch-to-crotch in a crowded elevator. Then I dropped that first quarter. The overhead light went out as the movie came on. Men humping and sweating and gyrating. It was almost sexy. But mostly violent.

"So how much you got?" I asked.

"Ten inches. And fat. Come here."

He took my hand. "You like that shit, right? Yeah. Yeah."

I was rubbing his dick through his jeans. The top of my head fell at the bridge of his nose. Suddenly I wondered why I'd ever thought of him as a boy when there seemed to be nothing about him that spoke of youth or innocence. Then I looked down again at his shirt.

"Das it. Yeah. Take it out."

After pulling the shirt from his pants, I unzipped his

zipper and searched for the opening of his boxers. But I
was fumbling, so he undid his belt and pants himself and
lowered them over his buttocks. His penis pulsed toward
me in his underpants. I reached for it as it took the initia-
tive to part the slit in his shorts.

"Yeah! Let me pull on it, little boy," said the older guy
who lived down the block. "Uh-huh."

"It's startin' to feel funny," I said.

"Like you gotta pee?"

"Uh-huh."

"Then pee." And that's what I did for several years, because I was six and didn't know any different.

"How much you want?" I asked my Jersey hustler.

"Ten dollars."

"All right." I was starting to want it now, even though I
could imagine Bryan looking up from his piano, searching
the audience for me.

He opened his legs and moved his feet farther forward.
"Whas your name, man?"

"I don't want to talk."

"Ah'ight. Then maybe you wanna suck my dick."

"Mmm."

I went down on him and forgot he was a hustler, maybe
because he hadn't lied: He was at least ten inches. And I
rationalized that each one of them was probably worth
more than a dollar, so he was just about giving it away.

I sucked hard and fast.

"Ah yeah. Yeah, boy. Suck that shit!"

But I felt like I couldn't get enough of it into my mouth.
It was great to find a dick that was a challenge. I took it to
the back of my throat, let it rest on my gag reflex, lull it.
Then I opened my throat and pressed forward until my
upper lip brushed against his woolly pubes and my lower
lip was crushed up against his balls.

"Motherfucker, suck that shit!"

I gagged.

His hands were on my head, now that he knew I had learned to deep-throat the way most black men thought white guys did it naturally. He rocked his hips back and forth. He began to sweat and I smelled it. Strong. Like an aphrodisiac. Then I forgot that he was anything but a dick.

"John, you never say anything when we make love."

"I know. I'm just quiet."

"Well, sometime maybe I'd like to hear you grunt or call my name while you're cumming so I don't think I'm wasting my time."

"How do you know I won't call somebody else's name?"

From the sound of his moans, I thought he would cum. I didn't want him to ejaculate in my mouth, and not yet. I raised my head. "Wait a minute." I fumbled in my inside coat pocket to find the little GMHC envelope with the condoms and lubricant. "I want you to fuck me. OK?"

"Just turn around."

I pushed my behind at him as he applied the lubricant with two of his fingers. He shoved them into my ass and held them there. Wiggling them.

"You like that shit? Right?"

"Uh-hum," I smiled.

"Well, I'm a fuck you lovely. Ah'ight?"

"Yeah! Mmm!"

He plunged into me immediately. It was all I could do to remain quiet in the tiny booth. It felt like the first time, all those years ago, when I met a twenty-year-old man who said he would fuck me: but somehow I heard the word "love."

"I thought you said I had to let you do it. Or else you'd leave."

"That's right."

"Then why are you leaving me? I thought we were boyfriends."

"We are. But virgin ass ain't all it's cracked up to be, boy. And I can fuck anybody I want. Including you."

"I thought I was yours."

"You are."

I lost count of the strokes he leveled into me. It was damned sweet. He seemed to be able to hold out forever. But maybe that was because we had to stop every so often to drop another quarter.

"Fuck me, you no-named motherfucker," I thought. "You've got a dick like God!"

"Ah yeah! I'm gonna cum."

"Yes. Yes. Do it!" I panted. "Is the condom all right?"

"Uh-uh. I ain't wearing that shit!"

"Oh no," I muttered. "Oh no!" I could hardly get it above a whisper for a second. I struggled to turn around, but his strong hands held my hips as he buffeted my ass.

"Mmph," he grunted.

"Stop! Take it out." I was whispering what should have been screamed. I couldn't raise my voice, though, because it was illegal to have more than one person in a booth. I felt trapped—hot for the fuck while struggling against it, yet trying to remain quiet, all at once.

"Why are you driving so fast, John?"

"Because I'm in a hurry."

"But if we crash we won't never get there."

"Yeah, but we won't have to worry about gettin' anywhere else."

"At least buckle your seat belt."

"Why? I'm not afraid."

He pulled me closer, put one arm around my neck, and covered my mouth with his other hand as he fucked, humping upward into me.

"Take this dick," he whispered into my ear like a lover.

His tongue caressed my earlobe as he breathed. "It don't matter now, anyway." He fucked. "This gonna cost you more, by the way. Acting like you ain't know I ain't put that shit on."

I pushed him back against the far wall with a thud, as his head struck the screen. Still he held on—not even missing a stroke. He choked me. "You like it like that, right?"

It did feel damn good. But then I knew this fight wasn't about the feeling—it was about the fuck. He forced me forward again into a corner of the booth, kicking my feet outward and ramming even harder. I could hardly breathe.

"Ah yeah! Here it comes. Hold on, you motherfuckin' cocksucker. Yeah! Yeah!"

I bit his hand and gasped. Tried to push his hips away, but found my hands sliding on the sweat of his smooth skin. Frantic, I finally found the courage to scream, "NO!"

"Now, how you gonna raise your hand to your mother?" she asked as her hand fell across my face.

"I'm sorry, Mama."

"Go get me that belt so I can beat your ass!"

He tightened his arm around my neck and punched me in the head with the hand I had bitten. His hips surged forward a few more times, then he pushed me against the door, yanking his dick from my ass.

"Ouch," I thought. "Don't you know you never pull your dick out that fast?"

"You gonna pay me my shit, man," he said, as he started reaching into his inside coat pocket. Cum was shooting from my dick onto my pants at my ankles. My heart raced with orgasm and fear. As he withdrew his hand, I heard the click of a utility knife. "Now, motherfucker, you—"

In a moment of desperation, I kicked him in the groin, pushed him back, and quickly turned to open the door. I tried to run out, but sprawled facedown in the aisle because I'd forgotten to pull up my pants. I looked up and just saw faces. Men who'd gathered around because of the commotion they'd heard inside the booth. There were a lot more of them than when I'd gone in. And now there were some real beauties.

Above the clamoring, I heard, "I'm a fuck you up." And I looked up to see my trick walking proudly out, wiping his hands on a kerchief. "You gotta come out sometime, right?"

"Caught in the parking lot with some man! Who the hell is he?"

"I don't know."

"Get the hell out my house. Get out, you faggot! You don't belong around decent people."

"Where am I gonna go, Mama?"

"Straight to hell!"

I tried to pick myself up gracefully. The older men had managed to contain their laughter. The young boys, however, were holding nothing back.

"Get out!" the fat shop attendant yelled. His hair was Jheri-Kurled and turning orange at the edges. "There's only one person per booth. Take yo' stupid ass on outta here!"

"Can I fix my clothes first?"

"Fix yo' damn clothes at home," he said loudly as he adjusted the waist of his dingy sweatpants and pulled his T-shirt down to cover his protruding stomach. "This ain't no boutique. Now let's go."

"Shut the fuck up!" I yelled at him, trembling.

"What? Boy, I'm a call the police. We'll see how—"

"Go ahead. Call. Just leave me alone." The way I was

feeling, I just wanted to squeeze my butt cheeks together and pray.

Then from within the small crowd, I heard, "John?"

I kept quiet. Sometimes when I'm in distress I think that simple things like ignoring people will make them think that I'm not really me. That maybe I'm just a look-alike.

"Talk to me, John."

I knew the voice. "Hello," I said. It was my ex-boyfriend, Peter. He was standing there staring at me, trying to pretend that the situation was not peculiar.

"I won't ask what you're doing here, John. I guess I already know."

"Good," I said as I buckled my belt. "And I won't ask you."

He started to sort of tsk and hah, nodding his head as if he were confused.

"You left me for this?" he asked.

"You'll never understand why I left you," I said sharply. "And I'm certainly not going to stand here trying to explain it to you."

"Good enough. Have a nice life, John."

"Fuck you," I murmured, angry at so many things, including the fact that I still loved this man, yet felt the compulsion to drive him away.

"Maybe what they say is true then, John—that some people just don't appreciate what they get for free. And that seems to include love, huh?"

"I don't know," I said slowly, stepping around him to leave. "Maybe I'll call you when I figure it—"

"Didn't I tell you to get your tired black ass outta here!" the attendant burst in. "You must think you special because all o' New York know you got fucked by a 'ho. Upstairs!"

"Yeah, right. You'll call me." Peter dismissed me with a frown. He almost had to yell to be heard above the screaming attendant, whose loud voice was his only real weapon. Hoping to embarrass people enough to make them scatter. "Don't bother. I'm not about to wait on you. And I don't need to." He hesitated, then said, as if in triumph, "By the way, my new lover's name is Mike."

"Get out before I put you out! And you"—he turned to Peter—"if you ain't spending no quarters you can take a hike, too. Port Authority is across the street. Don't no buses come here."

I continued to ignore him as I talked to Peter. "Yeah, I know Mike," I said. "I've seen him down here before. He's got a n-i-c-e dick."

"You're sick, John."

"I know," I said loudly. "Even I can see that. But congratulations on the trade, anyway."

"Get into that closet! Tryin' to kill yourself again in my house."

"No, Mama!" I screamed, wishing she hadn't grabbed the knife from me. As she slammed the closet door shut, I heard the mirror crack. "Don't leave me in here!"

"This ain't your life to take, boy."

"Then you take it, Mama. I don't want it," I cried in the dark.

"I love you, but you wrong. And always been wrong. You ain't gonna die no time soon, you damned sissy. God'll keep you alive—to punish you."

I picked my cum-stained coat up from the floor and left. Outside, my young stud was waiting.

"Where's my money?" he asked threateningly.

I smiled. "Here," I said. I gave him thirty-five dollars and my telephone number. I hardly wanted to admit it to myself, but somehow this young hustler had known exactly what I'd wanted: finally to be taken advantage of by someone who didn't pretend to care about me. Not to be loved: to be fucked. I liked it and hated it, but told him to call me anyway, excited about what he might do with his concealed blade in my house.

As I walked along 42nd Street, I remembered slowly emerging from my mother's closet that night with every intention of running away. But as I closed the door, my own reflection in the shattered mirror frightened me. I stood before myself broken, segmented, and afraid. So I went back in and waited for my mother to let me out. She never came.

"I know you ain't out that closet!"

"Uh-uh," I yelled.

"I tell you what: You'll stay in there if you know whas good for you."

"I know, Mama. I know."

I inherited my mother's brownstone when she passed, and have lived there staring past her mirror into the half-open closet ever since.

MIRANDAS

Jesse Green

*T*he two Scotties lie in the corner, curled so intimately that, were they human, you could not bear to look at them. Their nubby pink stomachs are almost obscene, puffing out, deflating; but better asleep than awake, I say. Visitors somehow assume they're related, because they're both gray and annoying and live in the same house. But the male, George, was abandoned by some old lover of Abner's before I moved in. The female, Martha, arrived in the Castro years later, showed up whimpering at the screen door one day: in heat, so the joke goes, not for George but for Abner.

Abner himself lies curled in his four-poster bed, the contours of his body generalized by sheets, blankets, the stained chenille cover. Six layers—and this is June—yet still he's cold. Elsewhere in the house, windows are held open with the thickest and least-loved books available: almanacs, multigenerational novels, the Time-Life series on Unexplained Phenomena. It is an unexplained phenomenon why such tawdry books should be here at all, unless they too gravitated toward Abner, preferring to remain with him when their original owners left orbit.

In any case, here in the attic he rescued and redesigned over the years, Abner needs no books or breeze. His eyes are shut, his teeth clatter. Toby has sensibly bought him a cap—a 49ers cap; how unlikely! But it seems to have helped. Last time Abner spoke, he claimed to be hearing music inside it. "Marvelous sounds, Rosalind," he told me, though we weren't sure if he was being ironic or delusional. "Music you'd . . ." Then he shut up again, and hasn't spoken since.

Meanwhile, there is nothing to do. We eat like pigs. Toby has proceeded one recipe a day through Julia Child; even now I hear him downstairs, hacking away at a horrible fish he brought home this morning. These will be the weeks of seafood; July—I looked ahead in the book, preferring to know my fate—promises fowl of all kinds, when all I want is lettuce. I feel I'm being fatted up, like Mrs. Sprat. But Toby has become fanatical. We must go in order, he says: He's learning the classic techniques. It was only with the utmost charm and a scalp massage that I managed to dissuade him from rabbit ragout when it turned up in the rotation in April. "What about Scottie instead?" I suggested.

We eat; it takes hours. We use Abner's heirloom silver and clean each piece by hand. Often, friends—that is, Abner's friends—will dine with us, look in on our patient, help dry dishes. But there are always more hours to fill. Toby rents videos, which I watch until I fall asleep in my

chair. When I awake, my checkbook is balanced: precari-
ously, but beautifully. Toby used to be an accountant and
likes to keep in touch with numbers.

I, never having worked at anything so concrete, have
nothing to keep in touch with. I polish brass doorknobs
one floor at a time. I wash my nylons immediately upon
wearing them, which is rarely if ever at all anymore. I
wait to be useful. Right now I wait for the light to shift in
the attic windows, wait for the moment when Abner's
poppies will crane their tissue heads to follow the sun
west. I dare not crane my own tissue head: What if the
sun has gone down? I crane my ears toward his snoring
instead and am content. *Still alive.* Or is it the awful dogs
I hear? Their noses wedged in each other's crotches, they
sleep in the corner for hours on end, leaping up to yip up-
roariously if I move. I hate to wake Abner, but eventually
I'll have to descend to the kitchen, where Toby—I dread
this—will have liberated four tiny fillets from the largest
fish on earth.

When I first met Abner, he was thirty-five but looked
about twenty. We both belonged to an overpriced gym
and our schedules matched. He was big then, broad all
over, with white teeth like a poster boy. He walked
around house-proud in square, striped trunks. He hogged
the lap pool: swiming nowhere against its motorized current, his form perfect, as if he were motorized, too. When
he emerged, the water fell off him in flumes. He'd
laugh—I don't know why—and his laugh would echo like
a radiator beating. I would almost have hated him. But
you could follow his big flared watery footprints all over
the place, and he *was* nice to watch.

Eventually we started to talk, sarcastic but educational
conversations about lovers. In my case the sarcasm hid

ignorance mostly; for Abner it was the sarcasm of expertise. Nothing could surprise him any more; no twist of the
bedclothes, no fold of the flesh. It embarrassed me how
much more he knew about pleasure than I did. Nights,
after we talked, I would think about finding someone on
whom to try out what he told me, hoping it would work
for a self-conscious woman as well as it did for an obliv-
ous man.

He got me to start in the lap pool; we took turns swimming and chatting. Sagas unfolded in twice-a-week seg-
ments, like flowers blossoming in stop-time photography.
Abner met a man at a bar, and suddenly—much too suddenly, it seemed—they were a couple. A night of theater, a
Sunday at Candlestick, a week in Florence, and the man
moved in. But several episodes later he was demoted; he
moved from Abner's attic suite to the smallish rental on
the second floor. Then, suddenly—much too suddenly, it
seemed—he had to leave.

"Had to?" I asked, when my mouth came up above
water.

"Was compelled to."

I had to think of a two-syllable way to ask my next
question; that's all the time my stroke would allow me.
"By whom?"

"A voice."

"Saying?"

Abner considered. " 'You are no longer wanted here.' It
was *my* voice actually." He shook out his long, meaty
arms. "You have two more minutes in there, by the way."

I was unhappy living with two madly efficient nurses in
graduate-student housing near campus; their bustle, their
obvious worth to society, shamed me. A music major, I
couldn't compete. My dissertation was a rich girl's hoax.
"Pergolesi and the Music of the Spheres." Even my ad-
viser snickered when he saw it on my notebooks. And

while I could never make my work important, I could make the contrast between me and my surroundings less painful. Rich as I was, Abner was richer, and living with him could not possibly shame me.

"Will you be renting?" I asked, struggling out of the stream for a moment and holding to the edge of the pool. "The empty apartment, I mean."

"Yes, though I hate to. I mean, it's my house, why should I share it? One's parents never took boarders—did one's?"

"What about Toby?" I said.

I had been to a Fourth of July party at Abner's house the previous summer, and met for the first time the occupant of the ground-floor bedroom. Toby was chubby, with tight black curls of hair, his face sweet but so freckly you really had to grin. He seemed totally out of place in Abner's world, except there he was, installed like a viceroy. He ran the household. "Ask Toby," Abner kept saying to his guests, and Toby, at the barbecue, would answer all questions. "Corn holders? Okay. Kitchen, far left near the phone, second drawer, behind the corkscrews. *Don't let the dogs out!*"

Abner moved in stately pomp among his guests, but got edgy when trapped in real conversation. He referred all lengthy inquiries to Toby: Toby was keeper of the stories as well. "Yes, it's a beautiful dormer," Abner told me, "but have Toby tell you what happened during last year's storm." And Toby did, with bashful glee. He was wearing a T-shirt, gift of Abner, that said I'M WITH STUPID; when he bent toward the steaks, the WITH got swallowed in the fold of his belly.

"Oh, Toby's different," said Abner now, by the side of the lap pool. "Totally different. He's not like a tenant. He's like I don't know what. And where could I get someone else like Toby?"

I swam for a while. "Me?" I said, and wiggled, blushing, to the bottom of the hurtling stream.

He could not wait for my hair to dry: I must come see the house at once. "I call it the unpainted lady," he shouted. We were speeding, top down, in his maroon Aston Martin. I felt like I was on a date. I stared at him. His hair was magically dry.

"Renovating roof . . . shingles . . . widow's walk. . . ." I could barely hear him for the wind, but he chattered on merrily, half his words stolen.

"Terrible leak . . . "

I nodded.

"Vegetable garden . . ."

"I know!" I shouted. "I've been there, you know!"

He slowed for a stop sign. "I'm sorry, what? I couldn't hear."

"Never mind."

"That's a pretty smart pair of shorts you have on," he said, accelerating into the intersection.

When we got to the house we were immediately set upon by the awful Scotties. "You don't mind the dogs, do you? That one's George and that one's Martha."

"I love them," I said. They were leaping at my gym bag as if it contained meat. "How can you tell them apart?" I asked.

Abner stared at me.

"Oh, yes, of course."

"Don't mind the chewing. It comes with the territory."

"Yes, no, that's fine. I love dogs, I really do. I had a dog once. Rather larger, though, to be honest." It was, in fact, a yellow Lab, noble and fey, named Barnacle, though not by me.

Abner and I went directly upstairs. "This would be

your room," he said. "Closet behind you. Those Maxfield
Parrish posters can go, if you want. You can't imagine
what's passed through here. Bathroom through that door.
If you don't like the shower curtain—what's-his-name left
it—feel free to change it." It was a map of the world on
transparent vinyl, the countries in various grotesque pas-
tels. "Sri Lanka is spelled wrong," Abner added. "*Sir*
Lanka—a knight?"

Everything was immaculate. The world in the bathroom glistened and waved. "I'll take it," I said.

Abner looked pleased. "I'm tired of men," he said.

"I completely agree."

"Except Toby, of course."

"Totally different."

"And that reminds me." I was hoping to see his room
upstairs, but Abner now led me back down toward the
kitchen. "Let me read you your Mirandas."

"Okay," I said.

"You have the right to remain silent. We all have the
right to remain silent." He stared at me. "This isn't some
ashram."

"No. It isn't."

"Everything voluntary."

"Yes."

"Knock on my door; I'll knock on yours."

"No ashram."

"Exactly."

Toby was washing a springform pan in the kitchen,
having just baked some kind of spinach-and-rice torte—
he had not yet taken up with Julia Child. He dried his
hands carefully before shaking mine. "Nice to see you
again," he said.

"Again?" said Abner. "You two have met?"

"Fourth of July," Toby said.

"Really?"

"Of course, you toad," Toby said. He flung his hands in mock despair.

Abner reached down from his height and squeezed Toby around the waist. "Sorry, teddy bear." Toby accepted the endearment with chagrin, regretting its aptness. He curled into Abner's chest.

"And sorry, Rosalind." Now he squeezed me, with his other arm.

"No problem," I said.

The dogs, sensing intimacy that did not include them, dashed over and tried to leap into Abner's face.

"Oh, George and Martha," he said. "That's one rule I do have. They must be fed if I'm not here. Which I'm sometimes not."

"No problem," I said. "I really love dogs."

Abner broke up the happy grouping and looked at me critically. "Yes," he said. "You had one once."

I have had no lovers these three years in Abner's house, have felt no need. His illness, a disaster for him, has been clarifying for me and Toby. I have been a madly efficient nurse when necessary and not worried about my paltry life in between. The world is for once completely unthreatening. I am in a haze of approval, as if I were pregnant— but what will I be delivering, and when? The pharmacist nods sympathetically when I purchase Abner's bewildering drugs. He thinks I'm a modern saint.

Hagiography is a booming business in San Francisco these days. Aileen McCarthy, a reporter from one of the five-o'clock news shows, comes by to interview me for a segment of her series on "Homecare Heroes." Toby, though demurring for himself, encouraged me to appear, and now he hovers around the edge of the living room like a stage mother banished. The mood is more somber than I would like. The reporter, cameraman, producer, and makeup person all speak quietly, as if too much noise will cause me to cry. Yet the dogs are yipping all around them, gnawing at cables.

"Have you always been a helping kind of person?" McCarthy asks.

"No, never. I'm more the type that gets helped," I say.

This elicits a patronizing smile. "But your taking care of a dying man is so . . . so . . . *heroic!*" she says. "And you're not even related or anything!"

"You take things one step at a time," I say, attempting to imitate my mother's breezy modesty. She has often been interviewed about the redesign of some part of her house.

"But your typical day—I understand you've given up some promising work on a doctoral dissertation—must be a constant struggle with fear, grief."

I shake my head no. "Today, Toby and I gave him a bath. Then we played Trivial Pursuit on the sundeck."

"Cut!" says the producer, raising his hand. "Rosalind? Since Toby isn't in the segment, could you not refer to him? It confuses the viewers."

I rephrase my answer. "Today, I gave him a bath. Then I played Trivial Pursuit on the sundeck."

Aileen McCarthy eyes me suspiciously. Though I keep insisting I'm not a hero, she takes my disavowal as further proof that I am. Finally I say, "If you're so bent on finding a hero, why don't you bring your camera upstairs?" But everyone is appalled by the suggestion, and anyway, I don't even believe what I'm saying. Ravaged and stoic though he is, Abner is no more a hero than I am.

McCarthy and her crew pack up, disappointed; the night my segment is supposed to air, a different Homecare Hero is featured. Toby and I are mesmerized by a mother doing and saying the same things about her dying son as I have said about Abner. Except this woman really does seem a hero.

In September we come to red meat. Whether it is the improving menu or Abner's deteriorating health I cannot say, but Abner's friends, who have dropped by singly or in pairs all summer, tonight suddenly materialize en masse. For the first time, I'm panicked. Their campy exuberance, so successful previously at keeping things afloat, keeps coming to nothing. Here they sit, eight handsome men, obediently holding out their gold-rimmed glass plates while Toby and I serve the boeuf bourguignon. We might be on the Cunard line, except that the Scotties scamper beneath the table from one crotch to another, flicked away but unrepentant.

"Who gets George and Martha?" someone asks. We all look to the lawyer friend who has prepared Abner's will.

"Unless he changes his mind," he says, "it's Rosalind."

This is the first I've heard of the bequest, and I try to look pleased as I turn toward the platter. "Potatoes, boys?"

"That's nice," says Toby, seriously. "You had one once."

"Sort of," I mutter. Barnacle had actually belonged to my brother, who, leaving for boarding school, abandoned him to me. "Hey, Roz, you'll take care of Barney, there's a trouper," he had said, putting me in a headlock and knuckling my skull. For the next seven years I kept the home fires burning, as I imagined it, having seen too many Greer Garson movies, and adoring my brother too much.

"Well, you like dogs," says Toby.

But really, I think, no one on earth knows *what* I like, or could approve it if they did. My brother, when he announced his engagement, thought it was the newly dead Barnacle I cried for, and even now Toby says, "But what Rosalind really loves is her music." Well, it doesn't matter what I love, I think; what could possibly matter less than a woman's love? These kind, frightened men, they are my dearest hearts. One has said he will never have sex again: Him I would like to marry.

But nobody never has sex again. One day when Toby and I are giving him a bath, Abner gets an erection and smiles quite plainly. I stare into that smile. "Could he know?" I ask. "Could he possibly know?" Toby shrugs, and continues soaping the inside of Abner's tiny thighs.

And then Abner speaks. "Rosalind," he says. I clutch Toby's elbow.

"Oh God. Yes, Abner?"

"Go."

"What? What did he say?"

"Go."

"What is he saying?"

Toby says, "He's telling you to go."

"To go? But why?" And then I realize. "Oh, I'm sorry, yes, of course." And I leave the bathroom, shut the door, hurry downstairs until Toby should call me back.

Following this, Abner has occasional moments of lucidity. He strokes the back of my hand from time to time. I talk to him incessantly, of course, with no idea how much he gets. I thank him for giving me something to do in my life, and he shakes his head no. On Columbus Day, I ask him what he *really* wants done with the dogs. "You don't actually want *me* to have them, do you, Abner? Me of all people?" He nods his head yes. What does he mean? But Abner continues to exercise his right to remain silent.

"Me?" I ask. "*Me?*"

I walk downstairs so silently that I scare Toby in the

kitchen. He drops one end of the tray he is holding, and a dozen lamb kidneys go skittering across the floor. At once, the dogs come racing in, then slide around on the greasy linoleum. George gets a kidney before I manage to smack him away. "Drop it! Drop it, you monster!" I scream. But he's already swallowed and is lunging for more. "Disgusting *beasts*!" I grab a broom and literally sweep him and Martha outside.

Toby is crying, his head hanging down like the tray in his hand, both he and it dripping. "Oh, Toby," I try, but it's no use; I have never been moved by sadness, even my own.

We stand that way for several minutes. As soon as it seems acceptable to do so, I turn to the open cookbook and pretend to read what tonight has in store. I am glad and then discouraged to see, at the end of the recipe, a paragraph labeled "Variations." I close the book.

"Abner spoke to me," I lie. "He's changed his mind about the dogs. He wants his sister in Marin to have them. She's got a farm. Plenty of room."

Toby nods, then looks at the carnage. "Can I use these?" he says. "Do you think? Or start over?"

I do not want to slow him down now that we are finally nearing desserts. "Use them," I say. "Always use them." And as he starts plucking them off the floor, I rush to my room, hop out of my clothes as if they were burning, and jump into the shower. I unfold the world on the vinyl curtain as far as it will go, which is not very far. How transparent and revealing the oceans! How gallant Sir Lanka—dripping off the nose of India, a single pink tear. Not that the pink matters, I've finally realized, for the map is arbitrary, with a legend but no key.

IMAGINING LINC

Scott Heim

I am inside the igloo with Lincoln. Customers come and go, moving sluggishly in the 101-degree heat. They touch the cool white brick of Sno-Palace and peek into its window. I concentrate, trying to guess which of the 126 exotic flavors they'll order. Linc scribbles their choices on a pad. He grinds a forked implement over a giant block of ice. He whisks the froth into a cup, then covers it with a funnel. Three squirts of flavor, and *voilà*.

"It's all in the snap of the wrist, Ned," says Linc. He wipes his forehead with the back of his hand. His cowlick points sky-high. He looks great. I want him to push me against the air conditioner, to do it to me right here, during my lunch break.

On most days, I spend the noon hour at home. My mother prepares grilled cheddar on whole wheat. Split-pea soup. The first few days of this summer, I thought her system was nice. But after a while I grew tired: the lawns, then home for lunch; the lawns, then home for dinner.

Since I've known Linc, I've replaced sandwiches with sugar; soup with cups of ice.

A young couple steps to the window. I touch my temples and consolidate my thoughts. I guess pink champagne for the woman, and raspberry for the man. "Two small watermelon snow cones," the woman says, and I'm wrong again.

I met Linc three weeks ago. I was on my way to the library. I carried a box of overdue books. Inside were accounts of telekinesis and mental transportation. Biographies of Edgar Cayce and Uri Geller.

I stopped when I saw Linc. He leaned from the igloo window. He looked my age, but I knew I hadn't seen him at school. When I approached, he asked my order. "One medium passion fruit," I said. And then, even though I tried to stop it, I blushed.

The guy smiled. He handed me the cup, a blue spoon angling from the ice. "There are psychics," I said, "who bend utensils just by staring at them."

"But that spoon is plastic," he said, "and plastic doesn't bend." He pointed to his indecipherable name tag. "Lincoln," he said.

I ate slowly. I watched him work. After a while, he patted the seat of a chair beside him. "Come on in, if you want," he said. A little door opened from the igloo's side. I stepped into what felt like winter.

Linc lists the week's most popular flavors. "People want to taste the exotic. Guava or mango. Or boysenberries-and-cream. Or your current favorite, tiger's blood."

Since I've known Linc, I've eaten what seems like a hundred tiger's bloods. On the days I skip Mom's lunches, I order them in giant size. Tiger's blood mixes strawberry, coconut, and three other flavors Linc's forgotten. It's unbelievable.

Today, the lurid red of the liquid darkens my gums and teeth. Linc, after kissing me, says, "Tiger's blood tastes best as the stain on your tongue."

He says it like he means it. But it could be he tells me this to make me happy, since he's just told me things I found sad. For instance, Linc moved here alone. He currently lives with his uncle and aunt. His real parents are dead.

"Now, I'm with parents #4," Linc says. Since he was five, he's been juggled from uncle and aunt to uncle and aunt. "I could bore you with stories," he says, "but I won't."

He must be crazy, I think. After seventeen years with my father's tales of weird teeth he's fixed, whose stories could be boring? So I beg until Linc gives in.

"On the days parents #1 crashed, I knew fame," Linc says. He shifts his weight. He tells me how his parents enrolled him in the Jimmy Joyce Children's Choir. The Carpenters, then one of the country's biggest recording acts, requested this choir to join the chorus on their hit "Sing." Linc stood in a horseshoe-shaped configuration with other boys and girls in a brightly lit studio. While he forte'd and crescendoed, his mom and dad drove across Los Angeles. They headed for a costume store. Two blocks from buying matching jester's suits for Halloween, they collided with another car. A green Grand Prix smashed Linc's parents' Mustang.

"My name appears on the liner notes for *Carpenters' Greatest Hits*," Linc says. "But by the time the record came out, my parents weren't there to hear it." He shrugs.

There should be something to say here, I think. I open my mouth. He kisses it.

When I get home, I head for my parents' record cabinet. Mom has alphabetized the LP between Cab Calloway and Rosemary Clooney. I slide *Carpenters' Greatest Hits* from the stack. It doesn't take long to find his name. I leave the album jacket open and center it on the rug my mother has just vacuumed.

After my parents fall asleep, I tiptoe downstairs. They haven't noticed the record. I lie on the floor. I hiccup, tasting strawberry sometimes, coconut others.

I practice my concentration skills on the ESP cards I splurged for last month. The instruction box reads, "ESP builders: the stepping stones toward true psychic power." I'm thinking: *circle, triangle, square. Little wavy lines. Star.*

In one of those books, I read how Edgar Cayce invented scenes inside his head. He envisioned ancient buildings or lush landscapes; beautiful vistas from lands he'd never visited. He would concentrate and cover the lens of his camera, then touch the button to release the shutter. And here's the best part: When the film developed, the scene he imagined would magically appear. It was as if whatever he wanted to see became real.

I try to picture Linc as a little boy. I'm no Cayce. It's hard to see his California home, his bedroom, his mom and dad.

My parents' stereo console crackles and hisses. I'm surprised it still works. The volume has been set at 2, so I double it. I carefully lower the needle. The group of kids, Linc included, belt out the words in tinny altos. *Sing, sing a song, make it simple to last your whole life long.*

There's not a sound upstairs. I turn the volume knob to 5, then look back to my cards.

"Square," I say aloud. "Star." They're both correct. I'm improving.

Linc's festooned the top of my tiger's blood with a tiny, toothpicked umbrella. I tuck it behind my ear. While I eat, Linc sorts through mail he's brought to Sno-Palace. This morning, he received a package from Mother #2. Her name is Gert. Linc lived with her in Colorado for six years.

Linc refers to Gert in the past tense. He calls her "the next best thing to a mom." Gert kept framed photos of her brother, Linc's father. She taught Linc to play piano. She signed him up for Sunday Mass youth vocal solos.

Linc stands before the chilled bottles of flavorings. He unveils each item from the postmarked cardboard box. Tiny pieces of Styrofoam fall at our feet, scattering like chunks of snow on the igloo's floor. I ooh and aah as he shows me Gert's gifts: a treble-clef key chain; a giant-sized kazoo; a plastic toy Scooby-Doo which, when he pushes the bottom of the platform it stands upon, dances and spasmodically falls into a heap of bodily sections.

What Gert has saved for the bottom of the gift box was something forbidden in the days when pre-teen Linc was hers. "Aha," Linc says. He waves envelopes of cherry, orange, and grape Pop-Rocks in front of my nose. The candy consists of crystallized sugar and carbon dioxide. Back in the days of piano and voice lessons, Linc says, candy was a no-no.

I choose orange, and Lincoln, cherry. The CO_2 hits our wet tongues. The pebbles of candy start popping. Predictably, we giggle.

I see my chance. "What you need is some real food," I tell Linc. "And my mom is just the one to serve it to you."

I fiddle with the plastic Scooby-Doo and wait for him to object. But Linc doesn't need any urging. Tomorrow, he'll dine at my home. He'll meet my parents.

Linc says, "Touch my feet,"

I bend down. I press my palms against the toes of his high-tops. Linc's bones seems to collapse. Right there on the igloo's sticky floor, he mimics the actions of his new toy. He falls into my arms.

"Smack, smack, smack." I never thought kisses could really make that sound. But Linc's do. We crouch under the igloo window. Business suffers because of the weather. It's muggy and thundering. But we couldn't care less. Linc untucks my shirt and maneuvers his head inside. He tickles my chest with his tongue.

Then I say it. "Suck," I say. "Hard. Leave a mark." Linc complies. I feel his mouth against my skin, sucking the blood to the surface.

"Harder." Harder. "Higher." Higher.

Before Linc, I spent hours trying to imagine a scene like this. But the boys I fooled around with at occasional sleep-overs wouldn't do the things I asked. No one would pinch or bite. None of them put color on my skin. My parents went on thinking I was innocent. So today, I'm almost laughing as his fingers intertwine with mine. The rain pitter-patters above us. Linc's mouth moves from here to there, until his hard kisses have formed the shape of a question mark on my chest. And I feel capable of something miraculous. Perhaps I could move objects with the power of my gaze; perform mind-control to make someone think whatever I want.

At 5:30, Linc locks the igloo door. He and I hustle home. By the time we arrive, it's pouring. We are drenched, and late.

As usual, my mother has brought dinner to the table at

six on the dot. Steam rises from dishes of pork chops, beets, and turnip greens. There are four glasses of iced tea; pats of butter on china plates. Even a bowl of pears for dessert.

Dad already sits at the table. I look him directly in the eye. "This is Lincoln," I say. "A new guy at school." Neither parent seems to question this, even though school has been closed for five weeks.

I take a step closer to Linc. I clasp my palm on his shoulder and leave it there. My father looks at me, then Linc. He points his fork at us. "From what parts have you moved?" he asks.

"Here, there, everywhere," Linc says. We sit. "I've been staying with different relatives. Modesto, Colorado Springs, Laramie."

"I know people from Laramie," Dad says. This is news to me.

"There, I had a job similar to the one I work now," says Linc. He speaks to them easily, opening like an oyster displaying its pearl.

"What do you do?" Mom asks. "Is it more exciting than lawn-mowing?" She looks at me and winks. I think of the marks on my body, the skin that prickles from Linc's hickeys. Perhaps, I'm thinking, the top of the question mark is noticeable.

"I worked in an ice cream parlor," Linc says. "Parents #3 let me do whatever I wanted. Mom #3 did macramé, and Dad #3 made a lot of latch-hook rugs. So I did my thing, too. Didn't know anyone like Ned then, and I started doing things I shouldn't have. I went to work stoned a lot. It was no big deal there, because we only had ten flavors."

My father's face looks as though he's just swallowed crude oil. It's as if he's just discovered something secret, some chunk of information he didn't want to know. For a second, my stomach knots. I think it's terror, but then I realize I'm wrong. I'm loving this moment. Relishing it.

"That was two years ago," Linc continues. "I was fifteen. Now that I'm at Sno-Palace, I don't waste time. Imagine if someone asked me, being stoned, for kiwi-honeydew and I gave them lime. They're both green. It would be an easy mistake." He looks at me. My parents do, too. "Ned can testify to this," Linc says. "Their taste buds would want 'tantalize,' and I would give them 'snooze.' "

Mom and Dad chew as if their spoonfuls of diced veggies contain hidden bones. Linc smiles and eats. When my mother passes the bowl of pears, I say no thanks. "We're having snow for dessert," I tell her.

"Skin should be a flavor," Linc says, "to pour over shaved ice." His mouth explores the back of my knee. It's near midnight. Outside, the air swarms with heat. In here, the cool becomes cold. He and I have downed three rum-spiked snow cones each. I've never felt so naked, so care-less. It doesn't matter to me that the air conditioner's sputter reverberates across the avenue. Or that Linc has forgotten to lock the igloo's door behind us.

At home, Mom and Dad sleep under the whirr of their ceiling fan. Soon—I hope—they'll wake to find the hall light I left burning. My open bedroom door.

Linc's mouth moves along the inside of my thigh. "That tickles," I whisper. My leg kicks the table. Sno-Palace bottles topple to the floor. One lands on my bare stomach, just missing Linc's head. Sticky flavoring gurgles from the spout. It's too dark to see the label, but it smells like cotton candy. Other bottles spill over our pile of clothes. I imagine my mother sniffing them as she does laundry, detecting green apple or pomegranate on my T-shirt and socks.

Linc laughs. He rests his head on my shoulder. His hair

is dripping. He touches his cowlick; wipes his finger on his tongue. "Cotton candy," he says. "But it's not near as good as the real thing. Parents #1 knew how to make it, right at home."

I think: *the real parents.*

"I remember Mom #3 trying to spin some once, but it didn't work out. She was Mom #1's sister, but hers wasn't sweet at all. It came out lumpy, like a roll of t.p. No way would I eat it."

We stay motionless. I watch the tiny gold hairs on Linc's chest, rising and falling with his breath. I want him to say more. It's unbelievably quiet, and I notice sounds I would normally disregard: the dull hum of the ice machine; the tick of Linc's sticky watch.

"We should clean this up," I finally say. Linc nods. "But first things first." I point to my neck. "Bite me. Right here." Linc licks the dried flavoring from my skin. Then, I feel his teeth take the place of his tongue.

When I arrive home, the hall light still burns. I enter my parents' room. I open the bottom drawer of my father's bedside table, where he keeps his camera equipment. He snores next to me, his eyeballs troubled and quivering behind the lids.

I close my eyes and touch the button of Dad's antique Kodak. I imagine Linc: Linc without clothes, pressing his body against mine on the igloo floor. Linc lifting my ass from the ground and pushing himself into me. Linc coming on my chest; rubbing it into the skin where he's left his marks.

I imagine all of this. And then, concentrating, I release the camera's shutter.

The next day, Lincoln numbs my earlobe with shaved ice. He says it might hurt; I say I don't care. He pushes a safety pin through the skin. It makes a sound like a steak knife cutting gristle. He fastens the safety pin and leaves it there.

As I expected, my father shows up at Sno-Palace. He stands outside the igloo and shifts his eyes. "Having a good day?" he asks. One of the best, I say. "No lawns to mow?" I finished them all, I answer.

"How about some shaved ice?" Linc asks him. "Whatever you want, it's on me." Without taking his eyes off the menu board, Dad orders a small lemon snow cone. Zzzz, I think.

My father's gaze shifts somewhere close to the mark on my neck. It nears the vicinity of the pin in my ear.

He only finishes half of the snow cone. His tongue resembles the underside of a melon. Even better, that look's still on his face. "Be home for dinner," he tells me. Then he splits.

Linc shuts down early. Today, for the first time, he's invited me home. We're both damp with sweat. I smell of grass; Linc, of sugar.

Father #4 hasn't returned from work. But his wife, Linc's aunt, looks a little like her nephew. Her dark eyes sparkle, almost identical to Linc's. She sits barefoot on the couch, swirling the burgundy-colored contents of a brandy snifter. She reads a book without a cover. When Linc tells her my name, she offers her hand. "Charmed," she says.

Linc leads me down the hallway. "Holler if you need me," he tells her.

A cat sleeps outside the door to Linc's room. "This is Beast," Linc says. He guides Beast's paw to wave at me. He whispers into its face. "This is the guy I've told you about," he says to the cat. "The good kisser." I kneel down to scratch its head.

The cover of a Harlequin romance has been tacked to

Linc's door. Its title reads, *The Missing Link*. He knocks.
He yells, "We're coming in."

I follow him into his room. "Here it is," he says.
"Home."

Linc's room smells vaguely like Sno-Palace, but everything else is different. The first thing I notice is the sad-
eyed basset hound on the latch-hook rug that covers the
floor. The second, orange and green musical notes printed
on his bed sheets. And the third, the row of photos above
his bed.

Linc sees me staring. "Oh, those," he says. He leans
over the headboard and points to the first picture on the
bottom row. "Parents #2." Within the frame, an older
woman smiles and peers from rhinestoned cat-eyes. I
know in an instant it's Gert.

The photo of Parents #3 shows them surrounded by
kids. The husband's hair pulls back into a ponytail. The
wife wears a headband and a wood-carved ankh medal-
lion. The members of the family laugh, their heads
thrown back.

"And here," Linc says, "are the current recipients of
little old me." This one shows the woman I've just met
and a slightly overweight man. They hold the cat from
the hallway. They stand next to a picnic table, hot dogs
splitting on a grill beside them.

I look at the larger picture, the one above the rest. A
young man and woman smile. Each uses a hand to support a sleeping baby, its body swaddled in checkered
cloth. Behind the trio, a studio backdrop exhibits a detailed beach scene. Waves crash, sunbeams glitter, and
palm trees sway. It's a scene more beautiful than I could
have imagined.

"Parents #1?" I ask.

"The ones. The only." Linc nods. "The genes that
pooled to create me. The one plus one equals one." He

turns to me. My face must look funny, because he smiles and touches my forehead and mouth, as if smoothing out lines. He touches my earlobe. Then he sits on the bed, his back turned from the photos.

Linc removes his shirt. I follow suit. Then—*bang*—he kisses me. Right between the eyes.

It's almost as if he's psychic. Today, he knows exactly how, what, and where. His fingers read me like ESP cards.

I'm hearing that song again. Linc and the rest of the children's choir overpower the voices of Karen and Richard. *Sing of good things, not bad; sing of happy, not sad.* I try to picture Linc at five. His evenly-spaced teeth in baby size, his cowlick more pronounced. I shift places to get a better look at his face, and the headboard bangs against the wall. Each of the four pictures rattles. I stop, afraid they will suddenly fall and smash into bits of glass. I look up, into the faces of Linc's aunts and uncles, Linc's mother and father, and the face of the infant Linc himself.

Then I look down. At Linc, here and now.

He smiles. He's perfect, just as I imagined him when I clicked the button of my father's camera. But surely my ESP will blunder. The picture won't materialize. I know this, so I let Linc strike again. I don't need a mirror to see what he does to my skin. From Adam's apple to navel is a new row of hickeys. This time, they form a perfectly shaped exclamation point. Linc stretches at the foot of the bed, admiring his work.

HARD-CANDY CHRISTMAS

Robert Trent

I know the kind of Christmas you have in mind.
Presents and family. That wonderful holiday
food and "Joy to the World." Whatever quarrels
you may have with the people you were assigned to,
Christmas is the one time in the year when everybody
likes everybody else. No, not likes: loves. And I agree, that
is a wonderful Christmas.

But can I tell you about the kind of Christmas *I* get?
The severe suburban kind. Well tailored and undemonstrative. Instead of roast turkey, peas, rhubarb pie, and
whipped potatoes drenched in gravy that somehow never
tastes so wonderful any other day of the year, we get *prix
fixe* at the country club. Okay, it's real food; but it looks
too perfect—it should be watched, not eaten. Isn't Christ-

mas supposed to be about being home? Not for us: We're
in that great empty dining room at a big center table trying not to stare at the Rutherfords, whose son died in a
plane crash two years ago. They still haven't come out of
the trance.

Now I'll tell you about the kind of Christmas I like. I
like Christmas at the baths. Of course, I like every day at
the baths. But there's something special about the baths
on that one day in the year when everybody else is doing
family Christmas. The baths can be as empty as that dining room; but then, the other people there aren't the
Rutherfords.

Take 1976 at the good old Everard. It *is* a little quiet
on this mother of all holidays, but in the steam room a
tall, lanky kid sits in the corner, looking half-asleep. Jets
of steam rise up around him, half hiding and half showing his sinewy legs, lean broad chest, wholesome angular
face and elephant's cock. He happens to be a legend
about town, known as Jolly Green Giant for his height,
his length, and because he likes everybody. His real name
is John.

Once, I met him on the street. Dazzled, I asked for an
hour of his life. He was smiling at my jazzy, collegiate
come-on till I told him I'd be happy to pay him for his
trouble. The smile went dead. "I'm not a hustler," he
said, looking sad and walking off.

Now, in the steam room, it's two years later and I wonder if he remembers me. Two older guys stand a few feet
away, looking at him. They hesitate—can I touch this?
They're timid; I'm insane. I walk past them and take
John's long, slumbering cock in my hand, stroke it until it
grows into that thickly veined monster I remember from
the porn movies he made.

You don't just blow someone this formidable. You slob-
ber him to death. John pulls me up to him, kisses me on

the lips—with passion, with tongue. I'm so excited, my hair hurts. The only thing better than sex with a stranger is sex with a stranger who once rejected you.

John flexes his arm; the biceps is much larger than you expect on a skinny guy. He leans back, I bury my face in his chest, forcing my tongue hard against the skin. I scour the armpit, raise my head and look over this gift I've been given—this *thing* from the Elgin marbles.

John laughs at my desperate, hysterical attempts to eat him alive. He says, "Isn't it better when you get me for nothing?" I say, "I'm glad you're here, John." We leave the steam room together—he's taking me to his room. I'm in shock: He thinks I'm as good as he is.

That was pretty fine, but Christmas 1981 might just rival it. My college singing group is in town for a reunion. We meet at the Williams Club, stand around the piano. While wives look on in polite appreciation for our closely harmonized renditions of "How High the Moon?" and "You're Gonna Lose That Girl," their kids try pulling down the drapes. Most of the guys are fatter and balder than those fleet youngsters I knew at college. But Dick Davidson, my sixth favorite man who ever lived, hasn't changed. He still has great, thick black hair, wire-frame glasses, and a deep bass laugh that makes you wonder when *your* voice is going to change. After the songs, I plead another engagement, jump into a taxi, and take myself to the baths.

Quiet again; it's Christmas, right? I scout all around, in case an Olympic gymnast is hiding somewhere. I check out one of the upstairs rooms and see some guy sitting on the bed, smiling out at me from semi-darkness. I must have Dick Davidson on the brain—people are starting to look like him. Then a rugged laugh pierces the dimly lit hall. "So, Reeve," says Dick, waving me forward, "you had another engagement, did you?"

I'm thinking: "Oh my God, there *is* life on earth," but I cover with a joke. (I usually do.) "I work here as a towel boy," I blithely announce.

"Come close, buddy," he tells me.

Kissing a man you went to school with. You think: Can I *do* this? Once, riding back from Vassar in the same car, I'd leaned against Dick, feigned drowsiness, and popped a complete hard-on all the way home. Now I've got him wide awake, laughing, and as I cup his balls in loving hands I say, "Why didn't we try this in school?" He says, "I was a one-man man, Reeve. My roommate and I were real close." What bliss in that dawn to be alive. How many other secrets did my delicious little college contain?

With a wicked smile, Dick gets up on his hands and knees. I plunge into him and we start dancing to our own *thwock, thwock.* Fucking is always sacred, but when we come, we can't hold ourselves back—we fall against each other laughing. We shower, dress, and leave the baths together. Dick has to get back to his family. "Good to see you twice, Reeve," he says, hugging me. As he hops in a cab, an old lady in a tattered coat walks by me singing "It Came Upon a Midnight Clear," and I head up Fifth Avenue in tears.

The system has a few kinks. For instance, Christmas, 1985: Disaster. The baths is so dead, there's only one possibility—a hairy, not unhandsome guy with incredibly muscular arms. He's somebody's dreamboat, just not mine. In walks a new man on the way to his locker. The back of his jacket says TOMMY BOY in big red letters. When he comes out of the locker a few minutes later, I realize who he is—Tom Taylor, the soap-opera hunk with the famous cowlick. On weekdays, Tom's an actor; but on Christmas, he's a parade: strutting towelless so everyone can take in his basket of fine fruit.

I'd always wondered about Tom. Is he gay? Could I get

him? Now that he's real, I'm afraid of the answers. Tom sees me, says, "Not too many guys here today, huh?"

"But we're the right ones," I tell him. Tom shrugs and wanders off—okay, the suave approach fell flat; now I'll flash at him. I go to my locker, work it up, step outside— where the hell is he? By the time I find him I'm half-soft again and he's standing against a wall watching the hairy muscle guy. At some obscure signal only beauties know, the hairy guy walks down the hall, followed by Tom. They go into a room. I hear murmurs through the door— murmurs, "Oh, yeah"s, and sighs. A few old guys pause and listen, too. One says to me, "Sounds like those guys are having a *heavenly* Christmas." "I hate you," I tell him; and I never watched Tom's soap opera again.

No baths for me this year. I've been snared in my moth- er's awful country-club Christmas with the institutional turkey and my mother scowling at her husband's three daughters from his previous marriage and especially at her husband. No—especially at me.

Why don't we get along? You think it's because I'm gay and she's a vicious homophobe? I am and she is, but that's not it. Or maybe because she's a cold selfish virago who lives to castrate and castrates to live? That's still not it, though I like the terseness of that description. No. The reason my mother and I don't get along is that I keep try- ing to get her to acknowledge me and she resents the pressure.

Sometimes, when I call her, she reacts with shock—as if she'd given me up for adoption years ago and how in hell did I track her down?

My friend Justin says, "Why do you even know some- one like that?"

"Are you kidding?" I reply. "My mother?"

"That doesn't give her special rights," he says, waving

away the very notion of blood ties. "If they're not nice to you, drop them," he says. "That's *my* motto."

But on Christmas she needs me and I need her to need me. "I can't face it without you, Ted," she tells me. "The table will be nothing but the enemy. Bill and those hideous daughters of his, plus Laura's horrible goon of a husband."

"Not Laura, *Nora*," I correct.

"Besides," she adds, "you're always so charming when you make those wonderful jokes. My handsome son, so talented and such a waste—but let's not get into that now."

Let's not get into that ever. "Be out here by two-thirty," she commands. The discussion is over. Her handsome son; and I'll do my best.

And for Christmas—this is Justin's fantasy—I am to bring her a lovely set of designer panties. She opens the box. She's thrilled, touches them—Wait! They've been strategically soiled by the sex-crazed brothers of Pi Sigma Gay fraternity at the University of Wisconsin, at one of their unspeakable toga parties!

"No, I bought her a silk scarf," I tell Justin, and I'm off to the station.

So I'm on line for tickets at Penn Station and I spot two men on the next aisle. They're in jeans, plaid shirts, and hiking boots. One wears a tweed jacket. He's got a duffel bag; the other, a suitcase and some packages. They look as if they might have been college roommates six or seven years ago, but I'm certain they're not chums. They're lovers. I know it from the quiet assurance on their faces, from the way they take each other for granted—his arm is mine, my coat is his. The guy with green eyes hands the other a camera case while fiddling in his pocket.

The second guy's jaw. Listen, friend: To have *that* face smiling at you in the morning, you'd never get to work.

They see me watching them, don't care much. I'm just some guy in glasses and a silly parka. I say, "Round trip, Manhasset," to the clerk, get my tickets and change, and when I look over again the two guys are gone.

On the train, I sit in the wrong direction again. I always forget which way Long Island *is*. I descend the stairs, board the train, and face what ought to be Montauk Point. Then the train moves the other way—say, to Philadelphia. But soon we race out of the tunnel into the deserted rail yards and decaying factories of Queens. Ancient cars sit on rusted tracks that crisscross amid the general grimness. I feel it—the dying—as I glide east into the heart of

Christmas. The car is packed—students, couples, kids running up and down the aisle as if they expect to find something wonderful in every seat. Wrapped packages are everywhere. Three teenage goons sing "Jingle Bell Rock" as loudly as possible. Slowly, too, as if they're on a chain gang. I've never seen so many red-and-green sweaters—it's as if the train has been kidnapped by Christmas terrorists.

Houses run past the window, then slow down as the conductor shouts, "Bayside!" A bunch of people get off the train. Jaw and Green Eyes are on the Oyster Bay line. Or so I imagine. They sit facing each other, their bodies drained. Last night, they did the Christmas Eve marathon. In between bouts of sex, they wrestled on the bed like Scouts at a Jamboree, then passed out on sheer joy.

I see them arriving in Greenvale. Jaw's mother waves to them. She's tired, too, but happy. Her life's a series of car pools, dancing lessons, P.T.A. meetings: getting *involved* in her children's lives. Mother drives the lovers to the house on Whitney Lane in Upper Brookville, there to be embraced by aunts, cousins, and kids. In the driveway, she kisses her two sons again—the real one and the adopted one. She accepts them as they are.

We get to Manhasset, I find a cab, ring our bell, and there's Bill: my mother's fourth husband and the first one she can't get rid of. "Hey, Teddy," says Bill. "How the puck are ya?" Bill likes hockey.

"Pretty good," I tell him. "I had a lot of sex on the train coming out here." With straights I figure the thing to do is go *into* the issue, not step around it. Bill barks a laugh. He's getting major heavy these days—Glenn Ford on a cake binge.

"Who is at my door?" An ecstatic, chirpy voice means *she's* leaving the back den and getting close. She thinks: My ally is here. I think: Theme from *Jaws*.

She's perfume, a dress, a beautiful face. My mother's arms surround me. She gives great hug—it gets me, damn it. And that melodious voice. "Hello, the Ted," she says, adding the "the," I forget why, and we always laugh when she says it, I forget why.

"It's me and you, kid," I lie as she releases me. She looks me up and down. She's smiling like a young girl. I think: She's not just the center of my life; she's the center of all life. Justin would be appalled.

"Merry Christmas, Mother," I say, handing her the box.

"A gift for me?" She beams, opens the package. Her head stills, she stares into the paper. Maybe there's a better present hiding underneath. "I suppose I could use another silk scarf," she says. "Thank you very much, Ted." She smiles, wan and weary. I follow her into the den. Why can't I ever give her what she wants?

Bill's somewhere else. My mother grabs my arm, pulls me near her. "You wouldn't believe what I've been going through," she says. "He criticizes everything I say." I look past her into the hall. "Don't worry," she says. "He's probably sneaking a drink." She says he's abusive. She pauses. "He used the f-u-c-k word the other day." She nods solemnly.

"Thanks for spelling things out for me," I tell her. "Can you leave him?" I ask.

She frowns. "And do what? Don't make idiotic suggestions, just listen."

A little dog runs up to us. "Hey, it's Closetina!" I say. My mother bends down, baby-talks the dog. "The Ted never calls Toto by her true name. Why *is* that, Toto?"

Closetina cavorts. She twists her poodle shape into a virtual Windsor knot to express her joy at seeing me. She looks at the bright Bergdorf box I brought, she thinks *presents* and decides to give me one—a tiny puddle, nothing fancy. Pretend-horrified, my mother runs for the Wisk as Bill comes into the room.

"How about a little toast to Christmas before we set out?" says Bill, handing me a glass. My mother returns, frowns at him. "Sure, I can already see tomorrow's headline," she says. "KNOW-IT-ALL DRUNK SLAMS CAR INTO TREE, KILLING WIFE AND STEPSON ON WAY TO CHRISTMAS DINNER." Pause. "Why bother doing such a messy job? You can kill us all with boredom when we get to the club." Bill sighs, and we head for the garage.

My mother has a few last words with Closetina as Bill and I get into the car. He shrugs. "I guess she's having a bad day," he says. "No," I tell him. "*I'm* having a bad day. She's having a bad century." He lets out a great peal of laughter as my mother gets in. "What's so funny?" she says. Neither of us answers.

Bill drives. We pick up the Widow Hudson, my mother's best friend. "Hel*lo*, hel*lo*," she sings as she plops into her seat and gently fluffs the back of her hair with her hand. "So, Ted," she says, lightly digging her elbow into my mother's side. "Are you seeing anyone in New York?"

"Constantly," I tell her.

"I mean: do you have a girlfriend?"

"No, but does she have a brother?" That shuts *her* up

for the rest of the ride. I relax and think about the one
thing in this world that really cheers a guy up. And that,
boys and girls, is

Sex. He's a hot nerd. Glasses, skinny, vascular body. A
turn-on who shouldn't be. We're under the tunnel near
the Eagle and he's blowing me. I pull him up to full
height. The moon shows his tight little muscles; his shirt's
a pile of cloth at our feet. He whimpers. We kiss, wind up
jacking off together, nothing too creative. Afterward, he
comes back to the bar with me. Justin and Chris wave to
us; we walk over. "You've just had sex again, haven't
you?" says Justin, smiling. I nod and grin. "You know
how to work this bar. Use it as a bathhouse. That's *your*
motto." He half-nelsons my neck and Chris shakes his
head at me. "Does it ever *stop*?" he says.

"Gentlemen," I say, freeing myself. "May I present . . ." I turn to the nerd. "I'm sorry. Who are you?"

"Jim," he says. "Bowers." He shakes hands with the
guys. Justin turns to me, says, "I'm having people over
for drinks tomorrow. Dennis and Mike, a few others. Can
you come?" Pause. "Can *you* come, Jim?"

Jim pauses, looks nervous. "I guess so," he says.

"You're coming," Chris tells him firmly, handing Jim a
beer.

After a couple of minutes, Justin and Chris wander off.
Jim turns to me, his voice a choked whisper. "Your
friends are so nice," he says. I put my hands on his shoul-
ders. "*I* like you, Jim," I tell him. "Why shouldn't *they*?"
His response is to hug me. Even his sweat is lonely. But
Gay is new brothers for the condemned.

Bill's daughters greet us in the clubhouse lobby. Caroline's
ten, sassy and dumb—her father's darling. Jane's eighteen
and struggling to make it through a course at Katharine
Gibbs—her father's darling. Nora's twenty-five, beautiful

and good-natured—her husband's darling. That's Tuck, the man on her right. Tuck's about forty-five, with a hot grin that knows things. I look past him into the dining room.

Yes, there are the Rutherfords. Bill says, "Poor Matt and Connie. To lose a son like that." He shakes his head.

My mother glares at him. "That kid was rude to me once. On the fifth hole—remember, Peg?" She turns to the Widow Hudson, who nods dutifully. "He was playing behind us, yelled 'Fore!' and 'Get off my green!' *His* green! I complained to the committee about him—they fixed him but good. He wasn't allowed on the course for a year." She smiles in triumph. We sit in teams: my mother, the Widow Hudson, and I on one side; Tuck, the girls, and Bill on the other. (A geometric miracle occurs: a round table, yet we make *sides* out of it.) I look directly at Tuck, one of the few hot heteros God ever made.

Tuck has big hands, gray eyes, and a funny cleft in one cheek. Not a flaw, really: It's a dimple in the wrong place. Tuck's wearing a jacket and tie, but he knows clothes don't matter. Skin does. Are his nipples large? Flat? Tasty?

"You're in a trance," says my mother, shoving my shoulder. "Do you want white wine or red?"

On Whitney Lane, kids drag Jaw and Green Eyes to the television screen. They're stuck in the Boss stage of the Ice Palace in *The Legend of Zelda*, unable to find the weapons to defeat Kholdstare. Green Eyes takes the controller, works out a combination of the fire rod and the sword spin-attack, and obliterates the foe. The kids shout "Yay!" Roland, a four-year-old clutching a teddy bear named Safeway, hugs Green Eyes's legs. See, I know how a real Christmas works.

"Merry Christmas, Mother Flo," says Caroline.

"I'm not your mother," says my mother coolly.

"In school we learn love is everywhere," the reckless child goes on. "Love comes from surprising sources. Yes, that's what Sister said."

Older, wiser Jane frowns. "Who taught you that? Sister St. Thomas?

Caroline nods.

"She used to beat kids' hands with a ruler, that's how much *she* knows about love," Jane observes.

Caroline says, "Yes, and you know what else? Billy Francis had a farting fit right in his pants during one of those lectures. Yes, did *he* get a beating."

"Farting fits *normally* occur in the pants," I note, as my mother closes her eyes. This is not the sort of comedian I'm supposed to be.

The Widow Hudson says, "Caroline, did you get some nice gifts for Christmas?" ("You're such a sport, Peg," my mother whispers to her.)

"I got the bunny book, Aunt Peg," says Caroline, sipping her Dr Pepper.

"The bunny book," says the Widow Hudson, smirking at my mother.

"Yes," says Caroline. "It's all about how peaceful life is in the bunny warren until Uncle Wiggly comes to visit and whispers a secret to the mother bunny. After Uncle Wiggly leaves, the mother bunny tries to eat all the children bunnies and they run away."

"With illustrations by Joan Crawford," I say. Tuck laughs. My mother's showing her *forbearing* look. She turns to me. "You know, Ted," she says, and I feel my stomach sink. "I didn't care for that Rutherford boy; but at least he managed to hold down a job. Are you *ever* going to work? I mean, we sent you to all those fine schools." She stares at me.

"I *am* working," I tell her. "In New York I conduct Socratic seminars on the pursuit of youth, beauty, and truth." Tuck laughs.

"That's wonderful, Ted," says the Widow Hudson. She turns to my mother. "See, Florence? He's a great teacher."

"He's not your son," says my mother grimly. I look away from her and discover that the room is empty. The Rutherfords are gone. The "O Holy Night" piping in from the ceiling has stopped. Everyone's gone except Tuck and me. He comes over to sit next to me. His leg brushes against mine. "Do you like to get fucked on your back or on your belly?" he says softly, his lips a few inches from my face. I can feel the

Tenderness, which is sex's sexiest secret. "I don't usually get fucked," I tell him. I like him so much because he laughs at my jokes.

"Sure, you do," he says. "Can I do you on your back like a woman?" His pants are gone and his trout-cock lies along his thigh, leaning toward me. "A guy likes to nuzzle into someone all hot and nervous like you," he says. "I'd like to settle you down." I put my hand on his cock while he kisses my cheek.

"I don't want to," I tell him.

"Sure you do," he says again.

"Oh, for *heaven's sake!*" my mother bursts out. She's sitting on my other side, in the blue dress she wore as Cinderella to a costume party when I was ten. "You do disgusting things with disgusting people—you're worse than an animal." She's close to tears. I look over at Tuck, but the chair is empty.

"You know what's disgusting?" I tell her. "Not loving your own child." She throws her hands in the air. "I have sex with men because when they touch me, I feel as if I matter to somebody."

"You matter to *me*." Her voice is a choked whisper.

"You're my only son. Of course I loved you. I gave you clothes and toys. You didn't even have brothers and sisters. You were a little king."

"I didn't need the toys. I needed you to be nice to me."

Now she's Queen Elizabeth, with a high ruff collar. "You really are crazy," she says. "Mothers *always* love their sons."

"Remember the day you turned the car around in that driveway in Munsey Park?" I ask her. "The tall boy playing basketball? He looked at us as you pulled in." Her eyes lock on mine—she remembers. "You said, 'You're afraid of that boy, aren't you? I hope you're not going to grow up to be a coward.' Was *that* love?"

She says, "I wanted you to be tough. You can't be afraid of life."

"I'm not afraid of life," I tell her. "I'm afraid of you."

Queen Elizabeth is gone. Now she's in her pink housecoat. She's wearing a black mask over her eyes to shut out the light. Her face is covered, but somehow she sees. "I think you slept all through my childhood," I tell her.

"It's a lot of work raising a child," she says.

"How would you know? My friend Justin says I should get rid of you."

"Justin, that idiot."

"You've never even met him."

She sighs. "You have a lot of complaints, don't you? I'd like to see how good *you'd* feel after four husbands."

"Yes, husbands are tougher than girl friends. They don't disappear after two-no-trump. But you can always slice little pieces off their cocks one day at a time—right, Mother?"

"I don't care about my husbands," she says. "I care about you." Suddenly, she smiles, takes my hand. "Remember when you played that Chopin nocturne at the recital, Ted? I certainly loved you that night," she says.

"You loved the performer. It was harder for you to love the child." She humphs. "That's why I'm here today—to give a performance, to help you avoid your husband and his daughters." She smiles evilly beneath her mask. "Husbands are already *men* when you get hold of them, Mother. I was a helpless *child*, for fuck sake!" She stands up in protest. "I was never big enough, never cute enough, never tough enough. I was never what you needed. I wonder what fabulous boy you *could* have loved." I'm crying, stumbling to be clear. "I wanted to be good enough for you, Mother."

She's gone. In her place, a little girl about seven years old sits scowling in a pretty pink dress.

"You haven't had your juice yet, Florence." My long-dead grandmother stands behind her, looking young and incredibly beautiful. She's smiling. She always smiled. The child says, "With *her* climbing down my spine all those years"—she shakes her head back, indicating my grandmother—"it's a wonder I didn't wind up hating you." My grandmother looks past her, sees me, and lets out a cry of shock and delight. "You're so *big*, Ted," she marvels.

"Nana? You look so . . . so nice to me." She reaches her arms out, I stand, move toward her—what relief to be held by her! But I clutch heavy arms, a man's build, and look up to to find Tuck, who cradles me against his chest. "That's my sad, sad guy," he says gently. I'm crying so hard I can scarcely see him.

"For heaven's sake, Ted, *sit down.* Everyone's looking at you." My mother is smiling, sort of; frowning, sort of. I'm standing in the country-club dining room—the object of everyone's eyes—even the Rutherfords'. As I sit, I look over at Tuck. He smiles—did we have the same dream? Nora smiles, too. Her face says: He's as hot as you think he is.

Mother is grim. The Widow Hudson watches her nervously. But Bill's oblivious, turns to her. "We could all go down to Bermuda with Tuck and Nora this spring and play some golf. Whaddaya say?"

Nora says, "You come too, Ted. We'll have fun." She smiles at me—really a great girl.

My mother doesn't answer Bill—her silence expands. But wine is Bill's cushion. He raves on, tells me family is what counts most in life. "Children," I tell him. "When you look in their eyes, you see yourself. You think you've beaten death."

"Not bad, Edward," he says. Finally noticing my mother's deepening squall, he turns to her. "Get into the Christmas spirit a little, will you?" he says.

"I'm sick of Christmas," she blurts out. "I'm sick of children." A glance at Caroline. "I'm sick of you," she tells Bill. She looks around. The waiter, alarmed at her black look, runs over. "Where's the goddamn dinner?" she barks. He runs off.

"Florence, this is Christmas," says the Widow Hudson, in her Cyrus Vance mode. "You have to have faith."

My mother glares at her. "You know what you can do with your faith."

The waiters are so terrified of my mother they bring everything at once. The soup, the coquille Saint-Jacques, a turkey, shiny potatoes, and stuffing that looks like purée of emeralds. We also get pies and ice cream—the table is a riot of plates and food. "Are you happy now?" says Bill, amused. My mother ignores him, starts digging into the painted potatoes.

"If we can't have sex, let's have food," I say. "That's my motto." Tuck laughs on cue—my true friend.

In Brookville they're opening gifts. Young Ned ignores his baseball mitt. He'd rather pull ribbons off Nancy's dress. She stands patiently for this ritual—she's a present, too. Mother absently strokes Green Eyes's hair—her second son. Green Eyes watches while Jaw opens his gift from him—a fiberglass fishing pole just eight inches long, a perfect bonsai. Jaw comes over to Green Eyes and hugs him.

Overwhelmed by so much food, we don't have to talk to one another. The Rutherfords pass our table on the way out. When they're gone, my mother stops chewing long enough to spear me with a glance. "Well, at least with a dead son," she says, "you can always dream about what great things he might have done had he lived." She shrugs. "With a living son, you *know.*"

We stand up—the official closing. My mother hugs Nora and Jane good-bye. Caroline gets a steely nod. Tuck and I shake hands. "Hang in there, Edward," he says, flashing the grin. As he and the girls walk to their car, I feel a nice little hole in my heart. My mother whispers to me, "I can't tell you how delighted I am to see the last of them." Bill drives the rest of us back to Manhasset.

There's no tree in our living room—my mother tired of that chore years ago. We're a bunch of adults sitting around on a day that happens to be Christmas. "Play the piano, Ted," says my mother. The Widow Hudson nods eagerly. Closetina wiggles blissfully near the piano bench I'm sitting on. I launch into "Losing My Mind" from *Follies*, vaguely aware that my mother didn't want a singing son. She wanted a senator. But when I look up at the end of the song, her eyes are wet.

In Brookville, Christmas dinner is always followed by amateur theatricals. One of the kids has to sing "I'd Do Anything" from *Oliver!* This year it's Nancy. She stands in front of the smiling crowd, little hands clasped tight before her, and belts away to Jaw's guitar accompaniment. On the line "For your smile everywhere I'd see," she blanks, punches Jaw's arm, curtsies, and sits on the teeming couch. Uncle Kid asks young Roland—still clutching Safeway—if *he'd* like to try. Roland thinks about it, panics, drops the bear, and runs into the nearest bathroom, locking the door behind him.

People try to coax him out, but nothing works: not the promise of candy or even the lure of an extra surprise toy. Finally, Mother gently tells Roland (through the door, of course) that the bear is starting to cry without the security of his trusted friend. Shouting "Safeway!" Roland races from the bathroom, grabs the bear, and, holding him as tight as a lover, promises he'll never leave him again.

Jaw remembers when he was eight and sang "I'd Do Anything." Everybody loved him. They love him now. Up the stairs he goes, good night ladies, to the bedroom, all Christmased out. He's a kid again. With Green Eyes he climbs into the bed Roland asks can he sleep here too the other kids drag their sleeping bags into Jaw's room the lovers in bed with Roland curled up inside Jaw's embrace and Safeway inside Roland's while Green Eyes watches all around him kids drift off to sleep sees foreheads here curtains there and everywhere

Home. "I guess Christmas isn't my best day," says my mother. An apology? Is Kholdstare exhausted? "I can't forget *you*," she says, handing me an envelope that says "The Ted" on it. I know it contains five one-hundred-dollar bills. "Merry Christmas," she says wearily. Merry Christmas and please stay my friend. I pocket the envelope, turn and wave to the cab pulling into our driveway, face her again. "I hate it that you're unhappy," I say. She rushes forward—I never know when she's going to do this—and hugs me.

"I'll be fine as long as you're on my side," she says. I think of Justin saying, "I love it when they cry."

"Count on it, Mother," I reply, caught up in satin, per-

fume, and confusion. I back out of the clinch, run down
the walk, jump into the cab, and ride away.

I get off the train, head home across Thirty-fourth
Street. The guy's standing in front of Macy's. He's in a
leather jacket, open to a blue T-shirt. He has slit eyes and
gray hair, but his face is young, unlined, and handsome.
He's Tuck twenty years ago. He sees me staring at him,
gives it right back to me. "What are you lookin' for?" he
says amiably.

"The day after Christmas," I tell him.

"I'm from Oregon," he says. "I'm here for a convention
at N.Y.U." He smiles.

"What convention is that?" I ask him. We're already
walking together, matching our steps.

"A very good convention," he says solemnly. I love the
little boy hiding in the man. It's what straights don't do
well. Their little boy is mean.

"My name's Adam," he says. We shake on it.

"I'm Edward," I tell him. "I've just had a day with my
family."

"Sounds like you didn't like it," he says.

We're at my door. "I knew what to expect," I tell him.
He clumps in after me. I put on some lights, draw the
blinds, and in a minute he's getting undressed. The body
is so clean it looks as if nobody's ever touched it. The
chest is large, the waist slim, and what's below is full and
friendly, a very good convention. He tilts his head a bit,
enjoying the way I'm drinking him in.

"Yeah, I know about Christmas," he says. "Grand-
mothers and kids and stuff. Right?"

"The Lord is come," I say, stepping forward into his
arms.

THREE

Michael Scalisi

THE CHOICE GAME

I was four when he was six. I was also nineteen
when he was twenty-one.

　　　We lived in a town about ten miles north of
the city. Our existence consisted of school, sports, and our
icon, Mother. We would stop at nothing to attract her attention. Sometimes a moment alone with her apart from
each other, a scolding, or just a glance in the afternoon
was enough to set us easy.

My brother and I would invent outlandish stories, and
each night before we went to bed we would tell them to
Mother. The stories usually involved Mother being threatened by some imaginary force, and, just on the edge of
terror, we would step in and save her. This nightly ritual
seemed to amuse Mother, yet in the moments leading up

to it she would behave with a certain formality, the same stark elegance she took on whenever she spoke of her days at the studio. We played out this undeclared competition week after week.

I remember one such story I told in a desperate attempt to win her approval. It involved the choice game, where the three of us were put in a situation that only two of us could emerge from. With Mother and brother seated in front of me awaiting my tale, I began, "Roman soldiers have arrived here after storming the town on chariots. They announce a new ordinance limiting our home to no more than two persons. I have been elected to choose who must go. If I am incapable of choosing, the decision will be made for us."

I thought of my brother, with his silver eyes, soft brown hair, and beautiful teeth, white as his bleached cotton T-shirt, framed by lips that looked as if they were about to burst. I then thought of Mother, with her blond hair, pink lipstick, and navy-blue eyes. She was a movie star. The idea of forfeiting my life so they could be together sent jealousy racing through my body like a shot of bourbon after an icy swim through rough water.

" 'I have come to the only possible solution,' I tell the soldiers. 'Please take my brother.' He screams as two large soldiers wrestle him to the ground, chaining his hands and leading him out. Mother and I sit for some tea."

When I was finished with my story, a look of anger and fear eclipsed Mother's face. She turned dramatically to face the wall and paused a moment before she spoke, cleverly using this time to prepare her performance in her mind. Slowly she turned her head to the left, catching a glimpse of her reflection in the glass doors of the discolored mahogany china cabinet.

Then she spoke: "This is completely unacceptable and irresponsible. How dare you even think of your brother as an appropriate choice for this tragedy?" She paused to light a Pall Mall, letting the blue smoke hover around her pink lips before inhaling deeply, then exhaling with a sense of urgency. "It is I who will be sacrificed for the happiness of my children, in a great and sorrowful moment that will be talked of for years to come." To my brother she said, "You must cherish him." She extended a beckoning hand, he came to her, and she kissed his mouth. "I will cherish him for your sake," said my brother, swelling with pride and power as one flying in a dream. Mother turned away from us, her eyes fixed on the mirror, and we two went up to bed.

Later that night my brother woke up and walked to the window. There he stood for about forty-five minutes staring out over the row houses and palm trees that flooded our neighborhood. The light from the streetlamp shone in on him, creating an angelic appearance. He was naked and erect. I lay in my bed admiring this vision, when, suddenly noticing I was awake, he calmly walked over to my bed. He stood next to me, his eyes veiled in the darkness. I recalled the day Mother and I left him alone for the afternooon, and in a rage he tore up the house and dragged my bed to the basement. Now my heart beat violently. Suddenly he leaned over me and kissed me open-mouth on the lips. His tongue thrashed around wildly inside of me like an eel caught in a net of fish, finally tightening the grip around my tongue and pinning it to the roof of my mouth. This lasted about two minutes. Then, without a word, he got up and went to his bed.

I thought about what had happened as the taste of him began to fade, despite my vain attempt to hold on to it. I replayed the act over and over in my mind like a wild stunt captured on a newsreel, analyzing each frame, slowly falling into a deep sleep. That night I dreamt that my brother made love to me in a steel mill two miles from our house. That was ten years ago. I haven't dreamt of my brother since and I haven't loved him more.

RAP WITH AN ANGEL

*T*he front steps of the Asser Levy Gym on Twenty-
third Street and F.D.R. Drive. Twelve-thirty on a
weekday afternoon. I'm waiting for a friend. He's
waiting for a john. Neither will show. After a few minutes,
he decides to notice me.

HE: Whas up?
I: Nothing.
HE: Hector. (He extends a large, vascular, tight grip.)
I: Michael.
HE: You workin?
I: No, I don't work. You?
HE: I'm waitin ta work, but he late.
I: What's it like?

HE: Wha, hustle?

I: Yeah.

HE: It ain't nuttin. (His soft pink lips slightly part.) This rich fag come over, I let him suck my dick, he jerks off, maybe I fuck him an dats it, a C note, boom! (He slaps his fist into his palm, then runs his hand through his thick black hair cut short against golden skin.)

I: That's it, huh?

HE: Yup.

I: Well, what if he wants to do you?

HE: Whatchoo mean? (He pauses, his eyes a solid shape.) Fuck? Na, I dont get fucked. (He laughs.)

I: Never?

HE: No way. I dont like guyz, dis is business. I need coin, I gotta girl.

I: Does she know what you do?

HE: You crazy, B? Where I'm from it don't matta how much pussy you get, you sleep wit one guy n you a fag.

I: You live with her?

HE: Na, I live wit a guy, he awright. Older rich white guy, he teach me tingz, he know bout art, muzic, and business, he real good at makin money.

I: You have sex with him? (His magnificent black killer eyes scope me like a hawk narrowing in on a field mouse.)

HE: Watchoo be axin deez tingz fo?

I: Just curious. Sorry, you don't have to answer that, forget it.

HE (reconsiders): Na, its awright, he treat me right. And I do what he like, fuck him, he play wit my dick, he suck it, he even lick my asshole. Damn, that be feelin real sweet.

I: You high?

HE: Na, but I'm goin to get mine now. C'mon I'll walk ya ta Tenth Street. (We begin to walk as he gives a nervous glance back.)

HE: I been here my whole life, been smokin bout four years. You get high?

I: No, no way, just not my thing, ya know?

HE: Thas good. I wish I neva tried it.

I: Can't stop?

HE: It's tough.

I: You got family, maybe they can help?

HE: Thas a joke. (He winces.) My family whack. My brutha n jail. Attempted murder of a cop, fifteen-ta-life. Second offense. My mutha alcoholic. I dunno rest of em are.

I: You're a good-looking guy, but you gotta get off the shit. (He pretends to be listening to my words, then without hesitation he anxiously fires a question:)

HE: You like Puerto Rican guyz?

I: Yeah, I do. (My response arouses him. He grabs his crotch and picks up his pace as his right arm swings wildly at his side.)

HE: You'd like my brutha. He diesel n real hansome, that nigga aint no joke. The women go nuts with him, but he crazy.

I: He know about you?

HE: Uh-huh, he mess around wit guyz too. He like white boyz. You been to Puerto Rico?

I: No, you go there a lot?

HE: Not no more. When I wuz little I r'memba goin wit my mutha to see family there.

I: Did you like it?

HE: Yeah, I wuz only like five yis old. I be runnin round chasin lizards in the rain forest. (A light chuckle spills out of him.)

I: Lizards?

HE: Ya, like, ya know, li'l baby lizards. I r'memba tryin ta catch em.

I: Then what would you do with them?

HE: Play wit em, let em escape, then try n catch em again. (We're both smiling; his story has pushed the image of a street hustler out of my mind. I am now with a boy. I want to take his hand. I imagine brushing the back of his neck with my hand, then running my fingers across his lips.)

HE: You believe in God?

I: Yup, and you?

HE: Yeah, but I dont think God believe in me. (A sullen look covers his face.)

I: Why do you say that?

HE: God jus don't have nough time for everyone so some people got to make it witout him. Theyz too many people for him. (His eyes wash over with a look of pain as his face battles to keep his emotions from erupting. But it's of no use. He stands exposed at the corner of Fourteenth Street, in full view of the approaching bus, the passerbys, the man in the pizza shop spinning dough, and myself. He realizes it's too late to try to rebuild the emotional wall he has just torn down.)

I: That's kind of sad. (He tries to revive his hard persona, but can only manage a soft laugh.)

HE: Ha, I like you, you awright, a cute white boy. You right, though, it's sad. Sometime I be feelin real down but I aint got no one to talk wit. I gotta be hard wit niggas on da street, ya know? (I listen silently.)

HE: I r'memba once I wuz in love wit dis girl, Michele, n we get into a fight n I slap her real hard. So she sez she dont want to see me eva again. I hurt so bad dat night, so I jet to my brutha'z n I cry. (He begins to relive the whole experience. He's heated and vulnerable.) All I wanted wuz to be held, thas it! But he jus look at me all scared n nervous, so I turn and run n run n run, all the way to the East River, then I got sick and jus fell asleep unda the bridge. (He calms as we walk in silence a few paces.)

I: That's heavy.

HE: Hey, you sad about dat? Don't feel sad, cuz Im strong now. I'm awright. See, feelinz iz eazy fo you, but homeboyz don't unerstand all dat, can't eva show dat side.

I: I think once you get off that shit and you find someone that loves you for this (I point to his heart) and not for that (I point to his crotch), you'll be alright. I think you're special. (He's stunned. He eases back a bit, taking slow short steps. A wide smile breaks.)

HE: Thanx, man . . . . I wanna give you a hug, but ya know we here on the street n shit. You make me feel real good. . . . I wish . . . I wish I knew people like you, maybe I wouldn be like dis.

I: This is my building.

HE: Yeah, right. Maybe I be seein ya on da street, we go shoot some pool or somethin.

I: I'd like that.

HE: Peace.

He starts off, then turns back, watching me as if considering whether to ask if he can come up. We are face to face. Everything is being said through our eyes. We both know that I exist in him and he in me. But the balance is a little off. He walks down First Avenue. I step into my building. Two boys rush by me in the narrow hallway. One yells, "Yo quiero helado!" The other answers, "Sí, chunky monkey!" They take three giant, joyful leaps and bolt through the front door. I go upstairs.

SATURNALIA

I am an American whore at the Paris Bar in Berlin. Across from me is a Parisian woman and a German man. I am between a liar from Spain and a beautiful man from Morocco. None of them knows who I am but they're all interested in what I have to say.

"So tell us about life in the States," the German asks me.

"Which life would you like to know about?"

"The sweet life, of course," says the Parisian woman. She is laughing.

"I've been to New York once," interupts the liar. "Truman Capote, Avedon, Nureyev, Jackie Onassis . . ."

No one is listening to him.

The German says, "In Europe we analyze too much. Americans construct. *We* deconstruct."

The Moroccan rests his soft hand on my leg. I turn to him, my eyes set hard on his. The liar spills his drink and screams, "Oh dear!"

I excuse myself and head to the men's room. A young boy with dark hair stands at the urinal next to mine. We release ourselves in silence. I visualize what he is holding. I feel what I am holding. Flash—a thought. I imagine we are at a carnival. We walk together as strangers. I see pink cotton, red apples, and blue ice. Through the crowd, between the concessions, we cross thick power cables, pinned up against the back of a trailer. We are just two.

My mind pulls me back to the men's room. The dark-haired boy places a yellow token on the urinal in front of me, then leaves. I read the inscription—an address—then bury it in my pocket. It's time to go home.

There's a water mark on the ceiling of my bathroom at the Residenz Hotel. It's in the shape of a giant angelfish with enormous, graceful fins. I notice this, then make my way down to the street to fetch a taxi. I hand the yellow token to the driver. He reads it, then glares at me with contempt. We jet to the address.

We speed through desolate streets, stopping in front of a town house. Its white paint is cracked and peeling, littering the ground. A pink light burns at the entrance. I knock twice and a large round face appears through the square window. I produce the yellow token and pass through the door, down a long narrow staircase lined with photographs. Jean Genet, Nazi soldiers, Jayne Mansfield, an Indian circus, a little boy crying.

At the bottom there is a small room with many people. It is a type of theater, with seats spiraling around an octagonal platform. A blood-red velvet curtain is suspended around it. People furiously push their way into the rows.

A woman with white hair saturated with jewels is knocked to the ground. Someone steps on her hand, causing it to crack; another kicks her shin. She smiles evilly, then lifts herself up and makes her way to a nearby seat.

My eyes scan the crowd, searching for the boy with dark brown hair. I hear the sound of a violin, the curtain goes up, the show begins.

A young boy stands in the center of the octagon wearing only a leopard-skin mask. His sex begins to grow with each stroke of the violin. I am bewildered, fascinated, apprehensive. The others are at ease. They wait, I watch, as a muscular black man, holding a riding crop, circles the boy. He snaps the leather against the boy's ass like lightning. He circles around to face the boy, then plunges his tongue into the small opening of the mask where the boy's lips are exposed. The audience is celebrating. The boy's sex is hard. The black man circles again, hitting him this time with spectacular force, then, quickly pulling the boy's forehead back from behind, he leans over him and shoots a load of saliva into his mouth. A thin line of blood runs down the boy's left leg as he ejaculates a steady flow of pearly white fluid across the floor. The crowd erupts with a deafening cheer mixed with applause.

A soft familiar hand rests on my shoulder; it's the Moroccan. I look into his clear, concerned eyes. "Does the show upset you?" he asks. "The show is over," I answer with a smile.

My cigarette burns as I huddle in the backseat of a fast car. We drive through the dark countryside. It is morning when we arrive at his house. We are welcomed by a striking woman who kisses him and smiles at me. She speaks. "Lunch will be served in an hour. We'll be eating in the garden. Perhaps our guest would like to freshen up?"

I agree, and he walks me through the house. The floors are marble, the ceiling is gilded, trendy masters adorn the walls—Picassos and Braques, I would guess. He shows me to the bathroom, directing my attention to the lavish collection of cosmetics, creams, perfumes, and talcs that crowd the shelves. "You'll feel better with these," he says quietly. She enters, hangs beautiful blue silk pajamas on the valet, and leaves.

I am standing face to face with the Moroccan, his tobacco skin a shocking contrast to his bright green deep-set eyes. His hand brushes my face, his thick fingers unbutton my shirt, he licks my lips, we strip. We are in the shower. Cool water rains on us as he kneels and takes me in his mouth. Blood races into my sex; his pink lips move over me, slowly, then fast. He fastens one hand to the back of my thigh while massaging himself with the other. He takes me deeper. I explode, then he. He looks up at me in praise, then lies at the bottom of the shower, running his fingers along his chest, letting the water fall on his face. The woman reenters and begins to explain the proper application of skin moisturizer. She speaks clearly, emphasizing each word, as I towel myself. "Won't you stay?" she pleads. "It would be so pleasurable to have a nice American boy with us." She waits for a response. I am silent.

I dress and walk out, leaving the two of them behind. Strolling across the marble floors, looking up at the gilded ceilings, I stop in front of a small, seductive painting of twin boys flipping a yellow coin. I decide it's a Picasso. Lifting it off the wall, I secure it under my arm and walk out of the house. I am hitchhiking with Picasso in my blue silk pajamas and high-top sneakers. My hair is slicked back; the sun is on my face. Only the rich will stop for me. I laugh, I whistle, the world is mine.

THE HUNT FOR
RED OCTOBER

Ethan Mordden

"No, I *like* Roy," Dennis Savage was saying. "Look, he's spirited and friendly and youthful and even smart, and those are useful qualities in a neighbor. I just don't understand why he's always going on about cock, and big-hung, and giant meat, and so on."

"Ask him yourself," I said. "He's coming up for a coffee date in about ten minutes."

"Well, haven't you noticed? I swear, he can turn any conversation over to his favorite—indeed, dare I suggest?, *only*—topic within three exchanges, *without a single non sequitur*. How does he do it?"

Roy is one of the new young gay guys who are starting to take over our building. When Dennis Savage and (shortly after) I moved in, sometime before the Spanish-American War, the entire apartment house was straight but for us and the closeted old grouch in 11-I. But during the last few years a striking number of gays have joined us, including a few lookers and one out-and-out hunk who seems to have sparked fantasies in our respective live-ins, Virgil and Cosgrove. He has become known to them as Presto.

"Then there's Roy's wistful little pal," Dennis Savage went on. "So polite, so yearning, so resigned. He's like a scream of agony too well brought up to let itself be heard."

"Well, Nicky's got a case on Roy," I said, getting out the cheese-and-crackers tray.

"A *case*? Like Israel had on Eichmann. He's up to his ears in the love of his life, and Roy doesn't notice and couldn't care less."

"What happened to all the cheeses I bought?" I called out from the fridge. "There was a Brie, a Gruyère, and a Stilton."

"I ate the little pie one," Cosgrove answered from the living room. "And Bauhaus was starting in on the Stilton."

"Who invited Bauhaus down here?" I asked Dennis Savage, while examining what was left of the Stilton. "He's *your* dog."

"You're not going to offer that to Roy, are you?" asked Dennis Savage. "God knows where those jaws have been."

"I'll just trim off the—"

"Nicky," said Dennis Savage, shaking his head. "If there was ever someone *born* to doom and gloom." He followed me and the cheese tray into the living room. "He reminds me of that pathetic little drudge in *Les Mis*, what's-her-name, who dies in the rain."

"Funette," Cosgrove put in.

"Yes, Funette. And such an *apt* name, because in fact she . . ." No, that didn't seem right, did it? "Funette?"

"I think you mean Eponine," I said.

"Of *course*, Eponine!" Dennis Savage whirled on Cosgrove, who was reviewing his CD collection. "So who's Funette supposed to be?"

"Now you'll never be sure," Cosgrove coolly replied, rearranging the CDs in the wooden display case he insisted I buy him—four feet tall, two feet wide, and I have no idea where we'll put it. Besides, Cosgrove owns only five CDs as yet—a Skinny Puppy single, the *8½* soundtrack, the Swedish cast of *The Phantom of the Opera*, the Riccardo Muti *Symphonie Fantastique*, and a Kate Bush album that Cosgrove swears he found lying on a sidewalk somewhere. He is very earnest about his CDs. He wants to become an aficionado, to be known for his taste, his energy in unearthing the arcane and wondrous. Having folded himself into my manner of living unquestioningly, he now wants to break out and discover something of his own. So he has refused to let me give him CDs or suggest key titles. He probes my expertise, yes, but mostly he consults reviews and catalogues and spends hours in stores and (his venue of choice) flea markets, examining, weighing, wondering.

I like this. I am sympathetic to anyone who surrenders his independence in worship of the unjust and vindictive god Demento, who rules over all obsessed collectors. Gods, of course, are the mythological idealization of fathers, and all known mythologies are heterosexually manmade. Yet Demento has his campy side. He likes to be thought of as dread, yet he'll materialize in a Sabu take-a-peek loincloth and Rochelle Hudson fuck-me-or-I'll-scream-the-place-down wedgies. Cosgrove fears and serves him. "Is it *rare* enough?" he worried when he considered buying the Swedish *Phantom* on a visit to the show buff's specialty shop, Footlight Records. I told him, "It's outlandishly expensive, it's incomprehensible, and it's available in only two places in the entire world: this store and Sweden." Still Cosgrove pondered. Then I said, "Just think, no more than five or six Americans will own that album. This is unique."

"I'm coming, Demento!" cried Cosgrove. He blew his bank account on it—double-disc CDs imported from Sweden run to fifty bucks or so. But Demento was content.

So was I, because collecting is building Cosgrove's confidence. When he and I first crossed paths, he had no façade, no protection. The slightest challenge dismayed him. Now, when I tell him that the Klondike people package their ice-cream sandwiches in boxes of four so that we can enjoy a treat on four different occasions—as opposed to eating right through the box in a single sitting, then testing one's bedmate by groaning and holding one's stomach all night—he says. "Demento lured me on." He says, "Too much is never enough." He says, "I suffered, you didn't."

Then there's his going-to-the-showers gambit—and, while we're at it, his "Great Moments from Movie Cinema" (as he terms it) act. Looking innocent, Cosgrove will approach the uninitiated, then suddenly wobble his hands about his ears as he writhes and screams, in the James Dean manner, " 'You're *tear*ing me *a*part!' "

I've told him how disconcerting this can be; but when he feels too deeply chided he marches into the bathroom and turns on the shower. The noise locks out a reproachful world, and he actually gets under the water, washing the difficulty away. Fresh and clean, he comes out as if nothing had happened.

"Funette," Dennis Savage muttered, one eye on Cosgrove. "He slips in Funette, and I bought it."

Doorbell; enter Roy. Roy says, "Did anyone see the gay porn clips on the sex channel last night? The guy with the whopper dick in the living-room scene? Did you *scope* that?"

Dennis Savage made a helpless gesture: See what I mean? Cosgrove pointed out his CD display case, Roy called it "nifty," and within twenty seconds he was going on about veins and how much they add to a "truly elegant dick structure."

"Cosgrove already scarfed up the Brie," I said, presenting the cheese, "but there's Gruyère and—"

"Watch out for the Stilton," Dennis Savage stage-whispered.

"Now, here's the true thing," said Cosgrove. "Should my next purchase be a complete opera, the kind that comes in this box with a booklet like a whole portfolio? Or should I catch up on my rock classics?"

"There's so much life here," Roy observed, as he crackered up some Gruyère. "That's what I like about you guys."

"For instance," Cosgrove continued. "Should I lay in some Wagner? is the question."

"Yes, laying in. The feel of some tightboy's enormous, jizz-spurting cucumber as it very slowly plays into you," said Roy, in the serenely reckless tone of the new-waver for whom sex talk, no matter how lurid, is to be taken as a formal element of liberation. "You're stretched out and ready. Psyched for it. Then . . . . first, that delicious trembling as the head presses against your rim. People don't think of this, but it's all geometry. The line of your body diagrammed on the bed, the triangular head and its tubular mass generating a logic of—"

"Where's Nicky?" Cosgrove asked.

Well, that stopped him. "How should I know?"

"You're always together."

"Are we? I hadn't noticed."

Dennis Savage cleared his throat. "You're more or less inseparable," he said. "At least, to the naked eye."

Roy laughed—a touch nervously, I thought. "Or to two naked cowboys," he said. "They were dozing, but then they get up and find a pair of thin white-linen drawstring pants. So one of them tries them on, and the other helps him, you know, adjusting the waistband, admiring the jut of his buddy's behind. So the guy in the pants gets hot, while his cowboy friend rubs his neck to loosen him up. Then his hands steal around and pull the string, and the pants immediately sag to the floor, revealing—"

"How can you tell they're cowboys," said Cosgrove, "if they're naked?"

"They'd still have their hats on."

"I," Dennis Savage began, in his careful mode, "always think these fetishist fantasies are like the haikus that fourteen-year-old girls write. For your eyes only."

"No, it can be very everyday as well," Roy replied. "Just your standard date. He says, 'Let's get naked.' And his zipper pulls down on a whopper, big-time. Instantly, the mind clears of its trash. The *truth* of the partnership is . . . Figure it." He paused, eyes half closed, savoring the moment. "This prince, this tyrant. This wolfling about to . . . to stuff your cream tunnel with—"

Roy halted as Cosgrove jumped up, went into the bathroom, and turned on the shower.

"Did I say something?"

"Try the Stilton," Dennis Savage urged.

The doorbell again. Now Virgil joined us, waving a brown paper bag like Churchill flashing victory fingers.

"Look at this contest I'm entering!" he crowed. "I could win fifty dollars!"

Out of the bag came a romance comic book; the contest, flourished on the cover and detailed on the last page, called for a brief essay on the theme of "My Dream Man."

"It's surely open only to pubescent girls," I put in.

"It doesn't say so."

"It assumes so, because that's who the readership is."

"I'm entering anyway. I even bought a composition book and an extra-fine-tipped pen. Hi, Roy. Where's Nicky?"

Flopping onto the couch, Virgil fished a spiral notebook and pen out of the paper bag, murmured, "My dream man . . ." and dug in.

"I wish people didn't lump me with Nicky all the time," Roy grumbled. "He's one friend out of many that I have. And he's so . . . you know."

Dennis Savage said, "No, tell."

"Well, sure, I'm fond of him in his way, but he's this kind of asexual, isn't he? Try standing around in a bar with him sometime. He never wants to talk about the guys and scope them out. You'll spot some really fly number and speculate as to the size and weight of the junk he carries, and Nicky just . . . he just . . ."

"Doesn't really care?" Dennis Savage asked. "Do you find that aberrant?"

"Oh, please. There are only two kinds of gays—size queens and liars."

"I'm not a liar," said Dennis Savage, "and I'm also not a size queen—although I can be impressed. I don't know how many kinds of gays there are, but even the four males in this room are completely different from each other."

"And wait till Cosgrove comes in," Virgil added, looking up from his notebook.

"Kinds of gays?" Dennis Savage went on. "I don't know if there are kinds of gays any more than there are kinds of people."

"I've offended you, haven't I?" said Roy.

"I'm always offended when someone assumes that his taste is my taste. I also find this romanticizing of size questionable in an age in which fucking and sucking are fatally risky. This is seventies material. It suits coming out and beginning to comprehend the expanse of male sexuality. But that was an experimental age. This is an embattled age. Today, your icon is poison."

I asked, "Who wants more coffee?," and Cosgrove rejoined us, prompting Virgil to do a little number on the Dream Man contest. Cosgrove expressed a thrill or two and we talked of any old thing till Roy blurted out, "Look, everybody, I'm sorry. I didn't mean to expose you all to my . . . I thought you . . . I mean, who doesn't feel this way? Isn't cock the center of male sexuality?"

Dennis Savage and I were silent, Virgil was deep in composition, and Cosgrove was reshelving his CDs, to study the effect from different parts of the room.

"I'm sorry," Roy repeated. "I should be more low-key about it, I guess." He shrugged. "Everybody's got something."

"That much is true," said Dennis Savage. "I gay-bashed a classmate on Halloween when I was a teenager."

Virgil came to life with "I hid my sister Anne's Barbie Goes Camping accessories in the Victrola in the garage and didn't tell her where they were for seven years."

"I peed off the roof last Tuesday," said Cosgrove.

I was lying low in the kitchen, safe from Truth or Dare. By the time I returned, with a bowl of miniature pears and Rome apples, the air had cleared and Roy was about to go.

"I'll have to give a dinner," he said. "Because you guys were so helpful when I moved in and all." As he shook our hands, he said, "It's a gay thing, right? Support group and like that."

"Make sure Nicky's there," Virgil called out from the

sofa, and Roy said, "Oh, count on it, because he'll do the cooking. He's very handy for those things the rest of us . . . you know, can't be bothered with."

Cosgrove was holding the door and Roy gave him a pat on the butt as he passed. Suddenly Cosgrove grew wary, enigmatic. " 'Is it safe?' " he asked, almost whispering to himself.

Now listen to Cosgrove's question: "Do we see it as valuable because it's rare, or is it rare because it's valuable?"

"Rarity is everything," I told him. "We don't want what we can have."

"How do we know what is rare?"

"The hard-core enthusiast figures it out. It's partly word of mouth from other collectors and sheer experience, and of course there are the catalogues and discographies, but it's mainly the innate expertise of the fanatic. The children of Demento live for what is rare, so they *have* to know about it. They find a way, burrow in deep."

Cosgrove was wearing a pair of my old glasses with the lenses pushed out, the effect designed to suggest Intellectual Profile. "Hmmm," he says. "Which is more important—when you find a certain rarity you had been searching for forever and ever, or when you crash into a rarity that you didn't know there could be?"

"That's up to the individual collector to decide. But one thing you must never do is pass up a rarity when you find it."

"Why?"

"You may never happen upon it again, for one thing. But there is also Demento to consider. Those under his fierce tutelage are not free to select their own personal assortment of rarities. *They must have them all.*"

Cosgrove loves these talks. It's totally risk-free sport, like getting into mischief so inventive that your parents never thought to forbid it and thus cannot punish you.

"And of course," I went on, "when Demento learns that you have scoffed at him by passing up some treasure, he will be revenged."

"He's everywhere," Cosgrove gloated.

"Once, I happened upon the original Brunswick *Show Boat* 78s in a thrift shop, in excellent condition, for forty cents! Remember, this is not only a super-rarity but, for its first half century, the only *Show Boat* album with *logo cover*!"

"You snapped it up?"

I shook my head. "I already owned the LP re-release. Two copies of the same album? Ridiculous. Then, two blocks from the store, panic set in. I raced back—the album was gone! Another collector had seized it. And, late that night, Demento paid me a call."

" 'They're coming to get you, Barbara!' "

"With a wave of his hand, Demento studded my Capitol *Pal Joey* with cracks, hisses, and skips, mildewed the cover of my Ann Sothern *Lady in the Dark*, and slit the binding of my mint copy of *The Saint of Bleecker Street*."

A knock at the door. It was Virgil, to announce that he had finished his essay on "My Dream Man" and sent it off.

"I still say they can't let a male win this contest," I told him.

"No, I outsmarted them. I signed it Kiwi Brown—that could be anybody. Anyway, I happened to browse through that comic book, and all the romances ended happily. So the guys who put it together must be very naïve."

"Virgil," said Cosgrove, "will you read us your composition, 'My Dream Man'?"

Virgil seemed a little startled; apparently, he hadn't been planning to share his vision with the rest of us.

"It's just this little contest piece," he said.

"Why don't you read it at Roy's dinner on Friday?" I asked.

"Yes," Cosgrove agreed. "A star-intensive event!"

"No," Virgil replied, with immense conviction. "No, I'll read it only if I win the contest." I could see him thinking, That could be twenty years from now, and they'll forget all about it.

I won't.

Roy was right: Nicky did cook the dinner: prosciutto, melon, and watercress salad followed by London broil with wild rice and mushrooms, and, for dessert, Grand Marnier over raspberries and sherbet.

"Primo!" Dennis Savage cried, as the salad appeared.

"Nicky always produces," said Roy.

"I want extra-well-done meat," Virgil warned us.

"Me, too," Dennis Savage added.

This is, for some, a problem in our group: We all like it more or less burned to death. "Yes," Nicky promised. "Yes, I will." But it clearly threw his timing off to put the beef back in the oven. Cooks assume that there will be a well-done zealot or two, not a house full of them. It wilted the mushrooms and dried out the rice, but Nicky was happy if Roy was happy, and Roy was happy.

"A toast to the kitchen," he said, raising his glass.

"Everybody likes Nicky," said Virgil, joining in.

"Let's not get carried away," Roy joked.

Cosgrove pulled in with a bag of CDs and his catalogues, breathless and brisk and in charge.

"Just hold on," he told us, "because I got British dance bands and a very suspicious-looking opera by Berlioz and look at this weird thing." He held up Lucia Popp's *Slavonic Opera Arias*. "That's sure to be rare, because who knows what 'Slavonic' is? Then I got Rachmaninoff's *Second* Symphony, not just his First."

"Who's conducting?" I asked.

Cosgrove examined the box. "André Previn."

"Victor, EMI, or Telarc?"

"One guy did all those? How am I supposed to know which—"

"I told you, the devotee commands the trivia."

"Quick, what are the differences?"

"Victor is incomplete, with shallow sonics. Telarc is excellent. But the EMI is one of the classic performances of Russian music—and it's out of print as we speak."

For a terrible moment, Cosgrove checked the box, then flourished it aloft—it was the EMI—for all to savor the cover shot of Previn conducting batonless, his hands floating and his features dim, lost to the rapture.

"You really scored," I said. "This is something no one else can have."

"And all for three dollars a disc!" Cosgrove exulted. "Yes, there I am, crossing West Tenth Street, innocent as a clam, when . . . What are they serving?"

"London broil," said Virgil.

"Very well done, my portion," Cosgrove sang out; in the kitchen, Nicky sighed.

"Take no notice," said Roy. "Nicky's always making little noises."

"Anyway, there was this street fair. So I saw a booth of used CDs and scooped them up!"

"I don't see what's so great about those little mouse records," said Virgil, who can understand any fetish except someone else's. "Bud's got a million records—why don't you tape some of his?"

"It only counts if you own them in the true format. Listening to tapes is like kissing your uncle instead of some nice friend."

"My uncles were okay," Virgil airily recalled. "Though one had this sort of ruthless streak."

"Still," said Cosgrove, admiring the jewel boxes spread out before him, "It's a giant haul in the Western world. A whopper haul for me, Cosgrove."

"I hope no one's all opposed to gravy," Nicky called out from the kitchen. "Or forks. Or plates."

"How come you sound so warlike?" asked Virgil, proceeding into the kitchen.

Their voices lowered, and I pretended to admire a Mucha reprint hanging in the vicinity, hoping to tune in on the conversation in my harmless yet resolute writer's way. As I had suspected, Nicky was feeling unloved and exploited and Virgil was comforting him. When Nicky said, "Sometimes I want to curl up and die," Virgil answered, "Dying is easy—*comedy* is hard," a phrase he picked up somewhere. I thought, No: Comedy is easy—*friendship* is hard. There's so much there there.

"So, Virgil," said Roy, as Virgil parked himself next to Cosgrove and his CDs, "how's that Dream Man thing coming? Bet you've got some major boner in mind, long and fat, with one of those pointed heads I love."

Virgil just looked at him.

"Yeah," Roy went on. "Some call them donkeys and some thumpers, but I—"

"No," said Dennis Savage. "No, if it's the taxonomy of cock size that we're addressing, can we please get our terms straight? The heavy endowments are called, in ascending order: exploso cock . . ."

Roy was intrigued.

". . . raw, long and quivering, suitable for any occasion—"

"Veined and pulsing, with a mushroom cap?" Roy asked. "So cream-filled, and bouncing high?"

"No, that would be the next larger size, the bazooka cock."

Roy was silent, pensive and shivering in his dream.

Virgil, eyeing him, whispered something unkind—or so I guessed—to Cosgrove. Cosgrove nodded.

"Bazooka cock," Dennis Savage went on, warming to his subject as a Classics scholar fields questions from the floor on Beauty and Truth in Petronius Arbiter, "is neither rare nor common. Certain connoisseurs claim the ability to detect the bazooka by a man's walk or the set of his shoulders, perhaps by his pronunciation of the word 'often.' "

"Bazookas pronounce the *t?*" Roy asked, hopeful, eager for a code.

Dennis Savage shook his head. "A legend," he pronounced. "The true bazooka is deceptive, elusive. You know the phrase 'a grower, not a shower'? The bazooka is like a strange and fearsome rumor that courses through the public ear, not only showing but then—so *implausibly!*—growing in power and purity till it must be revealed to one and all as an official proclamation."

"It is real," murmured Roy. "It is near us." He could have been in a trance.

"Someone in this room is a sleazoid," Virgil observed.

"And his initials," Cosgrove added, "are Roy."

"Exploso," Roy reviewed. "Bazooka. Yes, and then?"

"And then," Dennis Savage replied. I have to tell you, he had not looked this quietly yet consummately joyful since Hamilton College invited him up for an autumn alumni panel on "The Four Best Years of Your Life."

"Well, *what's* then?" cried Roy.

"What's then is last, and hugest, and perhaps more a magic than a reality. Yet it is truer than truth."

"Oh, Lord," Roy murmured, looking at me now. But this was Dennis Savage's scene, and I kept still.

"What's then is the Godhead, before which all humankind—the intelligentsia, the clerisy, the military, the press—make their solemnly frenzied kowtow . . ."

"Say it!"

". . . the seldom-seen but oh-so-devoutly-to-be-wished-for . . . Red October."

"*Yes!*" Roy cried. "Oh, *yes!*"

"Although," Dennis Savage concluded, with a wry chuckle, "I still wonder how appropriate such talk is in an age of epidemic."

"True, but it's all fantasy," Roy assured us, as Nicky began parceling out the laden platters. "I dream to the bitter end, but I don't do anything with anyone. Besides, who knows where the heroes are?"

"Well, given your field of interest, you must frequent Folly City."

"I've never been," said Roy, accepting his plate. "A strip joint is just a little too downtown for . . . Thanks, Nicky, the dinner looks fabou."

"It was kind of hard keeping everything together with so many demands for—"

"Right." Then, to Dennis Savage: "How far do they go? To the nude?"

"Each dancer does two numbers. First, a strip to the almost, then a dance in the, uh, full truth, entering—as tradition and the management demand—with a hard-on, as the crowd goes more or less wild."

"No!"

"Well, yes, actually."

"But are any of them . . . exploso? Bazooka?"

Dennis Savage nodded. "And, once in a blue moon, one glimpses Red October."

Roy let out a squeal.

"There's seconds on everything," said Nicky, joining us at last with his own plate. Nicky: average in every respect, pleasant, undemonstrative, resigned. Being treated as subsidiary by the man you love is preferable to not being treated at all.

"Of course," Dennis Savage went on, "the special feature of Folly City is that the dancers are available, at the going rate, for private shows."

"A show?" said Roy. He seemed pensive. "They dance for you at home?"

"If somebody wants to hire me," said Cosgrove, "I do the Russian kazatski."

"A private *show*?" Roy repeated.

"Well," Dennis Savage replied, "sex. That's where the dancers really make their money. I gather they've closed the back room where this used to take place, so now you take them home or to their hotel or whatever."

"You gather? You aren't a regular?"

"Oh, most gay men in New York know about Folly City. You don't actually have to go there."

"But do you?"

"I've never been."

"A likely story," Cosgrove whispered to Virgil—whispered, I should add, as Olivier might have whispered "Never came a poison from so sweet a place" to the top balcony of the Old Vic. "He probably dances there himself, when no one's looking."

"He'd have to," I observed.

"Why don't we . . ." Roy began, then halted, probably hoping somebody would help him.

I did: "Plan a trip to Folly City and see it for ourselves?"

"Well, don't you think we should?"

Nicky said, "Count me out."

"I'll be listening to Slavonic opera arias," said Cosgrove, showing Virgil the wondrous libretto booklet, with critical introduction and texts in four languages.

"I think it would be fun," said Dennis Savage. "Refreshing and so on. Like a field trip when you get to miss a day of school."

"How much do these private shows cost a guy?" Roy asked.

"It greatly varies. A full-fledged date would run you upwards of a hundred, but a quickie around the corner in a peep-show booth could fall as low as—"

"A peep-show booth?" said Nicky. "Is this a life?"

"They print all the words to the arias, see?" Cosgrove told Virgil. "So you can sing along at the significant moments."

"What's a good night for this trip?" asked Roy.

Dennis Savage wasn't sure. "I'll confer with certain sages of my acquaintance and we'll set a date."

Nicky sighed and Roy let out a tiny thrill.

"But I warn you," Dennis Savage went on, "there are cases of innocent and even noble men who blundered into Folly City on a dare and, overnight, became addicts, slaves to a passion that cannot be named among decent people. Can you risk that?"

"You mean, it's like crack or something?"

"I mean, it's like truth. It becomes its own Red October."

Roy was so intrigued he was virtually squirming in his seat. He said, "I think we should go and make our visit."

It took a few weeks to get everyone's free nights aligned, and by then Dennis Savage had bought himself one of those trendy haircuts where they shear off the sides but leave it extra full on top. I thought he might be just the tiniest bit Cretaceous for this essentially youthful look, though I said nothing; and Virgil wasn't sure how he felt about it. (As so often, it was Cosgrove who tendered the most direct opinion: Whenever Dennis Savage appeared, Cosgrove would cry, "Here comes Ragmop!")

It was Saturday afternoon, and I was hoping to get a little work done before we went to Folly City, for Cos-

grove had gone upstairs with his Gameboy to finish off
his and Virgil's Tetris championship. I once thought that
video games might become Cosgrove's fascination—we
have three hand-held systems, plus the Super Nintendo
hooked up to the television—but, as Demento's lifelong
adherent, I should have realized that something as street-
corner as video games could never tempt Cosgrove's need
to assert his individuality. Anyone can play video games.
Collectors seek the arcane—the fantasy, really. We're not
talking of an accumulation of matchbooks or butterflies.
We're talking about encircling something that most people do not know is there.

(Sometimes I think that's all that writers ever do. We
get so deep into our perceptions and analyses: but is anybody listening?)

Anyway, I wasn't getting any work done, because
Nicky had arrived, early, fretting and loquacious. He had
been absolutely opposed to this trip and absolutely determined to come along—"because," he explained, "sometimes you have to humor Roy or he gets all intense about
everything."

So I said, "I resent this derogatory nuance that has
been creeping in on that word lately. *Intense*, as if that
were the nth of bad style. As if we're not supposed to cul-
tivate passions any more."

"You think Roy treats me like sludge, don't you?" said
Nicky.

Okay. I like directness. "He does seem to take you for
granted."

Nicky nodded. "I embarrass him. Because I've never
figured out the, like, dress codes. I'm in black sneakers,
everyone else is in white. I still wear Lacoste shirts. Or the
I-put-too-much-honey-in-my-tea kind of thing. Roy's all
concerned about how people are judging him, always.
And I . . ." He shrugged. "I gave up a long time ago. But

here's what you don't know. He's very nice to me when we're alone. He gets all roughhouse with me, like frat brothers or something. He's affectionate. We take naps together, listening to music. We're dressed at the time, like schoolboys in a Victorian story. That's what I love."

Nicky was staring at me, as if expecting a question.

"Of course I have a crush on him," he finally said, filling in for me. "But Roy wants a boyfriend his gang can all respect. See, they have categories of—"

"Please don't say any more," I told him.

"Yes, there *are* certain categories of hotness which tell what people want in life." He leaned forward. "Don't you think everyone really knows what category they're in? Or do some guys try to fool themselves up somehow?"

"Gosh, I'm late for habanera class," I said, rising; and Nicky got up too, but he kept on talking: "Now, me, I know what category I'm in. But what I mean to tell you is, Roy is all inclined to promote me to a higher category as long as no one else is around to see. And what I mean to *ask* you is—"

Just then Cosgrove came in, and he and I got very involved in discussing Cosgrove's Tetris scores, and the significance of sound wrist coordination in the mastering of Tetris, and the overall history of Tetris from the age of Nebuchadnezzar to our own times. And by then Dennis Savage and Virgil and Roy had joined us. So off we went.

Now, Folly City may be many different things to different people. But it reminded me of that moment in *A Christmas Carol* when the ghost shows you a terrible vision of what you will become. In fact, once we had climbed the stairs, paid our way through the turnstile, and edged through a dank hall into the long, narrow "lounge" where mirthless aficionados schemed and lurked, Cosgrove took one look, vastly feared, and made a run for it. I had to pull him back up the front stairs by the belt of his pants.

There's something odd here. When you mention Folly City, no one says, "Who?" The place is very known. Yet where was our generation? Why was the operating concept that of degenerate age woefully fastening upon youthful beauty?

"And now," came the announcement over the speaker system, "let's welcome our next handsome dancer, Pietro."

We duly entered the auditorium, and out stepped a man of about twenty-three, trim and confident, throwing himself around to Annie Lennox's "Precious (little angel)." He got down to a vest and a jockstrap. Then he walked off through the backdrop of dark Mylar strips. The deejay put on "Dancing with Myself," and after a bit of a wait the same performer reentered, naked, with his dick turned on to full. There was applause, and some of the rows of seats began to shake.

"Those guys are beating off!" Dennis Savage hissed to me.

"Where are the kids?"

"They're in the back row, holding a Tetris championship."

"In this darkness?"

"Cosgrove brought that lighting thing that fits over the top. You could put them in the Black Hole of Calcutta, and they'd play Tetris. Where's Roy?"

"In the lounge. Where's Nicky?"

"With the kids."

"Now," said the announcer, "let's welcome Theobald."

The men hanging out in the lounge came to life at this; to a man, they hastened into the auditorium. I took a break in the lounge; Cosgrove wandered in after me to say, "This place is horrible."

"Did you see the Tetris machine?" I asked.

It was the full-size arcade version, of course, with colors and music well beyond Gameboy technology. It's a friendly machine, so eager to be played that it runs through a sample game as you stand there; and Cosgrove drew near. But how could you make contact with this great hulking monster of a Tetris? Why are the falling shapes so different from the ones in the Gameboy version? Even the music is alien, vicious. This Tetris was unsafe, and Cosgrove declined to play.

"Well, you seem to be new here," said some old guy.

Cosgrove, grim and tight-lipped, replied, " 'I tell you, that thing upstairs is not my daughter!' "

The old guy mulled this over and decided to drift away—wise move—just as thunderous applause broke out in the auditorium.

"Theobald must be quite some package," I told Cosgrove, who said, "When can we—" I'm sure that "leave?" would have been the rest of it, but just then Roy came running out, grabbing us and saying, "*Theobald* is the one!" and "What a *panther!*" and "Did you see the *whopper* on him? It must be . . . hmmm, not *quite* Red October. But surely a major bazooka! Now, how do I arrange for . . . well . . . "

"Stand there, by the telephone," I said. "He'll come through that door and voilà."

"Please don't French at me now, what do I—"

"Pounce."

"What's he excited about?" Cosgrove asked. "It's just people."

"Theobald!" Roy cooed, inching up, as the dancer entered the lounge looking wet, warm, and debauched.

"Hey, folks," said Virgil, joining us with the Gameboy. "I broke a hundred thousand. Nicky didn't do so well."

In fact, Nicky was doing quite badly, coming in to look

on miserably as Roy negotiated with the amenable
Theobald.

"He isn't really going to take him home, is he?" Nicky
asked me. "Wasn't this whole deal some joke or other?
Some silly nonsense?"

"Not to Roy."

The two of us watched as Roy spoke with Theobald.
Lucky Roy to have snapped him up, for other gentlemen
were crowding around, their eyes on Theobald, ready to
leap the second that his present conversation showed
signs of evaporating.

"Why did he bring me along if this is what it was?"
Nicky asked me. "Should I have to know about this?"

"This place has the worst potato chips," said Cosgrove,
passing by with a napkinful and a glass of punch.

"I told you not to touch the refreshments," I reminded
him. "Who knows where whose hands have been around
here?"

"Bartering for that guy!" Nicky went on. "As if nobody
had any feelings."

"Hey, Cosgrove." Virgil called out. "They just set out
the bread sticks!"

"Save some for me!" cried Cosgrove, avoiding my out-
thrust arm as he charged through the lounge.

"I don't mind what he does, but why when I'm right
there?" Nicky pleaded. "Why, to *torture* me?"

An employee came in bearing the refilled punch bowl,
and Cosgrove asked if he was planning to bring out any
chocolate-covered macaroons. "It's my favorite dessert,"
Cosgrove explained.

"That's my third favorite," said Virgil. "My second favorite is lime Frozfruit and my all-time is tiramisù, which
is probably not available here, I would imagine."

"You got that right," said the guy, as Dennis Savage
came into the lounge, noting it all in a single look. Roy's

presentations to Theobald appeared to have reached the bottom line: The two were head to head, whispering the intimate details that marry love and money on the fringes of the gay world. Theobald nodded thoughtfully, Roy made a gesture, and away they went without a glance behind them.

Nicky dropped onto the banquette that lines a wall of the lounge, distraught, beaten, the lover who dared not speak his name—an archetype as basic to gay life as any Theobald in full bloom. Dennis Savage and I flanked him, trying to soothe his pain, reason through it, and, perhaps, find some hope in it somewhere.

"I'm okay," Nicky kept saying. "It's not as if he signed a contract with me."

Munching a bread stick, Virgil came up and said, "If he's mean to you, just throw him away like tomorrow's sawdust."

"Theobald," Nicky mused. "Turns it on, turns it off." He shrugged. "Well, that's the style. They make sex the way a musician makes music."

"This ridiculous *collecting* mania of the randy gay male," Dennis Savage said.

Now Cosgrove horned in, with a new idea: "Why don't *you* take someone home, too, Nicky?"

"Oh, never," said Nicky. "This revolting trash."

"I don't mean Ragmop. Take home one of the dancers."

"You can't buy love, Cosgrove."

"But what if you can't *have* love? At least you can buy some nice company and not give way to secret tears that all can see."

"Oh, was I so . . . I'm sorry for all embarrassing you."

"Not at all," I said.

"Only a few people saw," said Virgil.

"And would you please," Dennis Savage asked me, "tell that thing to stop calling me Ragmop?"

"He's not a thing," said Virgil.

"Well, I'm not Ragmop."

"I'm not a thing," Cosgrove mused, "but somehow you are Ragmop."

Which got a giggle out of Nicky, at any rate.

"Let's get this boy home," I said.

"No, I . . . Can I come with you guys? Please?"

One could hardly have said no. Back on our own turf, as we piled into the elevator, a virile voice called out, "Hold that, please," and Presto joined us, with a stalwart grin.

"Could you push fourteen?" he asked.

Virgil and Cosgrove were very subdued, taking turns gazing up at their mystery love. Presto was not unamused by the attention; he held up his fingers to put donkey ears on the pair. Just then, Nicky burst into tears.

We all tried to comfort him as Virgil told Presto, "We're rehearsing a play."

"Looks like a real Greek tragedy" was Presto's opinion.

"No, *Gremlies Two*," said Cosgrove, master of the *fallacia consequentis*.

Well, we took Nicky to Dennis Savage's and calmed him down with a V-8. We said all the useless cheer-up things. We pointed out Bauhaus, who appeared at the bathroom door with one of his "Oh, them" looks, raced into the living room, dropped a little treasure upon the carpet, and sauntered into the kitchen. We cast aspersions upon Theobald, though most of us don't even know what he looks like. Then Roy came in to brag.

Oh, that Theobald! So wicked, so eager, his whopper flopping hard and ready out of his pants. His power, his readiness to do!

"This is an entirely different class of people," Roy told us. "They're not like, you know, the guys you meet in bars, guys you could have gone to high school with. They're . . . sex people. There's something inside them, like a motor. I see it now—these dancers and porn stars and so on, they're not doing it because you and I aren't available. It's because they're so hot that fucking is their vocation. Of course, I made sure we took the precautions. But can you imagine telling this . . . *monolithic* guy that you want to get pleasure-fucked, and he doesn't say, But do I like you?, or, Is it Thursday? No, he just sets you right up on the bed and proceeds to slide his big, fat, cream-filled joint right up your—"

Virgil, Cosgrove, Nicky, and Bauhaus dashed into the bathroom; the sound of the running shower directly followed.

"I blew it again," said Roy. "Speech is not free here."

I said, "The problem is that, in actuating a fantasy, you're threatening everybody's sense of stability. We all dream of encounters with the holy Lucifers of the sensual world, okay. But that's all they are. Dreams. Didn't you notice that all the men in the audience tonight were dreary old losers?"

"*We* aren't, are we? I'm not even thirty yet."

"But where were our coevals? I'll tell you. They're out seeking some more earthly version of the dream in socially reputable places. Because the only fit partner for Lucifer is another Lucifer. Anyone less total must feel inadequate. Threatened. Humiliated. Tell your friends where you went tonight and what you got. Tell them about Theobald. You think they'll be glad and plan their own trip to Folly City? On the contrary, they'll—"

"Good Lord!" cried Roy at something behind me; Dennis Savage and I turned to look. It was Nicky, nude and erect, walking in like a strip dancer launching his second number. And—I swear to God and all Her angels—he had a raging bazooka. Maybe even a bazooka plus.

"What's . . . what's going on?" asked Roy, as Nicky planted himself before his friend.

"Here's what you like, right?" said Nicky. "This gadget? You don't care about people, you just want a thing! Fine, now somebody put Annie Lennox on and I'll prance for you!"

"Has he been drinking?" Roy asked.

"He was swigging the V-8 like a man possessed," I said.

"Nicky," said Roy, as Dennis Savage went into the bedroom for something, "our friends will become alienated if you carry on like this."

"You don't like my boner?" replied Nicky, falsely coy.

"You're offending our hosts," Roy insisted, though I noticed that he couldn't take his eyes off Nicky's erection. "You've virtually cleared the room with this . . . this outrageous stunt."

"No, I approve of this," I said. "It's mildly eerie yet presented in a farcical naturalism that gives the whole thing a deceptively quotidian feel. A *Symphonie Fantastique* or so."

Dennis Savage came back with a bathrobe, which he tossed to Nicky.

"No," Nicky said, shaking his head slowly. "No, because if I don't show a big dick, Roy won't like me."

"He *must* be drunk," said Roy. "He's never like this."

"You don't *know* what I'm like! You never listen to me, or ask me how I feel, or do anything except take me for granted!"

"Come on," said Roy, helping Nicky into the bathrobe. "I do, too, listen to you." He patted Nicky's shoulder. "Boy, and I thought you were this quiet type."

From the bathroom, Cosgrove shouted, "We're not coming out till everybody's dressed!"

"All clear," I announced; and even Bauhaus joined us.

"In all the fuss," said Virgil, "I never got to make my

surprise revelation, which is, Guess who won the Dream Man contest?"

"Virgil, we're rich!" Cosgrove exulted.

"Actually, I only got third prize. Fifteen dollars."

"That's still enough for one brand-new CD."

"So let's hear the award-winning piece," said Dennis Savage.

"It's weird how you can know someone for so long," said Roy, regarding Nicky, "and be ignorant of the most basic things about them."

"It's not basic, I tell you," said Nicky, almost pleading. "It's just a device. The real me is more than something that goes up and down upon the application of erotic stimuli."

"Woo," said Cosgrove.

"It's college," Virgil agreed.

"We have to talk," Roy told Nicky, patting him again. "Come on, let's get you dressed."

"Now you like me in public, is that it?"

"What, I always liked you, you silly . . . big . . . boy . . . "

"Let's hear your piece," Dennis Savage urged Virgil, and Cosgrove and I clapped expectantly. Nicky gave us all a weary grieving look, but he let Roy lead him back to the bathroom. On the way, Roy whispered, "Is it really big when it's flaccid, too? Because I think I love that effect most of all . . ."

"I must admit, I was not planning to read my essay," Virgil told us, looking after Roy and Nicky with some disapproval. "Of course, upon publication, copies were to be circulated." He took a bow, to Cosgrove's "Bravossimo!," to which Dennis Savage (no doubt still grudging the "Funette" episode) replied, "I wonder if you mean 'Bravissimo.'"

"Sure, Ragmop."

Dennis Savage was patient, elegant, so *comme ça.*
"Didn't I ask you," he asked me, "to arrange for our de-
lightful little Cosgrove to stop—"

"Let's go out for haircuts," said Cosgrove. " 'Barber,
I'll take the Ragmop trim, please.' "

Dennis Savage rose, saying, "Now I'm going to mow
you down."

"Stop fighting," said Virgil, heading for the bedroom,
"and I'll read my piece."

Dennis Savage poured out white wine for the grown-
ups and juice for the kids, as Roy and Nicky made their
departure with thanks and apologies, and Dennis Savage
lip-mimed "We have to discuss this" to me.

Then: " 'My Dream Man,' " Virgil read out. " 'By Kiwi
Brown.' " He looked at us: Dennis Savage and Cosgrove
on the sofa, me sitting on the carpet, leaning against the
wall with the aid of a pillow. His extended family, as we
call it. "Don't be critical," he warned us.

"Just read it," said Dennis Savage.

" 'My dream man is gentle but commanding,' " Virgil
intoned. " 'Sometimes he is rough on me, but I know it is
only to make me a better person. And then he always
hugs and kisses me to say, "It's all right, and we're still
best friends." ' "

Dennis Savage and Cosgrove eyed each other suspiciously. Who was rough? *Who* kissed him?

" 'My dream man is not very tall, yet he seems treelike
to me.' "

Cosgrove, at five-seven, glowed. Dennis Savage, just
over six feet, scrunched down on the couch the slightest bit.

" 'You may ask, "What color his hair, his eyes?" I say,
"It doesn't matter." We two are so close that, however far
apart we may be, I can feel what he feels, at the same moment.' "

This bewildered Dennis Savage and Cosgrove. What's going on, *The Corsican Brothers*? They traded a second suspicious look; Cosgrove even made a fist.

" 'My dream man loves me not for my special talents but just for myself. I don't have to impress him. But when I do succeed, he is the first to admire me.' "

"Wonderful essay," quoth Dennis Savage.

"I admire you more," said Cosgrove.

" 'My dream man has the respect of all who meet him, but no one respects—and loves—him more than I, for he is my very own pop, Seth Brown.' "

Virgil looked at us. "I surprised you, right? You thought it would be just some boyfriend."

"Some of us did," I said, getting up. "Now, I have to get some work done and Cosgrove has to do the marketing."

"I'll go, too," said Virgil. "We're fresh out of Puffed Kashi."

Dennis Savage followed me downstairs, eager to settle the case of Roy and Nicky. "Here's the question of the year," he said. "Why didn't Nicky just tell Roy that he had Schlong Control in the first place?"

"But think of the risk. Getting exploited and patronized on a platonic basis is bad enough—imagine how Nicky would have felt if Roy rejected him *sexually* as well."

"He wouldn't have."

"How do you know? Besides," I added, getting out a notebook, "I think Nicky's worse off now. Okay, he'll get into bed with the man he loves. Right. They may even have a longish affair. But sooner or later, Roy will tire of Nicky, and he will stun him, scorch him. Why? Because Nicky wants a lover and Roy wants a dream man." I uncapped a pen. "And dream men, by nature, are out of reach. Touch one, and he becomes meaninglessly real."

"What are you writing?"

I shrugged. "Some story."

He looked over my shoulder and read out, " 'The Hunt for—' "

" 'Alice Faye Lobby Cards,' " I finished, my hand covering the truth.

"All right, snarky, I'm on my way out."

Cosgrove got in quite some time later, but then most people can return from a vacation sooner than Cosgrove and Virgil can return from D'Agostino's.

"The most incredible thing!" Cosgrove cried, plopping the groceries onto the kitchen counter. "This guy had set up a little flea market right outside his building. There was a crowd going over, like, these books and clothes and stuff. He was saying, 'Estate sale! Estate sale! Everything must go!' So I just leaned over to see—and guess what?"

"CDs."

"Not just CDs. Rock imports that you can't get here! He won't take plastic, so I'm going to rush back and—"

"I thought it was something like that," I told him, turning around from my desk. "Because, you see, Demento was just here."

Cosgrove froze. "He *who*?"

"Demento came. Something about your having ungratefully passed up rarities that he had placed in your grasp. He unwrapped one of those Klondikes that you're so wild about and rubbed it all over your Rachmaninoff Second. With his awesome power, of course, I could do nothing to intervene. Worse yet, he said that no other copies of that extremely rare and desirable recording will become available till 1996, when a retired mortgage broker in Riverdale will move to Florida and—"

"You didn't," he said quietly. "Are you so heartless?"

"I? *Demento!*"

He marched right over to his collection, snapped open the indicated jewel box, examined the disc—of course it was unharmed—and replaced it.

"That was such a mean joke," he said. "It was the acme of cruelty, and then some."

"Aren't you going to rush back to that one-man flea market and—"

"No. He was asking too much for them, anyway. And now I have a little idea."

I went on working as he unpacked the groceries and returned to his catalogues. Making a quick trip to the bathroom, I wondered if I'd gone too far. But, look, if you can't tease your live-in, whom can you tease?

So I was confident as I came back out. Cosgrove was quiet, deep in catalogue and thought. "He was back," he said.

"Who was?"

"Demento." He looked up, cool and resistant. "What a surprise for us to learn that he moonlights as the protector of injured roommates. He set up your Super Mario World on the controller." Responding to the look on my face, he said, "Well, didn't I *tell* him you don't like anyone fussing with your Super Nintendo? I said, 'It took Bud seven months just to reach the Valley of Bowser. Push the wrong button and he'll lose it all.' And you know what Demento said? 'I will push the *right* button.' And he erased your entire game."

With that, Cosgrove went back to his catalogue.

"You can't fool me," I said as I coolly returned to the desk. (I did take a fleet swipe of a look at the controller. Super Mario was nested there, though I hadn't played it in weeks. Uh-oh.)

I did this and that in my notebook. Then I said, "You would not be so foolhardy as to erase my game. Surely you would not dare."

"But," he observed, "Demento dares all."

"I will not be taken in."

He looked at me.

I said, "Did you do something to that game?"

He was struggling not to smile.

"Did you?"

"Someone is worried, I see."

It was too much to bear. I jumped up, switched the game on, and triggered the playing screen. My game was intact.

"Victorious" does not describe Cosgrove in that moment. "Apocalyptically sated" might do.

"Now who's so great, Mister Smarty?" he asked. "Demento is my dream man."

My voice was low, dangerous, Teutonic. I said, " 'Consida dot a divawss.' "

MARTY

Richard Davis

"Why'd you show yourself at school this mornin'?"

Stanley's daddy had caught him off guard.

"Why'd you show yourself?"

Stanley pushed his fists into his eyes until bright stars shone in the black. His daddy's slap tore the stars apart. "Stan!" his momma cried, but she turned her face to the floor.

"Why'd you show yourself?" his daddy demanded.

There was no escape. "I dunno," Stanley said. He was crying. He *didn't* know. He didn't even know what his daddy was talking about. He'd been playing by himself in the corner, and now this.

"You dunno? You dunno?" his daddy mocked. "You dunno that you showed yourself off like some dirty-ended little girl at school today?"

What had happened at school that day? Stanley had met Marty, that's all he remembered. His daddy's voice jerked him back into the present. "Do you think if you got a whippin' cross your big butt you'd remember peeing your pants in front of your class and everybody? Do you?"

Stanley flushed with fear and anger. He looked at his momma—why had she told on him? She looked back at him, her lips pressed tight. Stanley tried to pull away from his father. "No! No! Daddy, please! No!"

But his daddy held Stanley tight, pressing Stanley's face into his groin. Stanley could not breathe. He gulped for air and his mouth filled with the taste of his daddy's sweat. Bits of hardened cement on his daddy's jeans scratched his face as he struggled to escape. The belt hit and Stanley felt his butt blow up like a giant red balloon. It got bigger and bigger until it burst with one big pop.

Stanley hid in his tree house. The stupids who lived next door called over the fence, "Crybaby! Crybaby!" But they could not see him up in the thick branches of the umbrella tree. He wiped his face on his sleeve and stopped his crying. Digging around in an old peach crate he used for a shelf, Stanley found a black mirror he'd stolen from his momma's dresser. He usually used it to flash signals from the sun to kids up and down the alley. But now he simply stared into it at his face. Suddenly it occurred to him that people couldn't see their own faces. Stanley had thought that he was the only one who could not see his face, except in a mirror. Up until that moment he had thought that the people around him could see their own faces all the time, even without a mirror. With a start, he realized that *everyone* had to look into a mirror to see. He kissed his image, smashing his lips and nose into the glass, smearing it all over with his snot. He pretended like he was kissing Marty.

Stanley had met Marty because he had peed his pants in class that day. He had been afraid to go to the bathroom at recess because he had had trouble snapping his new school jeans without his momma's help. As the year wore on, the snap became loose, but during these first weeks of school the snap was too hard for Stanley to work by himself. He had tried to hold himself in, and thought he was going to be able to, but then in relief and horror all the pee came out.

He told Miss Nelson that stinky Gail had peed her panties and that he had accidently sat in it. Miss Nelson sent him down to the boy's room under the guard of Mrs. Schmidt, her aide. Schmidt-Bitch, as the kids called her, had swollen ankles, and she waddled indifferently toward the closest boys' rest room with Stanley in tow. Stanley hesitated at the door. "That's the one for *sixth*-grade boys," he tried to explain.

"Oh, it don't matter. Get in there."

Stanley entered reluctantly. Adults were too old to understand what kids knew. This rest room was for the *big* boys—boys who would be in junior high next year, boys who would be wearing jocks, boys who sometimes already had hair *there*. Stanley was just a kid to them.

Stanley was relieved to see that the room was empty. During recess he kept his distance from this dangerous place where boys smoked cigarettes, stopped up the toilets, and mercilessly taunted any misfortunate who might actually have to use the bathroom. That very morning he had watched a crowd of kids jeer as a skinny boy was dragged out of the rest room onto the playground with his pants pulled down to his ankles and his butt unwiped.

There was a sigh, and Stanley started—he was not

alone, after all. At the very end of the urinal trough, a boy stood with his underwear pulled down over his butt, occupied. Stanley quickly ducked into one of the doorless stalls. He didn't have to pee anymore, but he stripped off his jeans and stuffed his wet shorts behind the toilet. He would have to explain to his momma what had happened. She wouldn't tell his daddy, he was pretty certain. But remembering his momma, Stanley felt afraid. He quickly pulled up his jeans and tried to snap them, but he couldn't. His fingers turned white as he tried.

Maybe that big boy will help me, Stanley thought. It was a risk, Stanley knew, since the boy might make sport of Stanley and then not help anyway, but it was better than asking Mrs. Schmidt. Stanley came out of the stall and cautiously approached the boy. He was still standing at the urinal, holding his dick, but no pee was coming out. Stanley marveled at the length of the boy's blond hair. Stanley's daddy shaved Stanley's black hair into a crew cut, so the kids at school called him "Baldy." The long-haired boy's face shone red with effort, but fine blond hairs along his cheeks made the red turn rose.

"What's wrong?" Stanley's whisper echoed louder than he intended in the bare, tiled bathroom.

"I dunno," the boy replied. "Sometimes it's just hard for me to piss."

"Can I watch?"

"Sure, I guess."

Stanley looked closely at the older boy's dick. There was a blond gleam along the base. The boy said, "It's coming now."

What squirted out was red and yellow. The boy's face was now as white as his hair.

"Does it hurt?"

"No. It's okay. I'm getting healed soon."

Stanley didn't understand. He quickly said, "I don't

think it's weird or nothin'. If it don't hurt. It's neat to watch."

"Yeah, I like watching the piss come out red like that."

But the boy pulled back suddenly and hiked up his shorts to go.

Stanley blurted out, "Can we be boy friends even though you're in sixth grade?" His chest was too tight. He realized he sounded weird and expected the boy to make fun of him.

But the boy looked seriously at him. "Yeah, that'd be good. What's your name?"

"Bud." Stanley made the name up on the spot. "Stanley" suddenly seemed like a stupid name. His Adam's apple choked him so that when he asked the boy, "What's yours?," his voice broke.

"Marty," the boy said easily.

The two boys looked into each other's faces, studying each other as they would a newly won marble. Marty threw his arm across Stanley's shoulders and Stanley let go of his pants to return the embrace. His pants dropped and Stanley stood there frozen.

"C'mere," Marty said, and led Stanley over to a sink. Marty leaned Stanley forward over the edge of the cold porcelain and shoved up behind him hard with his hips. Stanley's pubic bone ground against the hard surface and the boys heard a pleasing snap.

It was Friday. Payday. Fight day. Stanley's daddy gave Stanley's momma his paycheck, but it was never enough money, and his daddy cried like a little boy and yelled his wife's name, cursed her, and demanded that she make it right, but she never said a word. She just sat in the corner with her head hung back until he had to beat her with his fists, and then Stanley and his sisters crowded around him, holding on to his legs, crying, "Daddy! Daddy!"

And his daddy said, "Momma, why don't you stop all this?" But she would not stop it. Stanley hated her for not stopping it.

On Saturday evening, Stanley's momma worked swing on the line at the cannery, so Stanley's daddy cooked up a big pot of chili for their dinner. He served it to the kids in Tupperware mixing bowls. Stanley added fistfuls of saltines and a brimming capful of vinegar to his chili. Stanley's sisters took their bowls into their room and closed the door on Stanley. They were going to listen to their stupid rock music, so he didn't care. He ate his chili with his daddy while they watched *Big-Time Wrestling* on TV. Stanley sat in his shorts on the braided rug and his daddy lay shirtless in his recliner, black hair spreading over his belly.

The wrestlers were fat and muscular, with big butts and angry faces. They looked like Stanley's daddy. "One night," Stanley's daddy told him, "at the old Downtown Arena, when they still had wrestlin' up there, a riot broke out and they pret' near tore that place up." He laughed. "Boy, there was blood all over, you can bet!"

Stanley wished he had been there to see the blood. He thought about how he would bring Pepper Gomez, his favorite wrestler, a cool drink of water, and how he would wipe his bloodied face with a clean white towel.

Stanley brought the saltines out of the kitchen, and also a can of whipped cream. He sprayed peaks of cream onto the crackers and fed them to his father. Stanley dropped one of the crackers and it fell, facedown, onto his father's chest. Stanley picked up the cracker and licked up the cream off his father's skin. His father knocked him away, saying, "Stop that rudeness."

Stanley cut across the outfield on his way home from school. He heard a kid yell something at him and he looked up, scared. The road was too far away to run up to a house if the kid was going to beat him up. The kid yelled again, "Bud!.," and Stanley realized it was Marty running toward him. Two other guys were with Marty. As the three approached, Stanley felt his body growing out of control. His head was too big and bald with his crew-cut hair. His legs stretched out like Jack and his skinny beanstalk. His mouth was like rubber, spreading into a big, silly grin. His chest burst where his books—he held them like a girl—rubbed up against his tits. He sank down into his jacket and tried to hide his ungainly self, but the boys did not seem to notice.

Marty introduced his two pals to Stanley, just as if Stanley belonged to his gang. Gary was the redheaded one, and he played clarinet in the school band. Tony was a Portagee whose daddy worked on a dairy farm over by Crow's Landing. Stanley liked the way his jet-black hair shone with grease. "Mind if I pick my nose?" Tony asked.

Nobody minded, but when he wiped his fingers on his pants, Marty asked, "Don't you eat them? I eat mine."

"I only like to eat my scabs."

The four boys had come upon Capp's Market and they bought Milk Duds, Jawbreakers, Red Hots, Bazooka gum, peanuts, and sodas. Stanley bought a cream soda. That is what his older sister, Marie, always bought, so he thought it was more sophisticated. The boys sat on the curb in front of Capp's and ate their snacks. Gary poured his peanuts into his 7Up. "Last night after my parents went to bed I saw this really neat movie on cable with this girl in it that had really big titties."

"At dinner one night in this mansion," Tony told them, "they were having this dinner party but the cook forgot to fix any dessert, so he said, 'What am I going to do?,' and the butler said, 'Wait here for a minute.' So he run into the bathroom and he shit on a silver tray and he brought that out to the cook and the cook put whipped cream on it and served it to the people and the millionaire said, 'By George, this is the best chocolate pudding I've ever had!' "

The boys laughed at the joke. "This one's even better," Gary said. "There was this girl and she was having her period and she didn't have anything to serve to her boy friend for breakfast so she went into the bathroom and she got out her used tampons and she gave those to him to eat and he said, 'Gosh, these jelly rolls taste good!' "

Just then Tony made a loud fart, upstaging the end of Gary's joke. So Gary forced a fart, but it was a silencer—no noise but plenty of stink—and the boys made as if they were going to ditch Gary, all except Marty. He lifted his nose in the air and breathed in deeply, looking at them as if they were all a bunch of kindergartners. "Would you guys grow up?" he said. "All guys like to smell their own farts."

Stanley was stunned by this assured pronouncement, and though he was not sure that he did like to smell his own farts, he now very much wanted to smell Marty's.

The boys continued wandering, going out over the Seventh Street Bridge. It had been superseded by a modern overpass upriver, and the boys spoke hopefully of the possibility of the old bridge's imminent collapse, preferably while they were on it. The ramparts were guarded by two worn but still noble stone lions. Elegant ironwork railings graced the sides of the bridge. From mid-span the boys looked out over the alluvial plain of the Tuolumne River, its barren, autumn orchards violet in the approaching evening mist. The river flowed massive and muddy. Across the river the shrill and lonely call of a cannery whistle scattered little black specks, birds, up into the gray sky, like ashes. The oldness of the bridge and the wideness of the river caused Stanley to think aloud, "It will still be here when we're dead."

"That's creepy!" said Gary.

"Good morning, Sister Samlan."

"Good morning, Sister Angus."

The two elderly women smiled sweetly at each other across the aisle of the county bus. Sister Samlan looked toward Stanley as she asked, "And who's this fine young man?"

Stanley grimaced and hid his face in his grandma's soft white sweater. He smelled her powdery sweetness.

"We've missed you in church, Sister," Sister Samlan continued, looking directly at Stanley's grandma.

"Oh, I know, Sister," Stanley's grandma replied, looking straight forward, "and I've missed goin', but Dad you know's been sick."

"Sick, Sister?"

Grandma Angus pursed her lips and looked forward determinedly. Stanley did not like Sister Samlan and he was happy when she got off at a different stop than theirs. "She's a busy old bitch," Grandma whispered, half to herself.

Stanley loved to go into town with his grandma on the bus. Sometimes he knew she contrived a need for buttons and pins just to make an excuse to take him. At Woolworth's, Stanley read out loud all the names of the different colors marked on the spools of thread, more colors than even in the biggest box of crayons. He touched the brocade and velvet cloth until the saleslady chased him away. Grandma bought him some little papier-mâché fruits with sugary glitter meant for decorating a hat.

Honking cars were backed up for a block on J Street, where Stanley waited with his grandma in front of the

Covell Hotel and watched in wonder as his grandpa's huge pink-finned Cadillac made a majestic U-turn, cutting off both lanes of traffic. With a final flourish of horn-honking, Grandpa landed the automobile with its front wheels up on the sidewalk. Grandma was clutching Stanley's hand too tight.

Stanley felt swallowed up in the backseat of the big car. His grandpa was hidden underneath a felt Stetson. Grandpa pulled away from the curb with nary a backward glance, causing a succession of screeching tires. "Dad! Be careful!" Grandma said, gripping the dashboard.

"You shut up," he told her and she did, gripping the dash even tighter.

Grandpa and Grandma Angus's trailer was set back from the road behind a junkyard of old tires and blackened car parts. In a narrow strip beside the carport Grandma kept alive a rosebush, spared by mere inches as Grandpa veered tightly into the space. He banged his door against an already bent and scratched aluminum post, heaved his bulk out of the Cadillac, stumbled a few feet, and threw up.

The smell of corn pone and salt pork made the air inside the trailer hot and greasy as Grandpa sprawled across the floor after lunch, chewing his tobacco and reading to Stanley from his preaching book. Stanley turned the pages until he came to a picture of a businessman sitting behind an office desk reading a big book marked "Holy Bible." On the corner of the businessman's desk, a large hourglass poured out its sand. At the window of his office, a masculine angel held back the drapes, revealing a sky where huge sheaves of accounting paper were falling out of Heaven. On each page was stamped, "Prophecy Fulfilled!"

Stanley leaned over the picture as if he were looking over a great height. It gave him the creeps and he pulled back against his grandpa. Grandpa spit in his tobacco-juice can, laid one giant, gnarled finger against the text, and began his stern exposition in a state of catatonia. Stanley could not understand the details—the Pouring Out of the Cup of the Gentiles, the Winepress of God's Wrath, the Great Whore Mystery Babylon—but the meaning was clear enough: God was coming to kill everybody. Stanley only wanted to know, "When?"

"The moon will turn to blood, the stars will fall from the sky, and the sky will roll up like a scroll." Grandpa paused dramatically. "Soon."

"Hush that talk," Grandma said.

"Soon, I say!" Tears began to roll down Grandpa's cheeks. He lifted one hand up in the air and said, "Come, Lord Jesus, I have been saved."

"How?" Stanley asked.

"Why, honey," Grandma said, "both your grandpa and me was saved up in Springfield at the revival meetin' they had there on June fifteenth, 1939, when we was full-immersed baptized."

None of this made any sense to Stanley.

Marty knew a lot about religion. He had to go to church school during the last half hour of regular school because his parents had requested time-release for religious instruction. Church school was presided over by a retired minister and his wife in a van parked discreetly beyond the public-school grounds. Marty had won a white phosphorescent cross for memorizing the names of all the books of the Old and New Testaments, in order. He had let Stanley borrow it to play with under the covers at night.

Now Stanley waited impatiently for Marty to meet him after church school. The public-school grounds were lonely after all the kids had gone. The tetherball chains made a plaintive *clink! clink!* as they slapped against their poles in the wind. From over in the church van,

Stanley heard the kids sing with a high-pitched screech, "Deuteronomy!" Suddenly, Stanley was knocked to the ground and a kid was on his back. Stanley tried to buck him off, but he was too big. The kid reached up under his shirt and started to pinch Stanley's titties—it was Marty.

"Fooled you. I ditched," Marty jerked his head toward the rollicking van.

Stanley led his friend across the outfield to a place where the ground underneath the hurricane fence, which delineated the field from the wildness beyond, had been eroded away, permitting the two boys to crawl under on their bellies. Beyond the fence they crossed through an expanse of dried grass, chest-high. Ancient, leafless walnut trees lined the field like monstrous sentinels. Grasshoppers clicked in the air and the two boys tried to catch some and put them in Stanley's Flintstones lunch pail. But as soon as Stanley opened the pail for Marty to put in a new captive, any prior prisoner flew out. So they had to start ripping off the insects' wings. Ladybugs glistened in the golden grass and the boys swept the stalks, causing the ladybugs to sputter into flight. Soon the boys were wiggling, trying to shake the little orange-and-red beetles out of their shirts.

The field abruptly ended in a neglected sward of John-songrass that passed for a county park. As ugly as it was, Stanley thought of it as his secret garden, since nobody else was ever there. Indeed, it had all the appearance of being abandoned. The toilets were locked—their doorways reeked of urine—and the playground was in ruins. But this made it all the more fun for the two boys. They ran up the teeter-totter, which swayed in midair, dangerously unstable. Next, the boys gyrated on the rusted chains, which were all that remained of the swings. Making a Tarzan whoop, Stanley swung grandly out and leapt off into space. The earth jerked him down and he landed, hard, on his butt.

That is when he saw them. The man was lying on top of the woman on a dilapidated picnic table. The woman was grabbing at the man's butt. His pants hung low on his hips. Marty came up beside Stanley, laughing at his friend's big flop, but when Stanley tossed his head toward the couple and Marty saw, he stopped laughing.

The boys let out a big yell and they ran up onto a canal bank that bordered the park. They kept on running until they began to laugh, relieved and exhausted by their escape. They fell on top of each other on the sandy bank. "They were doing it," Marty said.

Two planks served as crossing boards above a canal lock, and the boys walked out over them and looked down at the trickle of water still splashing over the lock in a tiny rivulet, the ebb of the summer's dammed and channeled flow. On the other side, they tried to turn the black wheel that controlled the floodgate, but it would not budge.

Steep stairs descended into the cement ditch and the boys climbed down to poke through the remnants of the summer's flood—broken beer bottles, a car tire, a grocery cart, a bra, two unmatched shoes, a dead cat. On the canal bottom the sun stood askance in the sky, and the air, tinged with chill, made them shiver in the shadow of the bank. Isolated pools of water sparkled bright green with algae against the mud silt. Marty thrust his head under the waterfall splashing over the lock and jerked back with a yelp. Water flung from his hair in a flashing arc.

The boys hoisted themselves up onto the crossing boards and stretched out under the low afternoon sun with their feet pointing toward opposite banks and their heads side by side.

"Was he hurting her?" Stanley asked.

"Nope. Girls like that."

Stanley hesitated. "Do you think it's okay for boys to kiss?"

"Jesus said we're all supposed to love each other," Marty considered, "even if we *are* boys."

Marty's answer irritated Stanley. Even he could see that his friend was making that part up. Jesus did not mean *that* kind of love when he said *all*. But Stanley could smell the warm wetness of his friend's hair. Marty turned his face toward Stanley and kissed him, upside down as it were. Marty's lips tasted sweet and salty. They tasted warm. They tasted like Marty.

Stanley grew too big inside, as if he couldn't fit himself all inside himself. He jerked up and looked all around as if someone might be watching. It seemed as if his parents at home might be able to hear his heart beating, it was so loud. Nothing was secret; the sky had seen them kiss.

Stanley ran off the canal bank into a darkening orchard. The dry, hard soil was littered with the yellow crescents of almond leaves. Marty ran after him, skidding on the slippery leaves, calling, "Bud! Bud!"

Stanley slipped and flopped flat on the ground with a thud. The world seemed to spin around him. His eyes focused on something sparkling in the earth. Marty was kneeling beside him now and he reached over to where Stanley was staring and picked up a chain of luminous red beads. "Are they rubies?" Stanley asked.

"Probably," Marty said. "This is a rosary. Catholics use these to pray with."

"Really?" Stanley was horrified and thrilled. "My grandpa says Catholics recrucify Jesus every Sunday. Maybe the beads are like drops of Jesus' blood petrified!"

"Yeah! Let's say they are. Like they're magic."

The orchard had grown dark. The pretend was scary. Everything seemed secret again. Marty showed Stanley his pocket knife. "We can be blood brothers."

Stanley looked at the knife warily. "Are you sure it's sharp enough?"

"Sure! Look." He pricked his finger on the end. "I sharpen it all the time."

"Do we have to say anything?"

"Nah. We just do it."

"Okay," Stanley said, trying to conceal the gulp that had crept into his voice. He held out his wrist to Marty and squeezed his eyes shut. The blade slid effortlessly across the skin, a quick sting. A line of blood wrapped around his wrist and dropped onto the ground. Marty quickly cut his own wrist and clasped Stanley's hand so that their wounds smeared together.

The week before Christmas, Stanley's momma scraped the car against the side of the garage as she backed it out. His daddy grabbed her by the hair and dragged her into the house. After he beat her she sat in the middle of the floor, crying. Stanley and his sisters huddled around her in a ball while his daddy crushed the Christmas bulbs on the tree one by one in his fist. Bright glass shards hung by tiny wires from the branches.

When he had gone away, Stanley's momma played Christmas carols on the record player and cried. "No one loves me," she said.

Stanley wanted to say, "I love you, Mommy," but all he could think of was how she could have prevented the whole thing if she had been more careful with the car. She caused the whole fight. Why hadn't she been more careful? Now their Christmas was over.

Stanley's daddy did not come home for supper. Stanley was happy. He sat at the head of the table and told his sisters they had to do what he said. He giggled excitedly as he got into his pajamas after supper and mischievously jumped on his momma and daddy's bed. Hiding under the covers, he waited for his momma to come to bed.

When his momma came in she wrapped him close to

her under the covers. She tickled his toes: "Piggy! Piggy! Piggy!" Her fingers crawled lightly up his legs: "Spider! Spider!" She pinched his bottom over and over and he giggled and cried, "Stop!"

She crushed him close to her breasts and kissed him. Her fingers twirled around his pee-pee. She whispered, "Peter, Peter Pumpkin Eater!"

"Don't!" he squealed, laughing and squirming to get away.

The light turned on and his daddy stood in the doorway, red.

"Waddya doin' here? Get outta here! You don' belong here!" He picked Stanley up and threw him across the bed. His head hit the bed board with a crack, and blood spurted out all over the white pillows. Stanley's momma used up two of her good towels getting the bleeding stopped.

All that January, Marty missed a lot of school. He told Stanley it was because of the blood-piss. His healing had not come yet and he was feeling weak and tired all the time. Stanley hung out over at Marty's every day. Marty's momma was fat and she never kept up the house or anything, but she was always kind to Stanley and happy to see him come over. Gary and Tony did not hang out with Marty much anymore.

In February, when the orchards began to bloom, Marty said, "Stanley, we should plant a garden." Marty's backyard was just dirt anyway. Marty's daddy talked to them about spreading a mulch, leveling the ground, and setting out the rows. He was a quiet man and let the boys alone when they started working.

Stanley had to do the real labor, leveling and digging. Marty sat in the dirt and directed Stanley in all that his daddy had told them to do. He helped Stanley pick out the seeds at the garden department at K mart. All Stanley really wanted was watermelons, but Marty insisted they get tomatoes, lettuce, lima beans, squash, radishes, and carrots. For himself, Marty wanted sunflowers. It was going to be a big garden.

Spring comes early in the Central Valley of California, and as the seedlings began to sprout from the ground, Marty would lie close to them in the warming earth and pretend he could see them grow. The plants came up so fast a boy might think he could. Soon they were a feast for fat green caterpillars. These the boys ruthlessly crucified, hanging them on pins stuck into the seed posts at the head of each row, to serve as a warning to others.

Stanley was not as interested in the plants themselves as he was in watering the garden. He liked to stick the hose into the ground and push it down deep as the water dug out the soil like a drill. The upwelling water fascinated him. One day he grabbed Marty and pushed the hose down his pants. Marty yelled at the cold and laughed. He wrestled with Stanley but he could not get the hose away. So Stanley pulled it out and gamely put the hose down his own pants. The force of the water pushing out gave him an odd sensation of volume.

Soaking wet, they stripped down to their shorts. Stanley lay down on his tummy to dry out in the sun. Marty leaned on his elbow at his side. "Bud, have you ever looked at your butthole?"

"No. How could you?"

"In a mirror or something." He paused. "Maybe we could look at each other's."

Marty got on his knees and pulled down his shorts. "I can't see anything just like that," Stanley said. So Marty leaned forward on his head and spread his cheeks with both hands.

Stanley was surprised it was purple-colored. "Like grape juice," he thought, though that was weird. He had not seen enough when Marty insisted it was his turn. Stanley assumed Marty's head-down position. Marty poked his finger right into him. "Hey!"

"It feels warm inside."

Marty's finger felt odd to Stanley, something other than himself in himself. Marty wiggled it.

When Stanley made Marty bend back over again he saw that both of them had boners. He felt tight inside and hesitated, then he poked his finger into Marty. His friend was like a fire. Stanley could not push his finger in as deep as he wanted it to go. Eventually, they both used a small stick to poke up each other.

Afterward Stanley felt shy toward Marty, and he could see that Marty seemed a little shy too—like when they had first met—because they had looked inside each other.

After begging his parents all week long, Stanley's parents let him stay overnight at Marty's on the Saturday before Easter. Marty was too sick now to go out into their garden. From his bedroom he liked to watch the sunflowers turn in the sun. Stanley played Monopoly with him up on his bunk.

"Why don't you go to the doctor if you're so sick?" Stanley was worried; the healing was not coming.

"I told you about million times already. We don't believe in doctors. We trust God. It was prophesized in church that I'd be healed."

Stanley did not believe it, though Marty was certain.

That night when Marty's momma came in to listen to their prayers she read to them a Bible story about two friends, Elijah and Elisha. Stanley like the story, but he asked, "How come Elisha didn't get to go with Elijah up to Heaven on the chariot?"

"He wasn't ready yet, darlin'." Marty's momma spoke as she pulled the covers up for the two boys, first Marty in the top bunk and then Stanley in the bottom. She sat down on Stanley's bunk. "But remember, Elijah gave his holy mantle to Elisha so that he could do everything Elijah had done and more. Now say your prayers, darlin's."

The two boys said their prayer about sleep and death in unison, but at the end Stanley blurted out, "And Lord Jesus when I go to Heaven I promise to buy you a great big Bible, like the kind they had in the old days with jewels and gold on the cover, if you don't take Marty away. Amen!"

Marty's momma laughed. "Well, I don't guess God needs no Bible! But don't you worry about my darlin' "— she was standing now and she rubbed her son's head— "he's gonna do just fine. You see if he don't tomorrow in church. It's Easter, darlin', and I know something special's gonna happen."

Stanley was up in Marty's bunk a second after the lights were out. Marty had the flashlight out and he played the beam on the sparkles in the flocked ceiling. They made a tent out of the covers and sat cross-legged and ate some marshmallows Marty had hidden in his bed. Marty's bed was never too clean and Stanley could feel the grit of crumbs on the sheets. In the closeness of the dark, the bed smelled strongly of Marty. Marty switched off the flashlight and said, "Watch!"

Stanley could not see anything in the pitch-black under the blankets. He could feel Marty moving his arm back and forth in the darkness. Slowly he became aware of scribbled lines of ghostly colors hovering in the black. He quickly began to circle his own finger in the air, making luminous circles. He wrote "Marty," and watched to see "Bud" magically appear from Marty's invisible finger. His friend's name began to dim beside his own. Stanley's eyes had begun to adjust and now he could see Marty's face.

Marty pulled Stanley back without a word. For several

minutes the two boys lay side by side in silence. Stanley could feel Marty's blood pulsing where their arms touched in the dimness. A prickly tension formed between the two boys' skins. Stanley's heart had ballooned up into his throat and his ears rang with his own blood beat.

"Do you want to kiss some more?"

Stanley's voice cracked when he tried to answer. He coughed and said again, "Yes," sounding as if he were crying. Marty rolled over on top of Stanley, crying out "Steamroller! Steamroller!" as if he were joking around. He lay still on top of Stanley, a dead weight. Neither boy knew what should happen next. Marty pressed his closed lips against Stanley's and he kept on pushing hard, mashing his nose and face into Stanley's. When both boys happened to open their mouths at the same moment to gulp air, they froze for a second, shocked by the insides of the other. But then Marty blew his breath into Stanley, puffing out his cheeks, and they laughed.

"Let's touch our dicks together," Marty said. He turned on the flashlight. His dick was sticking straight out of the fly of his pajamas. Stanley had a boner also. They touched the ends of their dicks together, rubbing the pee-holes. This did not seem to accomplish much to Stanley and he wanted to kiss some more.

Marty said, "No, rub my dick back and forth."

Stanley held on to Marty's dick and pulled it like Marty said. Wet stuff came out of the top all of a sudden; it was thick. "Let go!" Marty said, so urgently that Stanley thought he had hurt his friend.

"What's that?"

"Bud, I shot jis. Jis comes out when you rub your dick."

Stanley said, "Oh." He did not understand. The bed smelled salty now, like when he and Marty took showers together. Stanley started to touch Marty again. "No, not now. Lay down."

Stanley listened to Marty's breathing as he thought about all these things and fell asleep.

Marty's daddy took them out for breakfast the next morning. The waitress remarked, "Not too many people out for an Easter morning."

"Not with this fog," Marty's daddy averred.

"Isn't it something," Marty's momma exclaimed. "I saw on the news this morning that there had been a big accident out on Five. Seems like some people hit the fog—"

"Be just like hitting a wall, I guess."

"—and, well, they just stopped!"

"No!"

"Yes! And a double-rig rammed right into the back of them."

"Lordy! Lordy!" The waitress let her coffeepot droop so that the coffee threatened to pour out the spout.

"She ain't told the half of it," Marty's daddy added.

"Another car came along and went right underneath that truck—it just sliced off the top of that car."

"Twenty-six cars was in it altogether," Marty's daddy concluded.

"Ain't that something! People just don't know this fog enough to drive in it." The waitress turned a big grin on Marty and Stanley. "What are you boys gonna eat? Oh, I know this little dude, too well," she said, nodding at Marty, "Strawberry waffle, extra whipped cream."

Marty looked green at the thought. Stanley had pigs in a blanket.

The church did not look much like a church to Stanley. It was a large, plain, flat-roofed building resembling a warehouse. Inside was a modern auditorium with wood paneling, thick carpets, and comfortable theater seats. In front of the sanctuary, video equipment picked up the service for broadcast on TV monitors placed throughout the far reaches of the big auditorium.

The first part of the service was mostly just music and talking and Stanley was bored. Ushers came up the aisles and passed across the rows deep bags of purple velvet hanging from highly polished wooden handles. Marty's mother gave both boys a quarter to drop into the bag that passed down their row, and the coins vanished silently into the velvet's luxurious depths. Throughout the auditorium came the rustle of paper bills.

The sanctuary choir began to sing: "Oh, there's pow'r, pow'r, wonder-workin' pow'r in the Bloooood of the Laaaaaamb! Yes, there's pow'r, pow'r, wonder-workin' pow'r in the Precious Blood of the Lamb."

"Yes, yes, there *is* power in the Blood of Jesus," the pastor spoke into a hand-held mike at the front of the sanctuary. "Amen! Isn't that a wonderful promise? I said, Amen!"

Stanley was startled by the loud "Amens" shouted throughout the auditorium in response. Although the congregation belonged to the pastor already, he fine-tuned their enthusiasm, demanding, "Say *Hallelujah!* I *said*, say Hallelujah! I said, *say* Hallelujah!"

The congregation rose spontaneously to its feet as each person attempted to out-Hallelujah the other. This shouting match lapsed into strange groanings, babbling, and singsong sounds. People clapped their hands unrhythmically. In the choir, tambourines rattled in discordant climax. Even Marty and his parents were making the strange mumblings. Stanley sank down bewildered.

Gradually the people quieted except for the occasional aberrant shout of "Amen!" The pastor took control again, "Amen! Praise Lord Jesus!"

He stepped off the raised sanctuary to stand directly in front of the people at the head of the center aisle. "You know, some people say Jesus *wants* you to be sick! They say that God *sends* illness. But what does *God* say?"

The pastor held aloft a huge, well-worn Bible. Flipping it open, he draped the supple book across his left forearm like a towel and, in a voice hardly needing the amplification of his microphone, announced, "Luke! Chapter eleven, verses eleven through thirteen."

Marty's momma helped the boys to search through Marty's Bible for the page, as the pastor proclaimed from memory, "If a son shall ask bread of any of you that is a father, will he give him a stone? or if *he ask* a fish, will he for a fish give him a serpent? Or if he shall ask an egg, will he offer him a scorpion? If ye, then, being evil, know how to give good gifts unto your children: how much more shall *your* heavenly Father give the Holy Spirit to them that ask Him?"

Stanley knew that his daddy had given him only serpents and scorpions and stones. If his daddy was evil, was God evil? What good would God do him?

"My God, my God, my God, what kind of Jesus do people think came down? Do you think some sick little boy is going to come up here to this altar today, praying for healing, and the Lord is going to say to him, 'Here! Have a brain tumor, too'? No!"

Stanley wondered what little boy the pastor was talking about. Marty's momma was shaking her head, no, no, and tears silently flowed from her eyes.

The pastor slowly shook his head at the hardness of the human heart. Then he thundered down upon them like the very righteousness of God, "By His stripes we have been *healed! Every* sin, *every* wound, *every* disease has been forgiven! *Healed! Bound! Already!* Through the Precious Blood of our Savior, shed for you"—he paused significantly—"and me, up there on that cross!" He flung his Bible-draped arm back toward a large, plain cross that dominated the back wall of the sanctuary. He was sweating now. He laughed incredulously. "Do you not see?

"Jesus has already healed whatever disease you've got. What more does God have to do to get through to you thickheaded people? All you gotta do is claim your healing, claim it in the Blood of the Lord, claim it now. *Claim it! Right now! Right here!* He wants to heal *you!*" He flung his microphone straight toward Marty like a magic wand.

Marty's momma muttered, "I claim it. I claim it." Stanley mimicked her, though he was not sure what he was claiming. He prayed, but he did not know what for.

The mood of the congregation had quieted. Six middle-aged men dressed in dark suits gathered in a somber semicircle behind the pastor in his garishly colored polyester. The pastor now continued in almost a whisper, "The elders have now gathered with me, and whosoever will may come forward and receive the healing touch of Christ by the laying on of hands and the prayer of faith." He now pleaded gently, "Won't you please come?"

Marty's momma touched his shoulder and smiled at him, slightly nodding. Stanley's stomach dropped in fear. He grabbed Marty's arm. "Don't!" he whispered. Marty smiled at Stanley and put something into his hand. Then he quickly moved down the aisle, and the circle of men closed around him. Stanley stared in his hand at the red-beaded rosary he and Marty had found in the orchard the day they had become blood brothers. He prayed frantically, "God save Marty! God save Marty!"

The circle of men groaned with effortful prayer. A few of them uplifted their hands as if to draw down the power of God like a lightning rod. The pastor's head rolled back on his neck, and tears streamed across his fat cheeks. The men began to sweat and murmur, "Yes, Jesus, yes, Jesus, thank you, Jesus, I just want to praise you, Jesus."

All around Stanley the congregation began to stir like wind murmuring in a field of wheat. Laughter and clapping broke out like rain. The storm of noise swept up Stanley, growing louder and louder around him. Marty's momma slumped back, and across the aisle a man peed his pants. The ceiling seemed to crack open; light poured down. There was a cry, a scream from hundreds of people, and Stanley fell to the floor, flattened by the force of the sound. Then there was silence.

Stanley lifted himself to look.

"Healed!" the pastor cried out, and Marty dropped straight back from the circle of elders onto the carpet. He was still, pale, unseeing.

Dead. "He's dead," Stanley whispered. But then Stanley's eyes opened and he could see where Marty had gone. It was someplace Stanley could not go, a place of burning worlds, mirror-like seas, signs, portents, and beasts that spoke great boasts. Stanley screamed to Marty, "Eat! Eat!" Marty had to eat something. A man stood in the midst of a sea, slain yet not dead. He held a gold key in his hand. Marty ate it and became like a mirror, him but not him, clothed but not clothed, there but not there forever.

Stanley never saw Marty again. But he did not ask where Marty had gone. He knew very well where he had gone. At school, Tony got into a fight with Gary when Gary said Marty was dead. But Stanley knew.

He rode his bike around Marty's house. The windows were empty. The sunflowers in the garden had dried up and fallen. It was a ghost house. Stanley pounded on the door, and the pastor opened it. Stanley ran.

On the first morning of summer vacation, Stanley got up very early and rode his bike out into the old, deep orchards, beyond Whitman Road. The trees had long since lost their blossoms and were now deep green. Stanley coasted his bike slowly along the flat, hard orchard floor, deep into the coolness of the trees. Far into the orchard and hidden from the road, Stanley dropped his bike and lay flat on the damp, sandy earth. He looked up through the leafy ceiling.

Stanley idly trailed Marty's rosary across his tummy as he daydreamed about Marty. He lifted the beads up to stare at them closely. He did not know how to pray to saints with them. As he thought about Marty and all the things he had said, Stanley sucked on the red beads. Wet, they slipped from his mouth and fell like drops of blood onto the ground. Stanley covered them over with dirt and hid their brightness in the earth. Someday he would find Marty again.

It was now full day and hot. Stanley walked his bike back to the road and began his long ride home.

And it came to pass . . . that Elijah said unto Elisha, Ask what I shall do for thee. . . . And Elisha said, I pray thee, let a double portion of thy spirit be upon me.

And he said . . . If thou see me when I am taken from thee, it shall be so unto thee. . . .

And it came to pass . . . that, behold, there appeared a chariot of fire, and horses of fire, and parted them both asunder; and Elijah went up by a whirlwind into heaven.

And Elisha . . . cried, My father, my father. . . .

And he saw him no more.

ABOUT THE CONTRIBUTORS

MICHAEL CUNNINGHAM'S novel *A Home at the End of the World* was published by Farrar, Straus and Giroux in 1990. "White Angel" is a chapter from the novel.

RICHARD DAVIS grew up in the Central Valley of California and has lived in Montana and New York. He currently resides in San Francisco, where he has studied writing with Jim Brogan, Dorothy Allison, and the late Bo Huston. He sells newspaper advertising for a living, and is working on a novel about con artists in rural California. "Marty" is his first published story.

BRAD GOOCH is the author of a novel, *Scary Kisses;* a book of short fiction, *Jailbait and Other Stories;* a collection of poems, *The Daily News;* and, most recently, the biography *City Poet: The Life and Times of Frank O'Hara.* He lives in New York City.

JESSE GREEN, born in Philadelphia, was graduated from Yale University in 1980 and worked for several years as a music coordinator on Broadway shows, before turning to full-time writing. A journalist and National Magazine Award finalist, he has published articles in *The New York Times Magazine*, *Premiere*, *Mirabella*, *GQ*, and the late, lamented *7 Days*, for which he created, with novelist Meg Wolitzer, the popular Nutcracker puzzle column. A collection of their most diabolical efforts was published in 1991 by Grove Weidenfeld. His short fiction has appeared in *Mademoiselle*, *Mississippi Review*, and *The American Voice*, and his novel, *O Beautiful*, was published by Available Press/Ballantine Books in 1992. He lives in New York City.

JOHN EDWARD HARRIS grew up in Iowa City. Currently living in New York, he is the editor of *TheaterWeek* magazine and writes theater reviews for *Christopher Street*. He has just finished his first novel.

SCOTT HEIM is a native of Kansas, now living in New York City. He holds degrees from Kansas and Columbia universities, and his work has appeared in *Brooklyn Review*, *Santa Monica Review*, and the anthology of "new queer writers," *Discontents*. As a poet, he published *Saved From Drowning* (Chiron Books, 1993). His first novel, *Mysterious Skin*, will be published in 1995.

G. WINSTON JAMES has been interested in "the seedier side of life" for as long as he can remember: "watching people in the raw and all." Poetry is his favorite medium of expression; he has published in the Lambda Award–winning anthology *The Road Before Us: 100 Gay Black Poets* (Galiens Press, 1992) and also in *Sojourner: Black Gay Voices in the Age of AIDS* (Other Countries, 1993). He is currently co-editor of *Kuumba*, an African-American lesbian and gay poetry journal. It is only recently that he discovered the great power of the short story, especially in disclosing "the unspoken realities of gay black life.

A former California police officer, REX KNIGHT now works for a law firm. He'd like to be a gay Joseph Wambaugh, but lacks the discipline to get on first-name terms with his word processor, preferring to go for a twenty-five-mile bike ride or play baseball. An aficionado of pre–World War II British dance music, he recently restored a 1960 Ford pickup, barbecues killer steaks, and is the only guy left in Southern California who still smokes cigarettes. "The Number You Have Reached" is based upon an actual occurrence.

JIM PROVENZANO has contributed to *The Advocate*, *Frontiers*, *Ten Percent*, and other lesbian and gay publications. A former dancer, performer, staff member of *OutWeek*, and editor of the shortlived *Hunt* magazine, he is also the creator of the 'zine *PUP*. He was born in New York City and raised in Ashland, Ohio, and he now lives in San Francisco, where he is a staff member of the *Bay Area Reporter*.

A native of Stoneham, Massachusetts, MICHAEL SCALISI came to New York City in search of a more interesting life. He has found it.

ROBERT TRENT is a graduate of the Locust Valley Friends Academy, Williams College, the University of Virginia, and New York University (with a Ph.D. in English literature and a specialty in the poetry of William Blake). Like the Tyger, he burns bright. He has devoted his life to the notion that all success is contained in aggressive cruising technique. He was like that even in high school. I swear.

ABRAHAM VERGHESE is a physician and writer and lives with his wife and two children in El Paso, Texas, where he is Professor of Medicine and Chief of Infectious Diseases at Texas Tech Medical Center at El Paso. He is a graduate of the Iowa Writers' Workshop, and his stories have appeared in *The New Yorker*, *Black Warrior Review*, and elsewhere. His essays have appeared in *Granta*, *Sports Illustrated*, and *The North American Review*. His first book, a memoir about coming of age as a physician in the rural South during the era of AIDS, has been published by Simon and Schuster, and will presently be issued in paperback by Vintage Books. In Dr. Verghese's own words: " 'Lilacs' was inspired by a patient with AIDS whom I took care of in Johnson City, Tennessee. He had monstrous lesions of Kaposi's sarcoma on his face and a manner so obnoxious and so deliberately antagonistic that it made it tricky to recognize his particular form of bravery. Other elements of the story borrow from my experience with HIV clinics— particularly the waiting rooms—in Boston and Iowa. I began with the character and his anger and went along for the ride. Bobby's endurance and determination were all that he had left that was of any value to him; he had no medical options, and no amount of money could buy him more time. His diatribe with Clovis surprised me, much as it must have Clovis. It was, however, despite its cruelty, an act of love, a legacy to another young man from the rural South who had escaped to the big city to find anonymity and freedom only to encounter this unforgiving virus. Bobby's actions in the story exceed all permissible boundaries. But what are permissible boundaries when you are dying of AIDS? The story came out in one quick rush, then underwent several revisions, most significantly when I changed to the present tense, to convey a sense of urgency. My agent, Mary

Evans, and Daniel Menaker, at *The New Yorker*, helped me considerably. I think we were all cautious about tinkering with Bobby, fearful that, in his testy, irascible state, Bobby would tell us to butt out."

JOHN WEIR, gently merry, is the author of the novel *The Irreversible Decline of Eddie Socket* (Harper & Row, 1989). A New Jersey native who now lives in New York City, he has also written for *Details*, *The Advocate*, and *OutWeek*.

THE CULTURE OF DESIRE
PARADOX AND PERVERSITY IN GAY LIVES
by Frank Browning

Nowhere has America's gay culture been observed with greater intelligence, liveliness, and sensitivity than in this provocative and deeply personal book. Taking in Cuban couples in Miami and farmers in Kentucky, AIDS activists, sexual theorists, and dedicated hedonists, *The Culture of Desire* is an intriguing insider's guide to gay America and a sharp look at the conflicts that arise when who we are is defined by whom we love.

"Absolutely cutting edge—a portrait of modern sexual politics [that] should be required reading."
                                                            —Armistead Maupin

Gay Studies/Sociology/0-679-75030-4

FAMILY VALUES
A LESBIAN MOTHER'S FIGHT FOR HER SON
by Phyllis Burke

When Phyllis Burke's lesbian partner bore a child by donor insemination, it seemed natural for Phyllis to adopt him: baby Jesse, after all, was calling her Mama. But Burke soon discovered that, even in liberated San Francisco, there were forces that would deny lesbians the legal right to be mothers.

"An important book...about motherhood, identity, honesty and love for a child. It is about homosexuals and it is pro-family. A strong challenge to prevailing 'mainstream' sensibilities."
                                                            —*Chicago Sun-Times*

Gay Studies/Sociology/0-679-75249-8

THE QUEEN'S THROAT
OPERA, HOMOSEXUALITY, AND THE MYSTERY OF DESIRE
by Wayne Koestenbaum

The Queen's Throat is at once a passionate love letter to opera and a work that triumphantly overturns our received notions of culture and sexuality. It is an innovative, profound, and wildly playful book that reveals the ways in which opera has served as a source of gay identity and gay personal style.

"[A] high-spirited and very personal book...laced with moral reflections and warmed with comedy.... A work of formidable and curious learning...a dazzling performance."
                                                    —*The New York Times Book Review*

Gay Literature/Music/0-679-74985-3

OUT IN THE WORLD
by Neil Miller

In this eye-opening and vastly entertaining book, Neil Miller travels from the black townships of South Africa to the sex clubs of Bangkok to deliver a front-line report on the lives of gays and lesbians around the world.

"Sharp, informative, and always engaging, this is first-rate work." —*The Advocate*

Vintage Departures
Gay Studies/Travel/0-679-74551-3

CLOSE TO THE KNIVES
A MEMOIR OF DISINTEGRATION
by David Wojnarowicz

David Wojnarowicz's powerful and iconoclastic memoir takes us from a violent childhood in suburbia to eventual homelessness on the streets of New York City, to recognition as one of the most provocative artists of his generation. Street life, drugs, art and nature, family, AIDS, politics, friendship and acceptance: he challenges us to examine our lives—politically, socially, emotionally, and aesthetically.

"Wojnarowicz has caught the age-old voice of the road, the voice of the traveler, the outcast, the thief, the whore, the same voice that was heard in Villon's Paris, in the Rome of Petronius. Pick up his book and listen."

—William S. Burroughs

Nonfiction/Literature/0-679-73227-6

VINTAGE ✺ BOOKS